THE
RUNAWAYS

Ruth Thomas

RED FOX

Also available in Red Fox by Ruth Thomas

The Class that Went Wild
The New Boy
The Secret
Guilty!
Hideaway

A Red Fox Book
Published by Random House Children's Books
20 Vauxhall Bridge Road, London SW1V 2SA

A division of Random House UK Ltd
London Melbourne Sydney Auckland
Johannesburg and agencies throughout the world

First published by Hutchinson Children's Books 1987
Beaver edition 1988
Red Fox edition 1990

20

© Ruth Thomas 1987

Printed and bound in Great Britain by
Cox & Wyman Ltd, Reading, Berkshire

RANDOM HOUSE UK Limited Reg. No. 954009

Papers used by Random House UK Limited
are natural, recyclable products made from wood grown in
sustainable forests. The manufacturing processes conform to
the environmental regulations of the country of origin.

ISBN 0 09 959660 1

Contents

To Justin

1

Nobody likes me

The air was clogged with heat. Through open windows streamed the dusty sunlight of another city afternoon. An undercurrent of fretfulness rippled round the room. The children were irritable and niggly and Mrs Henrey couldn't stand them in the classroom any longer. Class 8 were going to the park for the last hour, to play rounders.

Only two of the twenty-four children didn't want to go, and one of those two was Nathan Browne, sitting at the front. Nathan looked like an ill-natured goblin. A small, black boy, glaring at the world through thick-lensed glasses, and hating most of what he saw, Nathan had no friends. He sidled out of his seat now, and put his request. 'Please, Mrs Henrey, can I stay behind?'

'No, Nathan, you can't,' Mrs Henrey snapped. 'We're all going.'

'I could stay in Mr Abbott's class,' he suggested.

'No, Nathan. Last time you stayed with Mr Abbott you picked a fight with two of his boys.'

'I didn't! It was them. Can I stay then?'

'NO!'

1

Recognizing defeat, Nathan slunk back to his seat. He regarded Mrs Henrey with scowling dislike. She looked, he thought, rather like a lady pig, with her small eyes, fat cheeks and pursed-up mouth. She had a mole near her chin with a few piggy hairs growing out of it. Nathan imagined Mrs Henrey snorting round a farmyard with a lot of other lady pigs, and the thought made him feel better. He made a face at her back, and that made him feel better still.

Julia Winter, also sitting at the front of the class, saw the face and called out, pleased to be the supplier of important information. 'Mrs Henrey, Nathan made a face at you!'

Mrs Henrey didn't want to know about the face Nathan had made. 'Don't tell tales, Julia. That's a nasty habit you've got. I've told you about it before.'

A shamed blush covered Julia's long, thin cheeks. Her eyes, pale as dishwater, blinked rapidly. Her lips went into a pout, and she tossed back the straggly pigtails of sandy hair which reached just below her shoulders and petered out to a meagre wisp beyond the elastic bands which secured them. Julia would never understand the grown-up world, she decided. They wanted you to be good, but when you showed them how good you were, by pointing out how bad other people were, then they didn't like it.

Julia didn't want to go to the park any more than Nathan did, but Julia didn't ask to stay behind because she was afraid Mrs Henrey would be cross. She was afraid of Mrs Henrey being cross because she wanted Mrs Henrey to like her. Indeed, she wanted very much to be liked by someone, just someone in the whole wide world. But sadly, no one did like Julia, no one ever had.

Julia was an only child. When she first came to school she was five years old and had never played with other children, so she had no idea how to behave with them. She grabbed all the crayons for herself, pinched the other children, and whined complaints all day. So gradually the others turned against her, and no one wanted to play with her. Nowadays Julia no longer pinched people or took their pencils. Indeed, she was rather afraid of them. There were so many of them, and only one of her. But somehow she had never been able to live down those early mistakes. And now, with her face set permanently in an expression of slightly anxious unhappiness, and her shoulders hunched into a despondent stoop, Julia was a fairly unattractive sight as well. *She* thought she was ugly, which she wasn't. Not pretty of course, but not exactly ugly. Actually she had rather nice teeth, but since she hardly ever opened her mouth to smile, very few people had noticed. Julia herself had no idea how much difference a real smile would have made.

So now among the girls Julia was the funny one, the odd one, the gawky one who stood head and shoulders above everyone else – sometimes the object of scorn and ridicule, more often just ignored. At eleven years old, Julia had never had a friend.

'Line up with your partners,' Mrs Henrey told the class – and this was the moment Julia had been dreading. Because no one would want to walk with her, no one ever did. There would be fussing and pushing and the chaos would sort itself out into a column of twos with herself, as usual, left skulking at the back – left conspicuously, shamefully, alone.

Nathan also would be left without a partner, and that was the reason *he* didn't want to go to the park. One of the reasons. He didn't crave a friend, particularly. If that lot didn't want him he didn't want them, so there! But he didn't like being left without a partner.

So there were two outcasts whom nobody wanted, and worst of all, to each the crowning indignity, they would be made to walk with each other.

Mrs Henrey counted the pairs of children. Julia was the last but one, pretending to be engrossed in a comic as she stood in the line, pretending desperately not to care.

'Put that rubbish away, Julia. Are you the last? Oh no, there's Nathan. Nathan, Julia will have to be your partner. Well come and stand by her, then. Come along, we haven't all day, she won't bite you.'

Nathan, who had been sulking by the windows, kicking resentfully at the pipes behind him, shuffled unwillingly forward. He cast one look of murderous hate at Mrs Henrey, and another at Julia. He came to rest a couple of paces behind his allotted partner.

'Stand *with* her,' Mrs Henrey insisted, exasperated by the heat and by Nathan.

Nathan moved forward a step. 'Rat-bag!' he hissed at Julia.

Julia hitched away, sniffed and blinked and turned her back. 'Do I have to walk with him, Mrs Henrey? Can't I walk with you? Can't I be your partner?'

'No, Julia, you can't walk with me. Nathan is your partner. Denise and Sharon, Sanjay and Paul, you go and get the rounders things. Meet us at the gate. Now come along, the rest of you.'

Outside, the sun beat down, bouncing heat off the hard playground and the brick walls surrounding it.

'It's too hot for rounders,' someone complained.

'It'll be cooler in the park,' said Mrs Henrey firmly.

The crocodile straggled up the road. Nathan lagged behind, disassociating himself from Julia. A tabby cat on a garden wall greeted him with a plaintive yowl, and Nathan stopped to stroke it. He liked cats. Cats were much nicer than people. The cat arched its back with pleasure and rubbed its head against his hand. Then it leaped off the wall and began weaving round his legs. The feel of its silky fur against his bare calves made Nathan happy, just for a moment. Then Mrs Henrey's sharp voice was cutting through his enjoyment, shouting at him to keep up with his

4

partner. The class had halted, to wait for him.

Mrs Henrey wasn't the sort of teacher you could muck about with. You couldn't play her up like you could some teachers. Nathan moved forward, scowling and scuffling his feet. The class moved on again.

Nathan trod on Julia's foot, hard, to punish her for being his partner. 'Ow!' said Julia – her foot really hurt.

'Not so much noise, Julia,' called Mrs Henrey from the front.

'Nathan kicked me,' Julia whined.

'I never,' said Nathan – and trod on Julia's foot again to punish her for telling, as well as for being his partner.

'He kicked me again,' Julia wailed.

'Walk properly, Nathan,' called Mrs Henrey, without looking back.

Nathan aimed a third kick at Julia, which she dodged. Then he ignored her again, seeing the prospect of more sport ahead. Paul and Sanjay were walking decorously just in front, carrying the rounders bats. Paul and Sanjay were the goody-goodies, Mrs Henrey's toadies. Nathan gave them a hard kick each, from behind, for being goody-goodies.

'Stop it, Nathan!'

'It wasn't me, it was Julia.'

'It was you,' said Sanjay. 'I saw you.'

'Less noise back there,' called Mrs Henrey.

Nathan went to kick Sanjay again, to punish him for seeing, but Paul was too quick for him. Forgetting to be a goody-goody, Paul swung a well-aimed punch at the side of Nathan's head, to which Nathan responded with fury. Lovely, to be so angry – a good fight was just what he felt like. So Nathan went at Paul in earnest, head down to protect his glasses, punching and flailing and kicking, like a savage little animal.

'Stop it!' thundered Mrs Henrey, marching towards the

5

combatants like an avenging angel. 'Stop it, both of you. How dare you fight in the street! Paul, I'm surprised at you. I really thought I could trust you to be at the back.'

'Nathan started it,' said Julia, virtuously.

'I didn't ask you,' Mrs Henrey snapped. A trickle of sweat ran down the side of her fat nose. Her dress was damp, and sticking here and there already. She began to wonder if going to the park had been such a good idea after all. 'Nathan, come and walk with me at the front. Julia, you'll have to walk by yourself. Now – any more trouble from anyone and we'll go straight back to the classroom and do . . . er . . . *spelling*!'

Nathan grinned, maliciously. There was nothing he would have liked better than to go back to school to do spelling. He excelled at it. It was one of his best lessons. His other best lessons were reading, and writing stories. Nathan considered in his mind how he could do something so awful that Mrs Henrey would take them all back to school to do spelling. He didn't care about the others. Let them miss their silly rounders.

But while Nathan considered, the opportunity passed, and soon they had arrived at the park – shady in part, and green to be sure, but hateful to Nathan because of the horrible game he was going to be forced to play. The cruel, humiliating game of rounders, with the hard ball that would come at him out of nowhere. Even with his glasses, things like balls coming were hard to see. So he would miss it, and keep on missing, to the accompaniment of loud jeers from everyone else, from all those who were good at rounders. There was no one who played rounders worse than Nathan. Except Julia, of course.

'Sharon and Paul be captains, and pick up teams,' said Mrs Henrey.

'My foot hurts,' said Julia, with sudden inspiration. 'I can't run on it.'

'Run on the other one,' said Mrs Henrey, unkindly.

The choosing of teams proceeded, without pity. First the good players were chosen, then the average ones, then the downright bad ones. Finally, inevitably, the two unwanted ones were left – shamefaced and embarrassed, pretending not to mind.

'We'll have Nathan,' said Paul, the recent fight totally forgotten.

'All right, we'll have Julia,' said Sharon.

Sharon was a muscular black girl, good at games and immensely popular. Julia would have liked above all things to be friends with Sharon. She might as well have aspired to friendship with the Queen.

The outcasts mooched sullenly forward to their respective teams. Paul's team was batting first, which meant that Julia was on the fielding side. She positioned herself, unasked, at the far edge of the pitch, as far from the ball as possible. No one challenged her for choosing her own position. No one cared where Julia stood. There was a lot of activity round the bases, a lot of shouting and exhortation and jumping up and down, but it was all a long way away. Julia lapsed into a vague daydream about Mrs Henrey asking her to stay behind to clear up after school.

Suddenly everything was happening. There were cries of 'ooh', and there was the dreaded ball hurtling towards Julia off the end of someone's bat. 'Catch!' Julia heard. Willing, but without hope, she stumbled towards the flying ball. She missed it of course; worse than that her foot caught a tuft of grass and she fell headlong. Groans of derision stung her ears. 'Get it, throw it, here,' her team was still calling.

Her knees smarting and stained with grass, Julia scrambled to her feet. She found the ball and threw it blindly, clumsily, ineffectively. It fell short, as she knew it would, and as the others jeered she turned her back on them, swallowing fiercely, the tears burning her eyes. Would this horrible afternoon never be over?

It was Nathan's turn to bat. With a heart full of hate for

7

rounders, he swiped mechanically as the ball came towards him. He didn't expect to hit it, he hoped only that it would not strike him in the face and break his glasses, for the third time that term. As the ball flew past his elbow Nathan started to run. Not very fast. With any luck he would be out at first base and then he could sit on the cool grass, under the big tree, for the rest of the innings. He reached first base and someone was still calling, 'Run!' Nathan was confused. Where was the ball? Even though he hadn't hit it, he could still make half a rounder if he could get all round. He ran again. 'Not you, Nathan!' a dozen voices shouted – but it was too late. Nathan reached second base but Jennifer, who was just in front of him, and had been forced to run because he did, was stumped at third.

'Jennifer's out,' said Mrs Henrey.

'I think there's a new rule,' said someone hopefully.

But Mrs Henrey did not know about the new rule. 'Jennifer's out,' she decreed.

'You made me out,' Jennifer accused Nathan, furiously.

'I never,' said Nathan. He had though, and he knew it.

'Yes you did,' said Paul.

'You did, Nathan,' said three or four others together. Jennifer was the best batter on Paul's side. They were a hostile crowd, penning Nathan in.

Angry with himself, and needing to lash out, Nathan hit the nearest one who happened to be another black boy, a tough character called Wayne. Wayne hit him back and Nathan's glasses went flying. Nathan lost his temper entirely. Rage lending strength to his small arms, he punched Wayne to the ground, and went on hitting him even after Wayne's nose started bleeding. Mrs Henrey had to get Paul and Sanjay to help her separate them.

'Just look at you both,' said Mrs Henrey. 'Who started it this time?'

Everyone agreed that the culprit was Nathan.

'Right,' said Mrs Henrey. 'We're going back to school this minute. And, Nathan, you're going straight to Mr Barlowe. I've had enough of you and your temper. Line up, everyone.'

There were lamentations and pleadings, of course, but Mrs Henrey was adamant. Grumbling its resentment, the class assembled in twos once more. Nathan retrieved his glasses, which fortunately were not broken, and dragged to the back of the line.

Julia was relieved to be going back to school, but she found she was not yet forgiven for her own mistake. 'Why don't you throw harder?' Sharon hissed at her as they stood in the line. 'You throw like a baby!' Sharon was angry really because they were going back to school, but the boys would deal with Nathan, whose fault it was, and Sharon wanted someone to get at too. 'Why don't you throw proper?' she taunted Julia.

'Don't want to,' said Julia, pouting her lips and tossing back her stringy plaits. She noticed that Sharon was chewing gum, which was strictly forbidden. She sidled up to Mrs Henrey and whispered in her ear, 'Sharon's chewing gum.'

'Take that rubbish out of your mouth, Sharon,' said Mrs Henrey, crossly. 'And don't tell tales, Julia.'

Why couldn't she remember that Mrs Henrey didn't like tales, Julia wondered bitterly? And why did she tell tales on Sharon, when really she only wanted Sharon to be her friend? It seemed she couldn't help herself. Telling tales was the only way Julia had of getting back at the others when they hurt her.

The unhappy procession moved down the road. Nathan, once more supposed to be walking with Julia, trailed a long way behind, scuffling his feet and muttering darkly. Mrs Henrey halted the line to wait for him to catch up. Paul, his saintly image again forsaken, turned and mouthed at him as he approached. 'We're going to get you, Nathan, after school.' Wayne, his face still smeared with blood from the fight, turned to add his bit. 'Yeah, we're all going to get you. You made us lose our rounders.'

Nathan knew they meant it. He was no coward, but all of them together could do a lot of damage. He brooded. The procession was nearing the turning to a side road. Nathan saw his chance and took it. Without warning, he bolted round the corner, and the next anyone saw was the back of his small figure, head forward, feet pounding, rapidly disappearing down the side road and round the next turning.

'Nathan's gone, Mrs Henrey,' shouted Julia, again forgetting not to tell tales. But for once she had done the right thing, and the others supported her. 'He's gone, Miss!' 'Shall we catch him for you?' 'I can run fast, shall I go?'

'Leave him,' said Mrs Henrey, grimly. 'Mr Barlowe can deal with him in the morning. And if I have one more sound out of any of you, there'll be no playtime for a week.'

She didn't mean *that*, everyone knew quite well. Mrs Henrey was strict, and she often got cross, but she was quite kind really. She was just at the end of her tether now, after an exhausting day. Nevertheless, fractious with the heat and the disappointment and the boredom of the half-hour's silent reading which Mrs Henrey imposed on them, Class 8 was not feeling well disposed towards their teacher. Usually there were plenty of willing helpers ready to stay behind and tidy up after the bell, but today there were none. Everyone discovered they had pressing engagements elsewhere. Except Julia.

Mrs Henrey did not like Julia. She was clumsy and she was sneaky and Mrs Henrey usually discouraged her. But today she was grateful to have as much as one child, even Julia, to help put up the extra chairs and pick pieces of paper off the floor after everyone else had gone.

'Can I do anything else for you, Mrs Henrey?' Julia enquired anxiously, her eyes begging. 'Can I clean the board? Please let me clean the board.' She was enormously pleased that the day had ended so well. Mrs Henrey had actually let her help!

'Thank you, Julia. Yes, you can clean the board if you will.'

She *has* got a nice side, I suppose, Mrs Henrey thought. I really must try to be nicer to her. She hasn't got much going for her, poor soul. Mrs Henrey had long ago despaired of ever actually *teaching* Julia anything.

'Can I do your desk, Mrs Henrey? Can I tidy your desk for you?'

Mrs Henrey thought it might be less than wise to let Julia touch the papers on her desk. Julia was notoriously clumsy and accident-prone. 'That's all right, Julia,' she said. 'I can manage now, you go home. Thank you for your help.'

Mrs Henrey left the room, carrying a pile of reference books. Julia supposed she was returning them to the library, at the other end of the corridor. She looked again at Mrs Henrey's desk. It was in a terrible mess. There were papers everywhere, and someone had even left a jar of red paint with two brushes in it, right in the middle of the papers. Julia thought she could at least remove the red paint and carry it to the paint tray beside the sink, where it was supposed to be. She reached across the table from the front, and picked up the jar of paint. As she did so she noticed another mucky pot, this time with blue paint in it, standing on a ledge just behind Mrs Henrey's desk. She might as well take the two pots together, Julia thought.

In her eagerness, Julia did not notice the leg of Mrs

Henrey's chair, cunningly protruding from behind the large desk. The red paint in one hand, she lunged forward to pick up the blue. She stumbled against the chair leg and tripped, bruising her arm painfully against the ledge, and her chest against the back of Mrs Henrey's chair.

The red paint leapt in a stream from Julia's extended hand.

The paint poured over the papers on the desk. It poured over Mrs Henrey's beautiful white cardigan, draped over the chair. It splashed over Julia's dress and spattered her face and her hair. It dripped on the floor, it was everywhere.

Horrified, too stunned to cry, Julia regarded the disaster for a moment, then ran from the classroom. She clattered on ungainly feet down the stone staircase, through the vestibule and the open school door into the playground. Shoulders hunched forward, she began to run heavily, up the road towards her home.

The tears broke as she turned the corner into her own street. They coursed down her long pale cheeks; she was racked by great ugly sobs. By the time Julia turned into the hallway of the house where she lived, she was bawling loudly.

Julia lived on the upper floor of a converted terrace house. As she lamented her way up the stairs, her mother came on to the landing, to see what the commotion was all about.

'Gawd, whatever's the matter with you?' said Julia's mother, surveying her unattractive daughter with some distaste.

Mrs Winter was very smart. Her dyed blonde hair was beautifully arranged, her well-proportioned figure immaculately clothed, and her face, pretty in a hard sort of way, carefully made up. Julia, plain and unprepossessing, had turned out a great disappointment to her.

'For gawd's sake stop that noise,' said Mrs Winter unsympathetically. 'Nobody's dead, are they? What's up then?' She did not wait for a reply because she had just noticed the red paint on Julia's dress. Her voice rose to a screech. 'Look at your clothes, you great nuisance! What have you been doing to get in that mess?'

'It was an accident,' wailed Julia.

The blotchy tear-stained face, mouth open and downturned in misery, did nothing to soften her mother's anger.

'Accident! You're always having accidents. Do you think I've got nothing better to do than clear up after you all the time? I've got to work, you know. This is supposed to be my day off. Oh, get in that bathroom and wash yourself. And put that dress to soak. More ironing for me again, I suppose. You'll wear me out, Julia, and that's the truth.'

'You don't care about me. You don't care nothing about me. You've never cared about me,' Julia screamed at her mother.

She banged the bathroom door behind her. She had stopped crying now, and in her heart was something very like despair. Loneliness she was used to, but never before today had she felt more bitterly the need for someone to confide her troubles to. If only she had a sister. Or a grandma. Or a kind dad at home like other people. But Julia's gran had died years ago, and her dad had left home when she was a baby, so she didn't even remember him. Now there was only Julia and her mother, together in a small converted flat, getting on each other's nerves.

Julia dropped the stained dress on the bathroom floor, deliberately not putting it to soak as she had been asked. She's so horrible to me *she* can do it, Julia thought viciously.

If Julia was wretched at having no sisters, Nathan's problem

13

was exactly the opposite. He had, in his opinion, far too many. There were four of them, all older than he was, and they filled the house with their clothes and their loud voices and even louder music. There was an older brother who didn't live at home, and when he came to visit things were worse, because the older brother quarrelled with the sisters and with his mother and father, and there was a lot of shouting and angry scenes. Sometimes the sisters quarrelled with each other as well. And as though all that were not enough, there were two younger brothers who took up space in the bedroom, and disturbed Nathan's peace. Nathan valued peace, when he could get it, almost more than anything.

On this day, after he had run away from the class, Nathan had not gone home; he had gone to his secret place. No one knew where Nathan's secret place was, but he had been going there regularly for some weeks now.

So Nathan came home late, and no one asked him where he had been, because there were always so many people coming and going in his house it was easy not to notice if one person was missing. Nathan pushed his way through the crowd of sisters, and sisters' friends, and his own little brothers. His mother was in the kitchen, he supposed, cooking something for the evening meal, which they would have when his dad got in from wherever he spent his unemployed days. Nathan went into his bedroom and found it blessedly empty. He looked for his library book, and curled up on his side of the bed for a quiet read. Good job his glasses hadn't got broken when Wayne knocked them off. He couldn't see very well to read without them and reading was his joy – what he liked doing best in the whole world.

The book Nathan was reading was *Treasure Island*. He didn't understand it all, and some of the words were too hard for him. But he could lose himself in the magic of the story – he could *be* there, on the ship, sharing all the adven-

14

tures of Jim Hawkins, the fear and excitement that Jim felt.

Nathan was happy.

Later, in the night, the weather broke. The glaring hot day had given way to a leaden, sultry evening. The first rumblings of thunder could be heard at about midnight, and an hour later the storm was overhead, crashing through the room where Nathan lay in bed with his brother Gary. The air around the boys shattered itself and splintered into great terrifying cracks. Gary woke, sobbing with fright, and clutched at Nathan for comfort. Nathan pushed him away. 'Shut up,' he said roughly. 'The thunder ain't going to hurt you. Go back to sleep.'

'I'm scared, I'm scared,' Gary whimpered.

Nathan kicked him for being scared. He thought, with an almost unbearable longing, of the time that would surely come one day, when he would have a bed all to himself. A *room* all to himself.

The storm passed over. The street slept.

2

The day of the money

Morning came, cool and drizzly. Julia, who had slept badly, got dressed as slowly as possible, wondering what excuse she could make for not going to school.

'Hurry up, lazy,' her mother called. 'You're going to be late!'

Julia came slowly into the kitchen. Her mother was still in her dressing gown, her hair uncombed. Julia's mother looked quite different without her make-up.

'I got a headache,' Julia whimpered. Actually, she didn't look very well.

'Hard luck,' said her mother. 'Get on with your breakfast anyway, and get to school. I'm not having you mooching about the house all day, making extra work for me.'

'I'll do the washing up,' Julia offered. There was a fair accumulation of it waiting to be done.

'Ha-ha! I've heard that one before. No, my lady, you'll go to *school*,' said her mother. 'Oh come on, cheer up. Eat some breakfast and you'll feel better.'

Julia ate her cereal, found her plastic mac, and began to walk down the road, her steps dragging. She had no idea where she was going, but one thing was quite certain – she was *not* going to school. Mrs Henrey's displeasure over the spilled paint was a prospect too terrible to contemplate. She would probably never go back to school again, Julia thought.

She was cold, and her hair was getting wet. The plastic mac had no hood, and Julia had forgotten to put a cardigan on over her thin summer dress. She turned into another road, so that her mother on her way to work wouldn't catch her not going to school. She stood under a tree for shelter, and wondered what to do next.

Since it was already late, there were not many children about, and those that were scurrying urgently to get to their classes before the register took no notice of Julia. Miserable and helpless, Julia leaned against her tree, fighting back the tears. She had never played truant before. Suddenly she noticed a small figure coming down the road. Another child, but not hurrying this time. Coming slowly, feet scuffling, spinning out the time. Julia recognized Nathan long before he recognized her, and she went round the other side of the tree, turning her back, hoping he wouldn't see her at all.

It was actually the fact that she was hiding that drew Nathan's attention. Nathan had no interest in Julia as a person, but this was odd behaviour, and he was mildly curious. He stopped. It was hard to see, because the rain on his glasses distorted everything. There was no doubt who it was though, lurking behind the tree. Stupid Julia Winter. Nathan stepped silently up behind her, and shouted in her ear. 'BOO!'

Her nerves already tense, Julia yelped with fright, and turned on Nathan angrily.

'What you do that for?'

Nathan grinned. I made her jump all right, he thought with satisfaction. 'Just wanted to. You bunking off then?'

17

'No.' Julia tossed her head and pouted her lips. Then, 'Yeah,' she admitted, miserably.

'I am too,' said Nathan – and regretted it immediately. He must be mad, confiding in this stupid girl, the dunce of Class 8. Then he decided to make the best of a bad job. There might be amusement in it, something to make the long day go quicker. The long day without a book, without anything to read. He had forgotten to bring *Treasure Island*, and he couldn't go back for it now.

'What you doing here then?' he asked Julia.

'Hiding, of course, what's it look like?'

'Well you can't stay in the street.'

'Why not?'

'Don't you know *nothing*?' said Nathan, contemptuously. 'They come out looking for you after Assembly. Mrs Peters – the Welfare Assistant – 'comes out in her car, and she goes all round the streets looking. We got to hide properly.'

'Where?'

'I know a place.' Again, Nathan half regretted what he had said. 'You got to promise not to tell, though.'

'A secret?'

'Yeah – it's a secret place. You got to promise not to tell.'

Julia gaped at him. She had never been asked to share a secret before, and she was enormously flattered that someone was asking her now – even if it *was* only horrible Nathan Browne, whom nobody liked either.

'I promise,' she said, trying to sound casual.

'Come on then, Rat-bag.'

Dumbly, Julia followed; round the corner, and into the next street. A derelict house, the garden full of weeds, and the windows long since smashed and splintered, defaced the otherwise neatly kept terrace. A train rumbled past, somewhere behind the row of houses. 'It's here,' said Nathan. 'In here.'

Julia was disappointed. 'That's not a secret place,' she objected. 'Everyone knows *that* house is empty.'

'Nobody knows I go there though,' said Nathan. 'It's *my* secret den. Wait a minute, what you doing?' Julia had made to take a step through the weeds, but Nathan stopped her. 'We got to make sure nobody sees us going in.'

He made a great performance of making sure. First, he paraded nonchalantly backwards and forwards, looking everywhere but at the house. There was a woman with a shopping basket at the end of the road, but too far away to count. Then the windows of the nearby houses had to be studied. 'See if anybody's looking out,' Nathan instructed Julia. He spoke in a conspiratorial whisper, and Julia began to enjoy herself very much. 'Nobody's looking,' she assured him, entering into the spirit of it.

'Right – now!' Nathan hissed, making a dive for the half-open door of the empty house. Julia followed. The two children stood together in the fusty passage way, smelling of damp and rotting wood. The small black boy with the glowering face and the poor eyesight, and the gawky white girl with a stoop. They looked at one another warily, mistrustfully. Then without a word, Nathan plunged deeper into the recesses of his secret den, Julia creeping at his heels.

They sat on bare boards, hardly warmer than outside, but dry at least. Another train went past, louder now, shaking the building with vibrations.

'If you really want to know,' said Nathan, 'it probably isn't just *my* den. It's probably a pirate's den as well.' His head was so full of *Treasure Island* just at the moment that he dreamed of pirates all the time.

'Don't be silly,' said Julia. 'Pirates are by the sea. There ain't no seaside here.'

'There's the river,' said Nathan, unwilling to relinquish his dream.

19

'What river?'

'You know, where the Houses of Parliament is.'

'Oh, *that* river.'

Julia had been to Westminster Pier once, last summer or perhaps the summer before. But it had taken so long to get there by public transport that she hardly connected the River Thames with her own home area. It was actually about four miles away.

'Come on, come on, come on,' said Nathan suddenly, in a different voice. For a moment, Julia thought he was talking to her. He had gone mad, perhaps. Then she saw the round eyes, gleaming in the dim light, as a shaggy black cat crept out of the shadows and into the children's view.

'Come on, come on, come on, I got something for you.' Out of his pocket, Nathan produced a torn plastic bag, and out of the bag some scraps of food – a piece of bacon, some cheese, a lump of gristly meat saved from last night's supper. He held out the bacon, and the cat stepped warily forward, but would not take the food from his hand. It stood two paces away, its gaze intent, quivering with longing. Half one ear was missing, and the nearest eye totally closed.

'He's really wild, this one,' Nathan explained. 'He don't trust no one.'

He placed the bacon on the floorboards and shuffled back a few feet. The cat sprang to the food as if it had not had a square meal for months, as indeed it probably had not.

'I call this one Sooty,' said Nathan. 'There's another one somewhere. Tiger, Tiger, come on Tiger!'

A second cat appeared, in no better condition than the first, but not nearly so scared. This one came right up to Nathan, mewed a greeting and took the lump of meat from his hand. Nathan divided the cheese between the two cats and, fed, the one with the ginger stripes allowed him to stroke its head. Its purrs echoed through the empty room.

'Took me weeks to tame him, but I eventually done it,' said Nathan proudly.

'Wish I had a cat,' said Julia. 'Would he let me touch him?'

'Shouldn't think so,' said Nathan. 'You could try. Mind he don't scratch!'

Julia stretched her hand out hesitantly. The cat eyed her with suspicion, but submitted to her caress. Nathan regarded her with the faint beginnings of respect, but he was none too pleased. 'Definitely peculiar,' he muttered. 'He's only supposed to like me.'

The children lapsed into silence for a while.

'Why you bunking off then?' said Nathan, suddenly.

'None of your business,' said Julia. 'Anyway, Nathan, *you're* in trouble. You got to go to Mr Barlowe, Mrs Henrey said.'

'She'll forget,' said Nathan, not worried.

Another long pause.

'What's this place got to do with pirates?' asked Julia, who had been thinking about it. 'Why d'you think pirates come here?'

He didn't *really* think they did. He just thought it would be nice if they did. It was an exciting idea that he could pretend to believe in when he was alone.

'I find things,' he said, mysteriously. 'I found a pipe one time, and a old shoe.' Indeed, piles of similar rubbish were littered all over the room, in between the cobwebs.

'Probably a tramp,' said Julia.

Probably she was right, but much more interesting to think it was pirates. 'I found a paper once with some funny marks on it. Most likely a message in code.'

Julia thought for a long moment. 'Don't pirates bury treasure?' she asked at last. 'Perhaps they've buried some treasure here.'

'Nah – they always bury it on a island, with a cross on the map to show where it is.'

'Don't they never bury it in a house? Shall we look and see? Shall we, Nathan?'

'Nah,' he said.

'Why not? We *might* find something. Where would they put it if they did?'

How stupid she was! She didn't understand it was a game, she thought it was real.

'Where do you think they'd put it, Nathan?'

'Under the floorboards, I suppose,' said Nathan reluctantly. It was silly to think the pirates were real, but of course, things that were buried in houses were always under the floorboards. Everyone knew *that*.

Half-heartedly, Nathan tried to prise up a board in the corner of the room which looked loose.

Julia frowned. 'Not there,' she said.

'Why not?'

'It's all thick dirt. Nobody's moved that lately.'

Nathan looked at Julia sharply. She couldn't be that stupid after all. 'Let's go in the other rooms,' he suggested.

They wandered through the house, peering carefully. It *was* only a game, of course – but on the other hand, you never knew. . . .

'There!' said Julia.

Nathan saw immediately what she meant. A piece of floorboard with fresh scratches on it, and the dirt scraped over to cover up the scratches. The board was quite loose, it came up easily in Nathan's hands. The hole revealed was empty. 'There's nothing there,' he said, disappointed but hardly surprised.

Julia lay full length on the dirty floor and thrust her arm into the space beyond where the piece of board had been pulled up.

'I got something,' she exclaimed, excitedly.

'What is it?'

'I dunno. Here it is.' She withdrew her arm, and in her

22

hand was a large brown envelope. The envelope was stiff and new, and hardly dirty at all. Julia was quite dizzy with triumph. Without speaking, she lifted the flap off the envelope and tipped its contents on to the floor. *Money!* Lots of real paper money, all in twenty pound notes. The two children stared at what they had found.

'Look at that,' Nathan breathed, his eyes round with incredulity. 'Just look at that!'

'You was right, Nathan,' Julia whispered in awe. 'It *was* pirates.'

Nathan shook his head. He was still struggling to grasp the reality of what had happened. This stupendous discovery that in one moment had put all the previous highlights of his life in the shade. 'It ain't pirates though,' he said. 'It ain't pirates.'

'But we found the money they buried.'

'It's the wrong sort of money for pirates,' said Nathan. 'Pirates' money is all gold coins. This is ordinary money.'

'Who put it there then?'

'I dunno. Robbers I suppose.'

'Where they get it from?'

'How should I know? Burglared a house most likely.'

'What did they put it under the floor for?'

'So the police won't find it in *their* house of course!' What was the matter with her – stupid thing? Didn't she ever watch telly?

'We found it, didn't we, Nathan! We found all that money! I can't believe we really found all that money, can you? How much is it?'

'I dunno. Hundreds of pounds anyway. Thousands, probably.'

'Thousands of pounds! How did the robbers get in here, Nathan? Suppose somebody saw them coming in?'

'You don't know nothing, man,' said Nathan, irritably. 'They come in the back of course, over the railway. It's per-

23

fect. I bet lots of these houses been burglared like that.'

The children's eyes, and their thoughts, went back to the money, lying between them, spilled over the dusty floor. Over the quivering excitement of having found it, an unspoken question hovered. Nathan prodded the money with his foot. Julia chewed the end of her pigtail.

'Nathan,' said Julia at last, 'is it *our* money?'

'Course. We found it, didn't we!'

'Do you think we ought to take it to the police?'

'I ain't taking my half to the police. You can do what you like with your half.'

'Oh.'

'What you going to do then, with your half?'

'Keep it, I suppose,' said Julia. 'Same as you.'

'Shall we share it out then?'

'Half for you and half for me?'

'Suppose that's fair. You found it, but it's my secret place.'

'Yeah, all right, that's fair.'

Dividing the money was easy. They dealt the notes like a pack of cards, and there were sixty-five each.

'We're rich now, aren't we!' said Julia. 'I can't believe I'm rich.'

'We mustn't tell nobody though.'

'Course not.'

'What you going to spend yours on, Julia?'

'I dunno yet.' Actually she was beginning to have an idea, but the idea was a private thing at this stage.

Nathan's plans were also private. He was thinking in terms of saving his half until he was grown up, and then buying a house. There would surely be enough money for that; there might even be some left over. He would put his notes in a very safe place meanwhile. And that thought raised another question.

'Julia – where we going to keep our money?'

Julia considered. 'Couldn't we keep it here? In another part of the house?'

'No, we couldn't! That's one thing we certainly couldn't do!'

'Why not?'

'Think, stupid! The one that put it here is going to come back for it, isn't he.'

'So. He won't find it in the place, it'll be gone. We could hide it again, so he won't know where to look.'

'But he might find us. He might come back any time and find us. Or somebody might see us going in, and tell.'

'Oh yeah – then he'd take it away from us again.'

'Then he'd *kill* us, probably.'

'Really? Really kill us?' Julia's pale eyes were round with horror and fright. 'When's he coming back, Nathan? Is he coming back now?'

'I dunno, do I?'

'Perhaps he's coming right this minute. Perhaps he's coming over the railway line now. Let's go, Nathan, before he comes to kill us.'

'Wait a minute, we got to think first.' But Julia's fear was infectious, and Nathan was already feeling uneasy and jumpy. 'All right, we'll go. Put your money safe first though. You can have the envelope. Have you got a pocket?'

The plastic mac had no pocket, neither had the cotton dress beneath it. 'Turn round, Nathan, don't look,' said Julia, primly. She stuffed the envelope with the money in it inside her knickers, where it felt scratchy but reassuring, against her skin.

Nathan wrapped his in the plastic bag which had contained the cats' food. The bag was a bit mucky and greasy inside, but no matter. Folded over, the parcel was small enough to slip into the lining of his anorak, through the hole in his pocket which had been there for almost as long as he had had the coat.

25

'Hurry up,' said Julia, hopping up and down with fear and impatience. 'Let's go quick. Let's go to the park. There's shelters there.'

'All right.' Nathan would never have thought of that. It was obvious really, but he had to admit he would never have thought of it. Clearly Julia was better at some things than he was. Stupid old Rat-bag she might be, but she did have good ideas sometimes. They ran to the park, and huddled in the shelter opposite the playground, wondering what to do next.

'Are you going to hide your money in your house?' said Nathan.

'I dunno. I'm scared my mum might find it.'

'Mine might too. Where can we hide it then?'

'Somewhere in the park?'

'Where though?'

Julia gazed around her. 'We could bury it.'

'The gardener might dig it up.'

'Not the grass bit. He don't dig the grass up.'

Nathan thought, scowling with the effort. 'He'll see where we hid it though. It'll show – like the board in the house.'

'Not if we cover it up. We can put the grass back, and cover it over with stuff. Under a tree would be best, with all those leaves and twigs.'

'We haven't got nothing to dig with.'

'A stone would do.'

Behind the shelter they found a large flat stone, and a piece of wood. Something was troubling Nathan. 'I won't look which tree you put yours under, if you don't look which tree I have.'

'All right.' Julia understood; Nathan didn't trust her. That suited her; she didn't trust him either. 'Who's going first?'

'Me. Hide your eyes and don't look till I get back.'

26

'Hurry up, then.' Julia closed her eyes and drifted away into a warm dream. Already she was seeing the finding of the money as the turning point of her life, the answer to all her problems. Next week her new life would begin, and she could hardly wait.

Nathan took the piece of wood and ran behind the shelter, flitting from tree to tree in the rain, looking for a suitable place to hide his money. He glanced back at the shelter to make sure Julia wasn't peeping, and then began to dig. The ground was harder than he expected, and he couldn't make a very deep hole, but fortunately the package was not very large. He took out one twenty pound note first, and put it into the lining of his pocket. Then he filled in the hole, and covered the evidence with leaves and twigs. The rain would soon wash away any remaining traces, and if anyone did notice, they would think a dog had done it. Nathan's money was safe.

Julia's task was even easier. Looking for a tree, she was lucky enough to find one with a hollow trunk. Her sharp eyes spotted the smallish hole, and when she thrust her hand through, she discovered there was a lovely big space inside. Standing behind the tree, she took the money out of her knickers. She hesitated, took out one twenty pound note, and put the rest of the money back in the envelope. Then she dropped the little package into the hole in the tree, and put the twenty pound note back into her knickers.

'I'm hungry,' said Nathan, when Julia got back to the shelter.

It occurred to Julia that she was hungry also, and missing the prospect of school dinners – which, if not exactly exciting, were at least always filling. 'We could buy something,' she suggested.

'Did you keep any of your money?'

'Yeah, did you?'

'Yeah, I kept one of them notes.'

'We better use yours,' said Julia.

'What's wrong with yours?'

'Mine's in my knickers, and I can't get it easy. Besides, there'll be a lot of change and I got nowhere to keep it today.'

'All right, but you got to pay me back. I ain't paying for your chips.'

'I'll pay you back when I change my note tomorrow.'

'What you going to buy tomorrow?'

'Never you mind.'

'Shall we go to Tony's Chippie?'

'Yeah, but—'

'What?'

'I'm *thinking*,' said Julia.

'What about?'

'The twenty pound note. Tony's going to wonder where we got it from.'

She was right, of course. 'What shall we do then?' said Nathan.

'I'm *thinking*, aren't I . . . I know, you stay outside and I'll go in by myself and say it's for my mum.'

Nathan scowled, and began to lag. He kicked viciously at a stone in his path. He muttered under his breath, and kicked the stone again.

'What's the matter?' said Julia.

'Nothing.'

'What you cross about?'

'Nothing, I said.' Nathan kicked the stone again, and wished he could kick Julia. He would like to kick her for being better at some things than he was. Resentment boiled up inside him. He didn't want this ungainly, bent lamp-post in his adventure. He wanted it all to himself, he didn't want to have to share any part of it.

28

'Rat-bag,' he mouthed at Julia's back, as they made their way to the chip shop.

He knew, all the same, that he couldn't do without her.

3

Found out!

The Day of the Money was Friday. By Monday morning
Julia was hoping Mrs Henrey had forgotten about the
spilled paint. In fact, Mrs Henrey had not forgotten, but she
had decided to be charitable. 'Are you feeling better, Julia?'
she enquired, with only a hint of sarcasm in her voice.

'Yes thank you, Mrs Henrey,' said Julia gratefully. 'I had a
bad headache,' she added, her pale eyes beseeching accept-
ance of the fib.

But Mrs Henrey had, in any case, lost interest in Julia and
her troubles. She had likewise lost interest in the abscond-
ing of Nathan, on the way back from the park. This morning, Mrs Henrey was only interested in teaching the class
how to do percentages. Next term they would all be going to
their secondary schools, and Mrs Henrey did not want
them to go, not knowing how to do percentages. Julia, of
course, was quite incapable of learning how to do percentages – but, mercifully, Monday was the day Julia was taken
off Mrs Henrey's hands for an hour.

'Don't forget your Class, Julia. Miss Payton'll be waiting

for you in the library.'

Julia flushed with shame, and shambled to her feet. On these occasions she always felt that everyone was looking at her, laughing at her because she couldn't read properly. Julia hated the Remedial Reading lessons – but today there was a crumb of consolation. Today she had a Secret – a lovely warm Secret, the substance of which lay hidden in her desk, wrapped in a plastic bag.

At playtime, Julia retrieved the bag and carried it self-consciously into the playground. She stood awkwardly in the middle of the yard, not knowing where to begin. Now that the moment had come she felt shy, uncertain. Jennifer rushed past, and pursuing her was Sharon. They were playing some game. Julia dived into her bag, and produced one of the dozen or so small objects that lay within. She stepped into Sharon's path and held out her offering. 'Want one?' she heard herself say.

Sharon stopped in her tracks and looked at the Mars bar in Julia's hand. 'For me?' she asked, suspiciously.

'Yeah – you can have it if you like. I got plenty.'

Sharon peered into Julia's plastic bag and saw that she had, indeed, a whole heap of Mars bars.

'Where you get all that from?'

Julia was ready for that one. 'It was my birthday on Saturday. My uncle gave me some money.' Both the uncle and the birthday were, of course, fictitious.

The girls crowded round Sharon, who repeated Julia's story between bites of Mars bar. Natalie, a sharp-faced girl with her eye on the main chance, left the group and approached Julia quite brazenly.

'You had your birthday then?'

'Yeah, want one of these?'

'Thanks, Julia. I like Mars bars.'

Then Jennifer called, quite casually as though she was going to do it anyway, to know if Julia would like to join

31

their game. A minute later most of the girls in Class 8 were happily chewing on Julia's Mars bars.

Nathan, from his solitary position against the playground wall, watched all this with a sneer of contempt twisting his face. Silly cow, he thought. Fancy wasting her money on that lot! They won't want her tomorrow – just let her see if they do! Tomorrow they'll be mean to her again.

But next day there were more presents. This time Julia had really splashed out, and bought little packets of felt-tip pens. The girls were delighted. Again, Julia was allowed to join in their game at playtime and what was more, when it was time for PE, Julia had a partner. True, her partner was only Natalie, and Natalie's motives were something along the lines of, 'The less she spends on the others the more she'll have to spend on me, so I'll get in and be best friends quick.' Julia was well aware that Natalie's arm through hers was no more than cupboard love, but it was a start. Julia had not had a partner in PE since anyone could remember.

Nathan observed Julia's success with mixed feelings. He did not want to spend his money on other people, he wanted to keep it all for himself. Furthermore, he had no particular interest in having a friend. Having friends was rubbish. It would be good to have a partner, of course. . . .

He held out, until the fourth day.

On the fourth day, Julia treated all the girls to a packet of chewing gum each, and gave Natalie 50p to spend on herself. Nathan also went shopping. He bought four packets of crisps on the way to school, and shared them with Paul, Wayne and Sanjay. The boys were totally astonished. Nathan never had money to spend, and he had never been known to *give* anything away in his life. Their astonishment, however, did not prevent them from accepting this sudden generosity.

Next day, Friday again, there were more presents. Nathan was now at the centre of a crowd of boys, and Julia was at the centre of a crowd of girls. Mrs Henrey noticed this altered state of affairs with increasing suspicion. Something was wrong. The two most unpopular children in the class suddenly the most in demand? There had to be a reason. Mrs Henrey decided to ask Pauline, a guileless child who would almost certainly tell the truth, whatever that might be. She detained her after morning school.

'I'm glad to see you've all decided to be nice to poor old Julia,' said Mrs Henrey.

'Oh, she gave us all presents,' said Pauline, innocently.

'Really! You mean sweets and things?'

'Yeah – and felt-tips.'

'You mean *Julia* gave you all those coloured pens? You didn't buy them for yourselves?'

'No, Miss. Julia got money.'

'Really!' Mrs Henrey thought for a moment. 'Pauline – has Nathan got money as well, do you know?'

'I think so, Miss. I don't know. I think so.'

Mrs Henrey sighed. What a bore! Now she would have to investigate. Now there would be all the tedious business of probing and questioning and listening to strings of lies, and finally exposing these children in some miserable theft or other. Humiliating for the wretched children, and it would all take precious time. Time that Mrs Henrey would infinitely rather devote to teaching – which after all was what she was paid to do.

'Who's got money missing?' she enquired wearily in the Staff Room. But none of the other teachers were short. Even the Dinner Money totals were all correct that week.

'You're thinking of Julia Winter and Nathan Browne, I suppose,' said Miss Phillips, who taught Class 1. 'I noticed them flashing money around in the playground yesterday. I meant to mention it, but I forgot. Wonder where they got it from.'

'No clues at the moment,' said Mrs Henrey gloomily,

'but I shall obviously have to find out.'

She tackled Julia first thing that afternoon.

'I hear you've had some money to spend, Julia.'

Flushed with success, and happy, Julia was unworried at first. 'Yes Mrs Henrey, it was my birthday.'

'When was that?'

'Last Saturday.'

'But Julia, your birthday is in April, and this is June – nearly July.'

Julia's face fell. The first uneasy premonitions of disaster cast their shadow over her bright world. 'It was Saturday, Mrs Henrey.'

'No, Julia. You were eleven on – let's see now – the fifteenth of April. It says so in the register.'

'It must be wrong in the register.'

'I can easily ask your mother.'

Julia said nothing. What *could* she say?

'So where did you get all that money from?'

Julia bit her lips together. When you were in a tight corner, that was what you did. You closed your mouth up tight, and refused to give yourself away.

'Nathan's got money as well, Mrs Henrey,' Paul called out. 'He's got a lot money.'

'Yeah, he has,' a few other traitors agreed. The bandwaggon was clearly over; it was time to come down on the side of the angels.

'Nathan?' said Mrs Henrey.

Nathan did not answer, but the expression on his troubled face showed the confusion of feelings that were boiling up inside him. Hurt and rage chased each other round and round in his mind. Hurt that his new 'friends' should turn against him so soon; anger at Julia, because her judgement had been wrong.

Nathan and Julia had not spoken to one another all week, except for a brief moment when Julia repaid the money she

34

owed him. But Nathan had been watching Julia closely, as much as anything for a lead as to what it was safe to do. And now she had been proved mistaken, Nathan felt bitter and let down. Julia was supposed to be good at these things. What was the use of her, if she wasn't good at practical things, like how to spend money safely?

'Stand up, Nathan,' said Mrs Henrey.

Nathan stood.

'Where did you get *your* money from? *You* haven't had a birthday, have you. Your birthday isn't till August.'

Silence. Nathan's face was now a sullen mask.

'All right – how *much* money have you got?' The piggy hairs on Mrs Henrey's mole went up and down as she spoke. Nathan watched the hairs dumbly.

'I seen a five pound note,' Sanjay offered.

'Nathan?'

No answer, no response at all. Looking from one stubborn face to the other, Mrs Henrey decided she was unlikely to break either Julia or Nathan unaided. Could they be in something together, she wondered? It seemed improbable, but you never could tell. Mrs Henrey decided to refer the whole matter to the headmaster. She sent a message via Paul, asking Mr Barlowe if he could manage to spare a few moments to help sort out something important. Paul was only too happy to carry this request, and the whole class waited in the pleasurable anticipation of seeing someone else, not them, in trouble.

Mr Barlowe came, looking harassed and impatient. It was Friday afternoon, and he was looking forward to his weekend. There was already a large backlog of matters to be dealt with before he would be free to go home, and a new problem was the last thing he wanted. He came into Class 8 now, smoothing sparse hairs over a shiny dome, and jingling the keys at his waist as he always did when he was annoyed.

'Yes, Mrs Henrey?' Mr Barlowe had a high-pitched voice,

which went higher in times of stress. The rising pitch of Mr Barlowe's voice was a danger signal which the children of the school had learned to recognize. Julia and Nathan heard it now, and braced themselves for the attack.

'Julia and Nathan have money,' said Mrs Henrey, 'which they don't seem able to account for.'

'Oh dear,' said Mr Barlowe. He frowned at Nathan, and the keys at his waist went jangle, jangle. 'Come on now, boy, let's get it over. You've got too much money, now where did it come from?'

Silence.

'Nathan, I'm speaking to you. Now don't waste any more of my time, please.'

The gaze from Mr Barlowe's keen eyes was unnerving. Nathan opened his mouth, muttered something, and closed it again.

'Speak up, speak up, I didn't hear you.'

'I said I got it from my Post Office book,' said Nathan, wildly and quite rudely.

'You haven't got a Post Office book,' said Paul.

'Yes I have,' said Nathan, stung. He *had* had one once, a long time ago. 'You don't know what I got, you don't know nothing!'

'He hasn't got one,' said Sanjay, in an audible whisper.

Nathan lost his temper. 'I have then!' he snarled at Sanjay and hurled himself across the desks to get at his tormentor.

Mr Barlowe grabbed Nathan by the scruff of the neck and hauled him, kicking and struggling, out of the room. Mr Barlowe was a short man, but his arms were enormously strong. 'You can come too, Julia,' he called over his shoulder. 'We can sort your problem out at the same time.'

Her lips drawn into a pout, Julia slouched after Mr Barlowe and Nathan towards the office, along the corridor and down the stairs, frightened all the way.

Although Mr Barlowe had his funny ways, he was not a cruel man, and when he wasn't worried by having too many things to do, he could be quite wise. By the time the three of them had arrived at the office, he had controlled his annoyance at having his work interrupted, and decided how he was going to tackle this matter. He seated himself in his chair, because that was the position of greatest authority, and made the two suspects stand in front of him. Miserable and defiant, they faced him across the table.

'All right now,' said Mr Barlowe. His voice had returned to its normal pitch. It was kind now – gentle and reasonable. 'All right now, I'm going to ask you once more. You've both got more money than you're supposed to have. A lot more, I'm sure, or Mrs Henrey wouldn't be worried about it. Now you understand, you're intelligent children, that we have to know where the money comes from. You're going to have to tell the truth in the end, so you might as well tell it now . . . Julia?'

Mr Barlowe's voice was quite soothing. His face was almost smiling. Julia relaxed, just a little bit. Perhaps she could fool him, after all.

'My uncle gave it to me,' she tried.

'For your birthday?'

'No, not my birthday. Not really my birthday. Just a present.'

'How much money did he give you, Julia?'

Julia thought for a long moment. 'Five pounds,' she said at last, hoping that would be a reasonable amount to admit to.

'Five pounds! Lucky girl – and your mother let you spend all that? My goodness, when I was your age I should have been made to put most of it in the bank. How much *did* you spend, by the way?'

Julia worked it out slowly, calculating on her fingers. 'I think four pounds and a bit,' she said.

'I see. Did you bring a bag to school this morning?'

'A bag, Sir?'

'Yes, you know, a plastic bag or a carrier bag of some kind.'

'Yes.' Julia was wary now, her defences up again. But the bag was safe ground. She had no need to worry about the bag.

'Go and fetch it, please.'

'Yes, Sir.'

Julia toiled back up the stairs and along the corridor, to fetch the bag from her classroom.

'Now, what about you, Nathan. How much money did you have?'

Silence.

'I'm waiting.'

'Five pounds.' It was as good as anything. Mr Barlowe had apparently accepted that from Julia.

'Oh *you* had five pounds as well. Where did you get it from, Nathan?'

Nathan's mind was a blank. Try as he might, he could not concoct a suitable story to cover himself.

'Nathan, five pounds did not fall from the sky, did it? You must know where it came from. Now, either you tell me or I can ask your father to come and see me on Monday. Which is it to be?'

Nathan was much more afraid of his father than he was of Mr Barlowe. Mr Barlowe could scold, suspend, expel even. But he would not take off his belt and lay about Nathan's legs and backside. Given enough provocation his father, Nathan knew, would do just that.

'Well?'

He could try the one about the Post Office book again, but that hadn't gone down very well when he tried it before. 'My uncle gave it to me, didn't he,' said Nathan desperately.

'Oh *you've* got a kind uncle too! Fortunate lad, fortunate

lad. . . . Ah, here's Julia back again. Let's see what's in Julia's bag, shall we?'

A scarf, a few pencils, a packet of fruit chews and three bags of crisps.

'I see you don't intend to be hungry, Julia. Turn out your pockets please, Nathan.'

Nathan did so. The contents of his pockets were innocent, but his heart was sinking nevertheless.

'Now your shoes.'

Nathan took off his left shoe and stood lopsided, his eyes behind the thick lenses pleading hopelessly.

'The other one please.' Mr Barlowe's voice was purring.

There was no escape. Nathan took off his shoe, and inside were two five pound notes and some coins.

'Well now – that must be pretty uncomfortable to walk round on,' said Mr Barlowe. 'And now I think we'd better have a look at your desk, Julia. Come on, follow me.'

Inside Julia's desk, hidden in the corner under all her books, was one ten pound note, two one pound coins and some odds and ends of silver.

'That's a lot of change from five pounds,' observed Mr Barlowe. 'Come along back to the office. My word, you've both got some explaining to do.'

Once more, the children trailed disconsolately after the headmaster.

'*Where* did you say this money came from, Julia?'

Silence. Julia's mouth was a tight, stubborn line.

'Nathan?'

Silence.

'All right. I'll tell you what we'll do. You leave all this money with me over the weekend. I'll look after it for you – it'll be quite safe. Then on Monday we'll have your parents in. They'll be able to confirm that the money was a present, won't they? Won't they, Nathan?'

Nathan took a breath, seemed about to say something,

changed his mind and shrugged instead.

'Have *you* anything to tell me, Julia?'

Julia sniffed.

'Back to your class then.'

They went, their steps like lead. Julia glared at the stairs, and Nathan glared at Julia. 'Rat-bag,' he hissed, angrily.

'What you call me that for?'

'Because you are. It's all your fault we got caught. What you want to buy all them things for?'

'You done it too.'

'Yeah well . . . you done it first.'

'So?'

Nathan was being unfair, but at that moment Julia hardly cared. All she could see stretching ahead of her, away and away into the future, was emptiness and loss. For a brief moment she had known popularity. The money had bought popularity, and if all the money was to be taken away from her, she would probably never have a friend again. If only it might be possible to hold on to the money in the tree.

'I'm not going to tell about the rest,' she said emphatically. 'I'm not giving none of that back. I don't care how much they ask, I'm not telling.'

Nathan gave her a grudging nod of approval.

'I'm not telling neither,' he said.

Of course he wasn't going to tell. The money was for his house, where he would be able to live in splendid isolation one day. Well – perhaps not *complete* solitude. He'd probably invite people to come in sometimes, but they'd have to go away again when he said.

'What we going to say on Monday then?' said Julia, pausing at the top of the steps.

'I dunno. Could we say we won the Pools?'

'Nah, children ain't allowed to do the Pools. Wish Mr Barlowe wouldn't tell our mums.'

'Yeah, so do I wish that. What we going to say then?'

'We'll think. We'll tell each other Monday what we've thought.'

Julia worried all through the weekend. She moped about and wouldn't eat and got on her mother's nerves. It wasn't just the possible loss of the money that was worrying her. Dimly she was beginning to suspect that she and Nathan could be in a lot of trouble for keeping it anyway. A *lot* of trouble.

'For gawd's sake, what's the matter with you?' Mrs Winter complained. 'You look like a wet week.' She had a new boy-friend whom she wanted to impress, and a miserable daughter drooping about the place would be enough to put anybody off. Not that Julia was a particularly attractive sight at the best of times. 'How did I ever come to have a daughter like you?' Mrs Winter said impatiently.

'I didn't ask you to have me,' Julia stormed at her mother. 'I wish you never had me. I wish I was dead.'

'Don't talk so wicked,' said Julia's mother. 'Come on, let's see what's on telly. Might be something that'll give us both a good laugh.'

Away from school, Nathan was not over-worried. The weather was fine again, so he took *Treasure Island* to the park. He sat where he could watch his tree, and read and dreamed most of Saturday away.

Sitting in church on Sunday, he suddenly remembered his cats. That afternoon, full of guilt at having neglected them for so long, he raided his mother's kitchen for some scraps to feed them on. That Rat-bag Julia would be scared of meeting the robber, Nathan thought, but *he* wasn't scared. He was going to feed his cats no matter what. He climbed over the railway line and went in the back way, to prove he wasn't scared.

41

In the room where he and Julia had found the money, there was fresh havoc. Someone had ripped up the floorboards over a large area, leaving a great gaping hole. Someone had searched frantically – and gone away emptyhanded. They wouldn't be back now. They wouldn't ever use this house again.

Happily, Nathan fed his cats.

By Monday morning he had almost forgotten there was trouble to be faced.

4

In trouble

'What's this?' said Julia's mother, picking the brown envelope off the mat in the hall downstairs. She had been on her way to work, but she stopped to read the letter first. 'Julia!' she called shrilly to the upstairs flat, 'It's only from your school, Julia! They only want me to go and see them this morning! What you been doing, then?'

'Nothing,' said Julia, appearing at the head of the stairs. She was late for school, but that was the least of her worries.

'Yes you have, you've been up to something. Now I shall have to ask for an hour off work. And it better not take more than an hour, neither!'

Nathan's father and mother had both been invited, but since his father was the one out of work, it was more convenient for only him to go to the school. Nathan's father was not pleased.

'What you been doing wrong now?' he worried. It was not the first time Nathan's parents had been summoned to see Mr Barlowe.

'Nothing.'

'You been fighting again?'

'No,' said Nathan, truthfully.

He was late for school too, and only began to worry about that when he remembered he had to consult with Julia about the story they were going to tell. What if she was already inside, and they had no chance to talk? Fortunately, they met crossing the playground.

'What we going to say then? Did you think?' Too late, he regretted not having bothered to think of anything himself.

'Say we found it,' said Julia.

'Where shall we say we found it?'

'On the pavement, on the way to school. They can't prove we didn't.'

'All right,' said Nathan, without enthusiasm.

It was an unimaginative idea, not to say a downright ordinary one. Unfairly, Nathan sneered inwardly at the ordinariness of Julia's idea.

Nathan's father was the first to arrive. He was closeted for about ten minutes with Mr Barlowe, and then Nathan was sent for. In a loud and angry voice, Nathan's father began accusing Nathan, the minute he appeared at the door of the office.

'What's this I'm hearing then? What's all this about money? You got no uncle give you money! What you say your uncle give you money for?'

Nathan hung his head and shuffled his feet. He was afraid of his father. He knew what he had to say, more or less, but he didn't know how to get the words out.

'It *wasn't* your uncle, was it, Nathan,' said Mr Barlowe firmly. 'We've established that much. So now – where *did* you get it from?'

'I found it.'

'Found it?' Nathan's father bellowed, 'Found it where?'

'I found it on the pavement.'

'What pavement?'

Nathan considered. 'Outside the school nearly. I was late and I found it.'

'How much did you find, Nathan?' asked Mr Barlowe. They might or might not be getting somewhere. In cases like these, Mr Barlowe was quite used to hearing a series of different stories. If one story wasn't believed, the child would try another one.

'A twenty pound note.'

'You find a twenty pound note, and you don't tell nobody?' Nathan's father shouted.

'Yes.'

'You find it on the pavement, and you keep it?'

'Yes.'

'What I always tell you to do if you find anything don't belong to you?'

'Don't know.'

'Yes you do. I always tell you take it to the police station. Why you didn't take it to the police station?'

'Don't know.'

'You keep money don't belong to you that's the same as stealing. You shame our family. Nobody going to shame our family stealing.'

'I didn't steal it. I found it.'

'You same as steal it.'

'Was Julia Winter with you when you found the money?' Mr Barlowe interrupted.

'No, I was by myself.' Nathan did not want to have to account for Julia's actions as well as his own.

'But Julia had money as well. You had twenty pounds, and Julia had at least twenty pounds. Where did *that* money come from?'

'I dunno . . . I suppose Julia found some as well.'

'Was the money you found just lying on the pavement, or was it inside something?'

'It was in a envelope.'

'I see. So you found twenty pounds in an envelope and

45

Julia found – what? Another envelope?'

'Yes . . . I dunno.'

'It seems strange though, doesn't it? You and Julia each find a large amount of money. Separately. On the same day – or at least in the same week. Are you sure the money wasn't all in the same envelope? Are you *sure* Julia wasn't with you?'

Nathan hesitated, confused. This was a question that seemed to demand the answer 'yes'. Clearly Mr Barlowe wasn't going to be happy with the idea that he and Julia had each found separate lots of money.

'Oh yes, I forgot,' he blurted, 'she was.'

'She was what? With you?'

'Yes.'

'And you forgot.'

'Yes,' said Nathan, lamely.

'You lying, Nathan,' his father shouted angrily. 'What you lying for? You hiding something? What you hiding?'

'How could you forget that Julia was with you? You must have talked about the money – shared it between you,' said Mr Barlowe, reasonably.

Nathan said nothing. If he said anything else he would fall into more traps. Once more, his face was a stubborn mask.

'Mr Browne,' said Mr Barlowe, 'would you like to leave this with me now? I'm expecting Julia Winter's mother at any moment. Perhaps she can shed more light on the matter. In any case, we'll get to the bottom of it somehow. Goodbye.'

'I see you at home, Nathan,' said his father. He was fingering his belt, but that was not all. There was an expression on his father's face that Nathan had never seen before, and didn't know how to read now. Anger yes, but more than anger, a deep hurt as well. Nathan felt profoundly troubled by that look.

'You can stay in the corridor, Nathan,' said Mr Barlowe.

'I'll send to your classroom for some work for you.'

There was a special desk outside the office, reserved for wrongdoers who were being barred from their classes for one reason or another. Nathan was to have no more chance of colluding with Julia. He wasn't even allowed to go out to play when the bell went.

Mrs Winter arrived just after playtime, and Nathan watched her being greeted by Mr Barlowe. He watched the door of the office being closed – and inevitably, some minutes later, a passing child being summoned to fetch Julia from her class.

She came, white and shaking, too frightened even to look at Nathan, sitting at his desk outside the office.

Julia's mother had applied an extra layer of make-up this morning, for going to see the headmaster, but the effect was rather spoiled by the anger which now distorted her face.

'What's this Mr Barlowe's been telling me, then? Come on, Julia, I want to know. About your uncle giving you money. It isn't Vince, is it?' Vince was Mrs Winter's new boyfriend. 'He hasn't been giving you money behind my back, has he? Spoiling you.'

Some chance, thought Julia bitterly. Vince had so far taken about as much notice of her as he had of the chair leg.

'He would hardly have given her so much, Mrs Winter,' said Mr Barlowe, soothingly. 'We found twelve pounds at least – and she'd been spending freely all the week.'

'Where d'you get it from, Julia? Gawd, you're a worry to me. Can't you do nothing right? She's a real worry to me, Mr Barlowe. Never puts a finger out straight to help at home. Always breaking things. And now stealing.'

'No, no,' said Mr Barlowe hastily. 'No one has accused Julia of stealing. It's just a mystery we need to clear up. Now Julia – you weren't actually *given* the money, were you. Tell the truth.'

'No.' Julia's voice was faint and wobbly. Her throat felt stiff, as though the sides were stuck together almost.

'Where did it come from?'

'I found it.'

'Were you by yourself when you found it?'

'With Nathan Browne. We found two twenty pound notes.'

'Inside something?'

'No – just on the pavement. They was blowing about.'

'So you kept one each.'

'Yes.'

'Why didn't you tell us this in the first place, Julia?'

No answer.

'Speak when you're spoken to, can't you?' said Julia's mother, sharply. 'Tell the headmaster.'

'I just didn't.'

'You realize you should have taken the money to the police station, don't you, Julia. Or brought it into school, and given it to one of the teachers.'

'Yes, Sir.'

'And of course, it'll have to go to the police now. What's left of it anyway. Unless we can find out who it belongs to. And you'll have to explain why some of it's missing.' Mr Barlowe paused. 'There's something else I feel I have to say, Julia, and I'm saying it to you in front of your mother. You and Nathan between you have told me a number of different stories, and even now your story and Nathan's don't quite match. I may be wrong, but I have the feeling we haven't quite got all the truth yet. We'll all have to do some serious thinking. Back to your class now, and thank you for coming, Mrs Winter.'

'That's all right, Mr Barlowe,' said Julia's mother, grimly. 'I'll get it out of her, don't you worry.'

'Good,' said Mr Barlowe. 'We'll leave the police till you've had a talk with her.'

Mr Barlowe didn't really want to involve the police at all; and in any case, he didn't want to do anything hasty. The children's story certainly did not have the ring of truth about it. Perhaps it was a family matter after all – money stolen from home – and the parents would find it out. In a way, Mr Barlowe hoped so.

But Julia, who had left when Mr Barlowe told her to, spent the day in mortal terror of the police. Every time the classroom door opened, she jerked nervously, thinking it was the police come to question her. She wanted to talk to Nathan, now back in the class, but he wouldn't look at her – just sat glaring at his desk. She didn't know what he'd said or anything, or if he knew Mr Barlowe was going to tell the police.

Home time came, and the police had not arrived, which was some relief. Julia looked for Nathan, but he was gone with the wind. So now there was the next ordeal to be faced. Her mother.

Julia did not know what her mother was going to do to her, but she was sure it was going to be something awful. She couldn't face going home just yet to find out what that awful thing might be. So she put off the terrible moment – she went to the park.

Nathan was there already. Thinking of that funny look on his father's face, Nathan also had decided to put off the moment of finding out what was going to happen next. There would be the belt, probably, but perhaps this time something worse as well. Nathan thought first of going to the deserted house and hiding there. But he had no food for his cats, and couldn't face them empty handed. He went to the park instead.

He mooned around on the swings, brooding and fearful. It wasn't just punishment he feared, it was losing the money as well. The grown-ups wouldn't let up, that much was certain. They would nag it out of him, or beat it out of him, or

49

trick it out of him. And however they did it the end would be the same, because the money would be taken away, and gone would be the dream of his house, all to himself, with nobody in it but him.

There was one way out, and it had been done before, Nathan had heard of kids doing it. But it was pretty drastic, just about as drastic as you could get, and terrifying as well. And what about his mum? She wouldn't like it, would she, if he did that drastic thing? Nathan liked his mum better than his dad, because she was nearly always gentle with him. When she had time to be. When she wasn't cooking, or washing, or ironing, or out at her part-time job. . . .

At this point in Nathan's ruminations, Julia arrived at the park. His first reaction to the sight of the awkward, shambling figure was one of irritation and resentment. Stupid thing – it *was* all her fault they got caught. His second thought, however, as she recognized and approached him, was that she might, after all, still have her uses.

Julia began her particular brand of weeping – great ugly sobs that shook her whole body, and sounded rather ridiculous coming from such a big girl. 'Mr Barlowe's going to tell the police!' she wailed at Nathan, from halfway across the playground.

'Shut up,' said Nathan. 'You don't want everybody to know our business.'

Indeed, a few curious heads were already turning in their direction. Julia came close and repeated, in a hoarse whisper, 'Mr Barlowe's going to tell the police.'

Nathan was dismayed at the news. This added a whole new dimension to the situation, a dimension full of dark possibilities and unknown terrors.

'What's he want to do that for?'

'He said we got to give the money to the police. And he said . . .' she sobbed again, '. . . he said the police'll ask us about the money we spent. And I'm scared. And I'm scared to go home to my mum, too.'

'Never mind about your mum – what about the police?'

'What will they do to us, Nathan?'

'I dunno. They'll make us tell, anyway– about all the rest of the money.'

'How, though? How will they make us tell, Nathan?'

'They got their ways, haven't they!' said Nathan, hinting at unimaginable tortures.

'Oh I'm scared. I'm scared.'

'You ain't the only one.'

'They was angry when they thought it was only twenty pounds. What're they going to do when it's hundreds and hundreds?'

'Put us away, perhaps.'

'Put us away? Oh yeah – in one of them boarding schools.'

'They might put us in prison,' said Nathan.

'They don't put kids in prison, do they?'

'One of them boarding schools then. Or something worser.'

'What could be worser than a boarding school?'

'I dunno, but there could be something.'

'I don't know which is baddest,' said poor Julia, 'the police or my mum.'

'There's my dad too,' said Nathan, remembering. 'I never see him look like that before.'

'What shall we do? What shall we do, Nathan?'

Nathan took a deep breath, and said it. '*Let's run away.*'
'What?'

'You deaf or something? I said, "Let's run away".'

'Where to?'

'I dunno, do I. Somewhere. We can take the money.

Then they can't make us give it back, and they can't do bad things to us neither.'

'You mean really run away, and live somewhere else, by ourselves?'

'That's what I'm saying, stupid. How many times you want me to say it?'

'We couldn't! We couldn't do that, Nathan.'

Nathan glared at her. 'All right then, stay here and see what your mum going to do to you, and the police, and get put away. *I* don't care.'

'Will you go by yourself then?'

A long pause. 'Nah,' said Nathan.

Another long pause.

'Shall I come with you, then?' Julia could hardly believe it was her voice saying such a thing, but it was. And having uttered the words she felt oddly calm. She was going to run away, she was going to escape from trouble. The prospect was frightening, but at that moment it didn't seem nearly as frightening as the prospect of staying behind.

'Come if you like,' said Nathan.

There was silence again, while each studied the ground, and pondered the enormity of what they were about to do.

'Shall we go then?' said Nathan.

'Now?'

'Might as well.'

'We'll go now then, shall we? Shall we get the money?'

'Yeah – won't somebody see, though?'

It was a fine afternoon, and the park was full of mums with young children.

'Don't matter if they see us getting it,' said Julia. 'They won't know it's money, and it don't matter if they know our hiding place 'cause it won't *be* our hiding place no more.'

'Come on then, let's get it.'

Julia hesitated. She was wearing only a thin cotton dress. No coat, not even a cardigan. 'I haven't got nowhere to put mine,' she said.

Nathan had his anorak. Rain or shine, he was rarely parted from his anorak. 'I could put yours in my pocket with mine,' he offered.

'No,' said Julia, emphatically, 'I want to keep my own.' She would have to put it in her knickers again. It would be awkward, managing that manoeuvre, but she wasn't going to trust Nathan with her precious money. 'We better watch out for each other, though. While we dig the money up, I mean.'

The earth was still loose where Nathan had dug, just ten days before. Wet soil smeared the plastic bag with the money in it. Dirt and all, Nathan stuffed it into the lining of his anorak, through the hole in the pocket. Then they went to Julia's tree. 'That's a good hiding place,' said Nathan, when he saw the hollow trunk she had found.

Julia held the money in her hand while she ran to the public toilets. She met Nathan again outside, and they scuffed over the grass a bit, trying to decide what to do next.

'We'll need some clothes,' said Julia.

'I don't need no clothes, I got enough.'

'Well I need a coat for a start. It's going to get cold later.'

'We can buy them.'

'Oh yeah, so we can. Not tonight, though. Time we get to the shops they going to be shut. We going to go home first then? Before we run away?'

'I don't want to go home,' said Nathan. 'My dad's going to strap me.'

'Well, you got a coat anyway. I'll *have* to go home.'

'Your mum might not let you come out again.'

'I'll just run out – she can't stop me.'

'All right, I'll wait for you.'

'Where will you wait?'

Nathan considered. 'What about the empty house, where we found the money?'

'But the robbers – they might kill us,' Julia objected, in horror.

'Nah.' Nathan told her what he had found the other day.

'You'll wait for me then,' said Julia.

'Yeah.'

'You won't go away? You won't go without me?'

'Nah. I said.'

Julia hesitated. She didn't trust Nathan not to change his mind and desert her. But then again, she *had* to trust him. She had no choice.

'Go on then,' said Nathan impatiently.

Julia went.

Outside her house Mrs McCarthy, the black lady who lived downstairs, was busy cleaning the front windows in the evening sunlight.

'Your mummy looking for you, Julia,' said Mrs McCarthy.

She was a nice lady, and Julia liked her really, but at that moment Julia was too upset to be nice back. 'Don't care,' she said rudely, pushing past Mrs McCarthy and into the house. Halfway up the stairs a thought struck her. 'Is my mum home?' she called back down to Mrs McCarthy.

'She gone down the road looking for you. She worried where you gone.'

'She's *not* worried,' said Julia. 'She don't care nothing about me.'

'You shouldn't talk about your mummy like that,' Mrs McCarthy called after her, up the stairs. 'Your mummy look after you very well. She work hard, you know, to make a good home for you.'

But Julia was not listening. She must hurry, hurry while

she had the chance. Her heart was pounding with fear and excitement. Now she had decided to go on this adventure, she was terrified that something would happen to prevent her.

Where to begin? The money first. Julia took the little parcel out of her knickers and looked for a safe way to keep it. A small plastic bag lying on the kitchen table gave her an idea. She put the money in the plastic bag, and found a piece of string to thread through the handles. Then she tied the string round her waist, underneath her cotton dress. The bag hung quite flat against her stomach, and showed no bulge through the full gathered skirt. She would have to have one of those notes handy for spending – in her coat pocket perhaps – but that could be organized later.

Next she rummaged on top of the wardrobe in her mother's bedroom, where the suitcases were kept, and found a small canvas holdall. That would do for her clothes. In her haste she knocked down another of the cases, which crashed into the bedside table toppling a lamp and a radio. It didn't matter – she would be out of the house before her mother came back to discover the damage.

In her own bedroom, Julia turned drawers out feverishly. What would she need? Clean underwear, of course, socks, a spare pair of shoes . . . two cardigans and her anorak. She thought that would be enough. She dragged at the zip of the holdall and it stuck. Fear was making her even more clumsy than usual. She wrenched at the zip, lurched against the bed-end and bruised her hip painfully.

The sound of her mother's footsteps pounding up the stairs almost stopped Julia's heart. Wildly, she tried to thrust the evidence, the canvas bag, under the bed. But it was too late. Her mother stood in the doorway, and her mother was very angry.

'Where've you been then? I been looking all over for you!'

Julia's mother had come home from work with a plan of attack already formed in her mind. She would not be rough on her daughter, not this time. She would be gentle, she would *persuade* the truth out of her. But finding the house empty, Mrs Winter was first annoyed, and then anxious. The stupid child wouldn't have done anything *silly*, would she? When the time went by, and Julia still didn't come home, her mother scoured the streets looking for someone who might have seen her.

Leaving the house, Mrs Winter had been quite worried. But arriving back, to find her daughter safe and sound after all, anger took the place of anxiety. She forgot her good intentions, she opened her mouth and launched into a tirade.

'Don't you go staying out like that again. You come straight home from school like I told you. Never mind if you're in trouble. I know you're in trouble. I'm in trouble an' all because of you. What's that you're hiding?'

'Nothing.'

'Yes it is. What's that under the bed?' Mrs Winter dragged out the holdall and tipped its contents on to the floor. 'What's this then? Where d'you reckon you're going with all this?'

'Nowhere,' said Julia, miserably.

'You put all them clothes back where they come from. Go on – do it this minute, while I'm watching you. I can't turn my back on you for a minute, can I!'

Helplessly, her mind a turmoil of frustration and fear, Julia did as she was told. Further screams of rage told her that her mother had discovered the mess in the bedroom. Julia thought of Nathan waiting in the empty house. She had no idea how she was going to get to him. Useless to 'just run out', as she had said. Too late she realized that she would only be followed and caught, if she did that.

'Have you finished?' Her mother was coming back to see.

56

'Right – then you can get in the lounge and stay there. Where I can see you.'

The 'lounge' was a section of the original upstairs front room, now partitioned into two. It was well furnished, as was all the rest of the flat. Short on sympathy she might be, but Mrs Winter had done her best, with limited means, to make a comfortable home for the two of them. The other part of the original front room was the kitchen, and since you had to go through the kitchen to get to the lounge, and since Mrs Winter had started to work in the kitchen and showed no signs of going anywhere else, Julia found herself well and truly trapped.

'I'm still waiting to hear where you really got that money from.'

Here it came, this was it. Julia sat in the armchair, bracing herself.

'Julia!'

No answer.

'All right, I ain't got time to get it out of you tonight. Vince is going to be here any minute. You made me waste a *hour*, a whole *hour*, Julia, looking for you! But I'll make you talk – don't you make no mistake about that. Put the telly on for now, and try and look a bit human, for gawd's sake!'

Julia sniffed, but did not move from the armchair.

'I said put the telly on.'

Julia went on sitting.

'All right, *be* like that! But I ain't having you around with that miserable face when Vince comes. Gawd, it's enough to turn the milk sour! You better go in your bedroom. You better go now. And don't think I won't be watching you stay there, because I will. I'll bring you down some supper later on.'

'I'm not hungry,' said Julia, getting up to go.

'Don't talk so silly. Of course you're hungry. You got to eat.'

57

Julia's room was at the end of the long passage which led to the back of the house. The stairs were in the middle. Julia's mother could see the top of the stairs from the kitchen as easily as she could see the lounge. Julia was still trapped.

Inside her cosy bedroom, Julia closed the door and tried to think of a way to get out of the house. She went to the window and looked down to the ground. But it was too far to jump, and there was nothing to climb down on, even if Julia had been any good at climbing. And anyway, there was only the tiny back garden below, surrounded by high walls with no access whatever to the road.

She lay on the bed in all her clothes, and presently she heard the doorbell ring, and her mother welcoming Vince in the hall downstairs. She heard their footsteps going into the kitchen, and then, a long time after, her mother's footsteps coming down the passage – bringing the promised supper, no doubt.

Suddenly, Julia knew what to do. It might not work, but it was worth trying. She turned her face into the pillow and began breathing, deeply and evenly.

'Julia?'

Her mother's voice was a sharp whisper. Julia went on breathing. She sensed her mother standing there, not sure what to do. Then she heard her mother going out of the room. Some instinct kept her lying on the bed, still pretending to be asleep, and a moment later her mother came back, and Julia felt a blanket being placed over her, carefully so as not to wake her up. Then footsteps tiptoed out of the room and Julia was alone, the bedroom door left slightly ajar.

Confused, and irresolute now, Julia went on lying there. She couldn't remember the last time her mother had tucked her up. Perhaps my mum does care about me after all, she thought. The home she was about to leave seemed extra cosy, suddenly, and secure. There were still the police, of course, but perhaps her mum would stand up for her – stand between her and whatever terrible things the police might want to do. If her mum would stand up for her, Julia thought, she would change her mind about running away.

Perhaps they were talking about her, her mum and Vince. Julia got out of bed and crept to the door of the lounge. She was not above listening in to other people's conversations, she had done it plenty of times before. She might get caught, of course, but so what? Things could hardly be worse than they already were.

Julia put her ear to the door, and heard her mother's voice. '. . . Anyway she's done it now, she's really done it now. She's always been naughty, Vince, you got no idea, but she's really been and done it now.'

Vince murmured something Julia couldn't quite catch and then her mother's voice, shrill and clear, came again. 'But what am I going to *do* with her? You tell me, Vince, what am I going to do?'

'How about beating her to an inch of her life, for a start?'

That was clear enough. Julia froze in horror.

'That's a good idea,' Julia's mother laughed. Of course she would never really allow Julia to be beaten but she thought Vince would expect her to laugh at his joke.

Julia crept back to her room. So they were going to beat her, and that was just to be the start! And her mother had actually *laughed*. How cruel! Julia looked for something to put her clothes in.

The canvas holdall, of course, was back in its place on top of her mother's wardrobe. The only container she could find was the plastic bag she used for taking things to school. It was large enough for her underwear and the cardigans, but she had to leave the spare pair of shoes behind. She put her anorak on, because the evening was quite chilly now. She took a fresh twenty pound note from the packet of money round her waist, and put it in her anorak pocket. She was ready.

There was a new sound now – the television had been turned on in the lounge. It was evidently showing a cops and robbers film, and there were a lot of screeching cars and loud American voices.

Carefully, Julia opened the bedroom door a little wider and crept into the passage. Her heart was a drumbeat – almost drowning the sound of the television in the lounge. Suddenly the screeching cars and the American voices were twice as loud, and a shaft of light from the opened lounge door beamed through the kitchen and into the passage. Someone was going to the bathroom.

Julia slipped back into her bedroom and stood behind the door, hardly daring to breathe, hoping no one had noticed her stealthy movements. She heard the toilet flush, and Vince's heavy footsteps returning to the lounge. Once more she crept out, and tiptoed this time to the head of the stairs.

Down the stairs. Why had she never noticed how loudly two of them creaked? The sound was like gunshot when you trod on them. Surely someone must come.

But no one did. The screeching cars and the American voices were coming from Mrs McCarthy's flat now. The thunderous noise obliterated any sound Julia made crossing the hall, opening the front door, and stumbling into the street.

As fast as she could go, on ungainly legs, Julia ran to the end of the road. It hardly mattered if anyone saw her. The time was only half past eight on a summer evening – not conspicuously late for an eleven-year-old to be out. Afterwards, when she was missed, when questions were asked, someone might remember seeing her. But by that time she and Nathan would be far away.

Now she was in the road where the empty house was. There were quite a few people in the street, and Julia knew she should be careful not to let anyone see her going in – but she was past caring, and come to think of it, that didn't really matter any more, did it. If only Nathan hadn't given up waiting for her, that was.

She pushed open the rotten door, and floundered into the passage. 'Nathan, you there? You still there?' she called.

He was there. He was crouching in a corner, on a pile of rubbish. 'Shut up, Rat-bag,' he told her fiercely. 'You want everybody to hear?'

The tears, shaming and unbidden, were rolling from under his glasses down his cheeks.

'Why you crying?' Julia asked, in a hoarse whisper.

'Nothing. I ain't.'

Naturally, he wasn't going to admit to her that he was crying with relief because she had come, when he had thought she wasn't going to. When he had almost given up hope that she would.

'Come on,' he said, gruffly, 'let's go.'

'Where?'

'Let's just go.'

Anywhere was better than here. Anywhere away from the strap, and the police, and the unknown horrors. 'They'll be looking for us soon, let's go quick.'

'All right, Nathan, I'm coming. I'm coming with you.'

It was all right now there were two of them. His confidence surging back, Nathan led the way out of the empty house, and Julia followed.

5

Taking off

They left by the back door. Ahead of them, at the end of the tiny concreted yard, were iron railings topped with sharp spikes. Beyond was the railway embankment, and in a deep cutting there were tracks where trains chugged or thundered past at intervals.

'We'll get on the line,' said Nathan. 'No one won't see us there.'

'Over that fence?'

'Course.'

'I can't climb that.'

'It's easy.' Lithe as one of his cats, Nathan sprang at the rails and vaulted the spikes. 'Come on.'

'I can't.'

'Come *on*. Someone'll catch us if you don't hurry up. They'll be looking for us any minute.'

'They won't be looking for me. They think I'm asleep in bed.'

'Well they'll be looking for me. Besides, we aren't allowed to be on the railway line.'

Julia looked for something to stand on. A tub which had once held flowers raised her high enough so that she could

62

lift one leg, fearfully, over the railings. 'Hold my foot,' she told Nathan. She threw the plastic bag on to the embankment, and grasped the railing with both hands.

'Jump now,' said Nathan. He could see she wasn't going to make it, but there was no alternative. Julia lurched clumsily, and her foot caught Nathan square in the face as they both crashed to the ground. There was the sickening sound of cloth ripping as Julia's skirt tore on the spiked railing. Nathan's glasses were kicked off, and Julia sat on them as she fell. Neither child was hurt, but the back of Julia's skirt had a long jagged tear and Nathan's glasses, when they found them, were cracked right across on one side. It was a bad start.

Julia stood up, to inspect the damage to her skirt.

'Get down,' Nathan hissed.

Julia sat in the long grass.

'Right down,' Nathan insisted.

'You said no one wouldn't see us here.'

'They will if we stand up. We got to keep down in the grass. We got to crawl.'

They crawled on their stomachs, the long summer grass waving around them. Anyone looking out of the windows of the houses opposite could have seen them quite easily, but there was at least the illusion of cover. It was uncomfortable going. The ground was soft from the recent rain, but there were hard stones under the grass which were rough on knees and elbows. Julia felt her knees being rubbed raw. She didn't think she wanted much more of this. 'How much further, Nathan?' she whimpered.

'Not far. There's a opening on to the road soon.'

'But where we going after that?'

Nathan had no idea. 'I dunno. Somewhere. A long way.'

'Are we really running away, Nathan?' She couldn't wholly believe it, even now.

'Course we are, stupid.'

A train pounded deafeningly past, only a metre or two from where they crawled.

'Where's that train going to?' asked Julia, who hardly ever went anywhere.

'Euston, I think,' said Nathan, who had sometimes crossed London, visiting other members of his family.

'Shall we go to Euston then? On a train?'

'All right.'

It was as good a suggestion as any.

They reached the gate which led to the pavement. Nathan raised his head and looked carefully round, peering as well as he could through one cracked lens and one whole one.

'Now!' he said, delivering the command in a theatrical hiss.

They bolted through the opening, which was ankle deep in litter. There were a few people on the pavement outside, but no one took the slightest notice of the children. They were used to kids playing illegally on the railway line, and anyway it was none of their business. The children were, of course, open to be spotted by any of Nathan's sisters who might have been sent out to look for him, but the risk was small as it was only a short step from here to the station.

When Nathan thought about his sisters he thought about his mum too– and then he made himself *not* think about his mum. He felt bad thinking about his mum. He even felt a little bit bad thinking about his dad. It made no difference though –he had to go, he *had* to.

'I'll get the tickets,' said Julia, 'and you hide. We don't want the ticket man to see us together, he'll think it's funny.'

Nathan loitered outside the station, while Julia went inside.

'Two tickets to Euston,' she said to the man in the little office.

'Halves?' said the man.

'Oh yes, halves,' said Julia.

'Returns, or singles?'

'What?'

'Are you coming back?'

'No,' said Julia. 'Singles please.'

She'd forgotten about halves and singles. She'd almost slipped up there. She had a story ready about her sister, who was just coming to join her on the journey to Euston — but the ticket man was not interested. He was not even interested in the twenty pound note. Julia had another story to cover her possession of the twenty pound note, but no one wanted to hear it. The ticket man handed over the two tickets and the change, without comment.

Julia went outside to give Nathan his ticket, and the two passed separately through the barrier and down the steps to the platform. The train came soon, and they joined the other passengers in the big, yellow-panelled open carriage with the green and brown seats. No one challenged them, no one noticed them particularly. Even the cracked glasses and the torn skirt attracted no attention, it seemed. Now they were really on their way, it was all being almost *too* easy.

'Are we *really* running away, Nathan?' Julia asked again.

'*Yes!*'

It was true. It was really happening. Julia's knees felt weak; she was glad she was sitting down.

'Are we nearly there?' Julia asked.

'Shut up,' said Nathan, scowling, 'What you keep asking that for?'

The train slowed down and they saw it: EUSTON, in big letters. 'What does that say?' asked Julia.

'Can't you read?' said Nathan, forgetting that indeed, she could not.

Julia blushed, and turned her head.

The station was quite different from the friendly sunlit one they had started from. This station was covered over, dark and gloomy and somehow forbidding. The children showed their tickets at the barrier, and walked up the long ramp to the entrance. The vast marbled hall they found themselves in amazed them – even Nathan, who had seen it before but forgotten how big it was. There was an appetizing smell of frying food coming from somewhere.

'I'm hungry,' said Nathan, who had had nothing to eat since lunch time, and Julia discovered that she was hungry too. They located a beefburger booth, one of several places in the station selling cooked food. They bought beefburgers and cans of Coke and looked for somewhere to sit down. There were very few seats, so they sat on the floor.

They ate ravenously, in silence. 'I'm going to have another one,' said Nathan. He was discovering the joy of having unlimited funds. You could have two beefburgers if you liked – three if you wanted them. Julia bought two bars of chocolate instead of another beefburger. She felt a little sick after she had stuffed them down, but she was beginning to enjoy herself. Running away was all right, she decided, though there was still a nasty sinking frightened feeling, somewhere in the depths of her stomach, nothing to do with the chocolate, when she remembered what an awful thing they were doing.

There were other people sitting on the floor besides Julia and Nathan. Some of them looked rather peculiar. 'They been drinking too much beer,' said Nathan, disapprovingly.

Those who had been drinking too much beer were taking no notice of Julia and Nathan. But one or two other people were beginning to give them funny looks. 'Let's go now,' said Julia. 'Somebody might ask us what we're here for.'

'All right. I'm tired now anyway.'

'Where we going to sleep?'

'Dunno. Somewhere.'

Until that moment it had not really registered in either of their minds that they had no bed for the night. They contemplated the harsh reality with some misgivings.

'Perhaps there's another empty house,' said Nathan, hopefully.

'Let's look,' said Julia.

Outside the station it was beginning to get dark. There were no houses, empty or otherwise, only high brick walls and, on the other side of the road, the green paling surrounding a huge building site. The cranes inside the building site towered over the top of the paling.

'Shall we see if we can get in there?' said Julia.

They crossed the road and walked around the building site, trying to find a way in. Through little cracks they could see that part, at least, of the area inside was roofed over. The floor looked dirty and hard, but at least there was shelter. 'There must be *some* way in,' said Julia, reasonably. 'The builders got to get in, haven't they!'

Suddenly they came to a little space. Not very wide, just big enough for them to slip through one at a time. There was a woman walking her dog, but no one else in sight. Julia and Nathan walked on slowly past the opening until the woman had passed. Then they doubled back quickly, and dived through. 'We made it,' said Nathan, grinning for the first time that evening.

They chose a pillar to lie behind, and cleared a space of rubble. They couldn't clear away quite all the lumps, and the hard floor was dismayingly cold. Julia's sharp eyes spotted a pile of old sacks in a far corner. She went across and fetched two, to make some sort of bed.

'What about me?' said Nathan.

'You can get your own,' said Julia. 'I'm not your slave.'

The sacks were very dirty, but it was better than freezing.

The children wriggled in them, trying to get comfortable.

'I don't like it here,' said Julia, after a while. 'It's spooky. I can't go to sleep.'

'Shut up,' said Nathan, sourly.

'No, I shan't shut up,' said Julia. 'I don't like Euston. And I don't like running away. I thought I did but I don't now. It's all horrible and scary. . . . What was that?'

There was a noise that could have been footsteps over towards the opening into the building site. Terrified, Julia clutched at Nathan.

'Keep still,' whispered Nathan, but he was scared too.

'Somebody's coming! Oh Nathan, I don't like it. Let's run, let's run!'

'Sh–sh–sh.'

'It might be a robber, come to steal my money.'

'Sh–sh–sh, they gone now. I *think* they gone.' How could he be sure though? Nathan swallowed the lump of fear in his throat.

'I want to go *home*,' said Julia in a small voice.

'We can't, said Nathan, suddenly wishing very much that they could.

'Yes we can. Why can't we? I don't care if my mum beats me. Anything's better than this.'

'But we done it now. We run away, didn't we. We made it worse. Whatever they was going to do to us before, they going to do worse now.'

'What, though? What can they do?'

'I dunno. Something bad though. Very bad.'

'Oh Nathan, don't say that!'

'They going to be so angry though. I can't think about how angry they going to be, it makes me feel all funny in my belly.'

Julia began to cry.

'No use crying. Come on, Rat-bag, stop crying, that ain't going to help. Listen, we'll go somewhere else tomorrow. Somewhere good.'

'Where is there good to go?'

Nathan considered. His fertile imagination had begun to build a lovely, fantastic dream – but he wasn't ready to share that yet, and anyway it was only a dream. 'Let's go to the seaside,' he said. The seaside was part of his dream, but it had its own merits too.

'Oh *yes*,' said Julia, forgetting some of her fright. 'Let's do that, Nathan.'

The thought of going to the seaside was quite soothing. It distracted her mind from the eerie sounds, both real and imaginary, all around them. Distracted it too from the hardness of the ground and the dank odour of the sacks, and the smarting of her grazed knees. She slept a bit, and so did Nathan. The hours of darkness passed.

After a restless night they finally woke – stiff, cold, and hungry again. And scared. They were really on their own now, weren't they? It was them against the world.

'What seaside shall we go to?' said Julia, bravely.

'I dunno. Any seaside.'

'I went to Brighton once. On a coach. Shall we go to Brighton?'

'All right. I don't mind.' Nathan had never seen the sea, only read about it. Any seaside would do for him.

The children were silent, thinking about Brighton. It was lovely, at the seaside. Even Nathan, who had never been there, knew that. Once they got to the seaside, everything would be all right.

'Let's get up now,' said Nathan.

They stood up, and brushed themselves down with their hands. They felt dreadfully scruffy, having slept in their clothes all night. They made their way towards the opening in the green paling, almost falling as they did so over a pile of rags that had not been there the night before.

The pile of rags stirred, sat up, and leered at them through a matted growth of filthy beard. It was a disgusting old tramp. Horrified, the children ran – though the tramp was clearly harmless.

'He *smelled*,' said Julia, with a shudder.

'That's 'cause he don't never wash.'

'*I* didn't wash last night. I shall smell like that soon.'

'You don't smell, Julia.'

'No, but I shall.' The thought was clearly troubling her. She found the Ladies' toilet in the station and stood hesitantly in front of the wash-basin. Even at that early hour, there were people coming in and out, so she couldn't wash properly. She splashed her face and hands, and that made her feel a bit better. She had forgotten to pack a comb in the plastic bag, so had to make do with smoothing her tangled hair with her fingers. She undid her plaits and did them up again more neatly. Looking in the mirror at her bleary face, she thought she looked awful. 'I'm really ugly,' she thought, not for the first time. 'No wonder my mum doesn't like me.'

Julia and Nathan breakfasted off Danish pastries and more Coca-Cola. There were crowds of people in the station by now. 'Shall we get our tickets for Brighton?' said Julia. 'You get them this time, Nathan – it's your turn.'

Encouraged by Julia's easy success the day before, Nathan approached the ticket office window without concern. 'Two half tickets to Brighton,' he said, confidently.

'To where?' the ticket man said, thinking he hadn't heard properly.

'Brighton. Two halves please,' said Nathan.

'Wrong station mate,' said the ticket man. 'You want to go to Victoria to get a train for Brighton.'

'How do I get to Victoria?'

The ticket man looked at Nathan sharply. 'Two halves, you said? To Brighton? Two kids on your own, is it?'

'Yes. I mean no, no. Me and my mum. My mum's over there.'

'Your mum travels on a half ticket, does she?'

'No. I don't want two halves. I want a whole ticket and a half ticket. I made a mistake before.'

'And your mum doesn't know the trains to Brighton go from Victoria? Just a minute, sonny.'

The ticket man turned and said something to another official in the ticket office behind him. The other man got up and moved forward. And Nathan ran.

Head forward, legs going like engine pistons, Nathan charged into the crowd moving towards the stairs which led to the Underground. Seeing him go, and terrified of losing him, Julia charged after him. The crowd carried both children along with it. There was a confusion of escalators and passages. At one point there was a ticket barrier – but there were so many people surging through that the woman who was supposed to be examining the tickets had given up trying to check everyone.

They were on a tube train, and the train was gliding out of the station. There were no free seats, so they had to stand. Julia was separated from Nathan by a fat businessman and a crowd of chattering typists going to work. She held on to one of the hanging straps as the train lurched and swayed. Nathan was too small to reach a strap, but he was held upright anyway by the pressure of bodies all around him. A few stations later, when the train stopped, Nathan thrust his way through the bodies and on to the platform. With trembling legs, and in a near panic, Julia followed him.

'Come on,' Nathan urged her.

Julia stood, bewildered. Nathan punched her in the back to get her going again, and they surged with the crowd through more passages, up and down more escalators, riding on more trains. It was a nightmare.

At last they were on a train that was comfortably half empty, and they found seats next to each other. 'Where we going, Nathan?' said Julia, piteously. Her heart was thump-

71

ing painfully, and she felt all the strength had drained out of her, from fright and exertion.

Nathan peered around him stealthily, squinting through the cracked lens. 'It's all right,' he pronounced at last. 'There's nobody following. It was a near thing though,' he added, grimly. 'We nearly got caught.'

In fact, nobody had bothered to give any sort of chase from Euston, but it was exciting to think they might have.

'Is this the train for Brighton?' Julia asked.

'Nah. We got to get to Victoria first.'

'Is this train going to Victoria then?'

'Nah. I dunno. I dunno where it's going.'

They got out at the next stop. The name of the station was *Bank*. 'Is this Victoria?' said Julia.

'Nah. I told you. We have to find out how to get to Victoria. We have to look at the Underground map and work out how to get there. It's not hard – I done it before.'

Nathan worked out the route, and they started their journey again on the trains that rumbled through the tunnels beneath the streets of London.

Now that they had attention to spare, Nathan noticed a sign on the side of the carriage which said that anyone found travelling without a ticket was in dead trouble, or words to that effect.

'I dunno how we going to get out,' he admitted to Julia. 'We haven't got no tickets, and they'll ask to see them at the barrier.'

'Can't we get out the same way we got in?' said Julia. 'I mean – can't we push through with a lot of other people?'

At Victoria they hung back until there was a crowd going through the barrier. Then they pushed in behind some grown-ups who looked as though they might be their parents, and as before the ticket collector didn't bother to count. They were through.

Julia was in no hurry to get the tickets for Brighton. Instinct warned her that there was danger in just walking up to the booth and asking for them. It was her turn, but Nathan had run into trouble and so might she. For some reason, grown-ups didn't expect children to be travelling to Brighton on their own. Perhaps because it was a long way. 'I want to think,' said Julia. 'I want to think of a good story.'

The children wandered round the shops and stalls inside Victoria main line station. They drank Coke, and Julia bought a little roll of sticky tape with which to mend her torn dress, because she thought it would look odd to be travelling all the way to Brighton in ragged clothes. Then she went to the chemist's to get a comb. She thought her hair must be looking very untidy, and people would notice.

And in the chemist's, Julia had her inspiration.

There it all was on display – lipstick, eye shadow, rouge, the lot! Julia knew what all the things were for, she had seen her mother using them often enough. She felt a bit silly doing it, but she made herself pick up some of each – any old colours, the first to hand – and take them to the counter. 'They're for my sister,' she explained, but the sales assistant was not really interested.

Feeling quite excited, Julia took her purchases into the Ladies' toilet, leaving Nathan sulking on the platform because she wouldn't tell him what she was going to do. There were a number of women in the outer part of the toilet, so Julia was glad she had remembered to buy a small hand mirror. She locked herself in one of the compartments, propped the little mirror on the seat, against the pipes, and knelt on the floor. With unpractised fingers, she made up her face as best she could. As nearly as she could

73

tell, peering this way and that into the tiny mirror, the result didn't look bad. She undid her plaits and combed out the thin, sand-coloured hair. It fell over her shoulders in little crimped waves. She had nothing to tie it back with, so it was over her face rather – but older girls often did wear their hair like that. She mended her dress with the sticky tape, and went self-consciously to find Nathan.

On her way out, Julia glanced at her face in the big mirrors over the washbasins, and her heart beat with excitement. She really looked *nice*.

Nathan was still waiting on the platform, and for a moment, he didn't recognize her.

'It's me,' said Julia, shyly.

'What you done that for? Put that stuff on your face for?' She couldn't tell from his expression what he thought about it – but at least he wasn't actually *laughing* at her.

'Don't you like it?'

'It's all right . . . It's good, you look older.'

'I know,' said Julia. 'It's to buy the tickets.'

Nathan frowned. 'The dress looks wrong,' he said.

'I know,' said Julia. 'It'll do for the ticket man though, won't it? He'll only see my face.'

Nathan considered. 'They'll see you on the train – and when we get the other end. Why don't you buy some different clothes?'

'Shall I?' said Julia, not sure that she would have the nerve.

'Yeah, go on, go on!'

Julia ran back to the toilet to get more notes out of the plastic bag around her waist. She didn't know how much the new clothes were going to cost, but she took three notes out to be on the safe side.

The children found a small boutique near the station. It looked a very grown-up sort of shop, and when it came to actually going inside, Julia's courage failed her.

'Go on,' said Nathan, 'what you waiting for?'

'I don't like to.'

'Go on, I'll help you.'

Julia still hesitated, so Nathan gave her a push. She stumbled into the shop, and now there was no going back. Julia took a deep breath. 'We was looking for some things for my friend's sister,' she told the salesgirl, but the salesgirl was bored and not really paying attention, her mind on other things.

Between them, the children chose a loose pink blouse, with great big sleeves, and a dark blue skirt with a slit up the side. In another shop they bought sandals with little heels, and a cheap shoulder bag to match the skirt. Then back to the Ladies' in Victoria Station, and Julia could not wait to get into her new finery.

This time, her glance in the mirror showed a complete transformation. With her height, and the make-up, and the new clothes, she looked sixteen at least. Wonderingly, she lingered by the mirror, turning from side to side, delighted by what she was seeing. She gave herself a small smile, and that made her look even better. Julia tottered out, on her little heels, to show Nathan.

'Looks good,' he said. He was grinning now, Julia could tell he was pleased. 'Why don't you get one of them bands, to put on your hair?' he suggested, so they went to the chemist to find one.

In the shop window, Julia's reflection showed her how badly she was stooping. The stoop was spoiling the effect of the new outfit. Julia pulled her shoulders back and held up her head. For the first time in her life, she was proud of her appearance.

The ticket man sold her one and a half tickets to Brighton, without a second glance.

6

Beside the seaside

They didn't talk much on the journey. For one thing, there were other people in the carriage to overhear, and anyway there was so much to look at. All that green – it was another world from dusty, grey old London.

Thinking about home was uncomfortable, so they tried not to do it, but every now and then the nasty sharp qualms shivered through them anyway. What awful, unforgiveable thing had they done? As the train carried them further, however, they remembered less and less often to be worried. And of course, they were going to the seaside, where everything was going to be all right.

It was early afternoon when the train arrived at Brighton. They were hungry, so they bought beefburgers and Cokes and ate them walking down the road to the sea. They were so anxious to get there, they couldn't wait to have a proper meal. Julia, teetering on her little heels, soon found the pain too excruciating to bear. She could only take little mincing steps, and that was too slow. To keep up with Nathan, she had almost to run, and she was afraid of toppling over. So she took the sandals off, and put them in the plastic bag with her spare clothes. It was the seaside, wasn't it! You were allowed to have bare feet at the seaside.

They could smell it before they could see it. The air was sharp, clean, different. A cool breeze met their faces as they hurried, cutting through the bright sunshine. And suddenly there was the sea in front of them, sparkling and endless, a million diamonds and emeralds under the clear blue sky. The children plunged over the pebbles towards the water's edge.

'Wait for me,' Julia called. The hard pebbles were hurting her feet. By the time she reached him, Nathan had removed his own shoes and was paddling in the mild surf. 'It's cold,' he squealed. He was staggered by his first sight of the sea. He had never quite grasped, in his imagination, that it was going to be so *vast*.

'It's lovely,' said Julia, joining him in the water. They splashed about for a bit, and then Julia said, 'I wish we could swim. I wish I brought my costume.'

'Why don't you buy one?' said Nathan.

'Oh yeah, so I could. Where, do you think?'

'There's shops back there.'

Julia limped back over the pebbles and found a little shop that sold seaside things. To be in keeping with her sixteen-year-old image, Julia bought a brief striped bikini. She was a little shy about the idea of wearing it, but anxious to try it all the same.

She hobbled back over the pebbles, and sat down next to Nathan, who had finished paddling and had perched himself on a little mound, staring keenly at the horizon.

'I don't see no big ships,' he said, 'only little ones.'

'There's a big ship over there,' said Julia.

'Where?' said Nathan, eagerly. He peered through the cracked glasses, straining to see.

'Over there, a long way. And another.'

'Oh good,' said Nathan.

'What you want to know about big ships for?'

'Oh, nothing.' He was not nearly ready to tell her his dream.

Julia began to struggle into her bikini, sitting on the beach and covering bits of herself with the anorak. 'Look the other way,' she told Nathan, primly. When she came to the money bag, still tied round her waist, she realized she had a problem. She frowned, pouted, hesitated, and finally turned to Nathan. 'You'll have to look after my money while I'm swimming,' she told him.

'All right.'

'I counted it,' she warned. 'I know how much is there.' This last was not quite true. Neither child was really sure how much money they had altogether.

'All right, all right,' said Nathan, offended. 'I ain't going to steal your money.' He would have been just as suspicious of her, but it was not nice to be accused.

Julia splashed into the water. Her 'swimming' consisted of three or four puffing breast-strokes at a time, with long pauses while she got her breath back. Nathan got tired of watching her, and turned his attention to the other people on the beach. It was the beginning of July, and although the schools had not yet broken up for the summer holidays, many families with children were taking their holidays early, and the beach was quite crowded. Behind Nathan, a woman and two boys were just arriving. The boys were younger than him, about six and seven, he thought. They were wearing school blazers, and they were calling to one another in rather posh voices. They had a ball which they started throwing and Nathan watched them, thinking they could throw quite hard for such little kids.

All of a sudden the ball went wild. Nathan, through his cracked glasses, saw it coming towards him and tried to duck. But it was too late. The ball caught him in the face and almost knocked him over. He recovered his balance, but his glasses went flying. The little boy, running to retrieve his ball, set a cascade of stones tumbling down the beach. Nathan's glasses were buried under the landslide and when he groped to find them he found that the one good lens was now shattered. He couldn't see anything through it at all. He tried looking through the cracked lens, but the shattered lens was for his best eye. His glasses were useless – he was better off without them.

The woman was coming towards him. As she came near enough, Nathan saw that she was looking very upset. 'Are they broken?' she was saying. 'Oh dear, I *am* sorry.'

She was a nice woman. Her hair and her clothes were quite elegant, and she talked posh, like the news readers on the telly.

'I've *told* Oliver,' she said to Nathan. 'I've told him and told him to be careful. His aim is just too unpredictable. Let me see your glasses. Oh dear, a complete write-off, I'm afraid. I'll pay for them, of course. Do you live in Brighton?'

'Yes,' said Nathan, warily.

'Well, that's good. You can give me your address and I can come and see your mother.'

'I mean I live in London,' said Nathan.

The woman looked at him, puzzled. 'I mean,' Nathan floundered on, 'I'm staying with my aunt in Brighton. For a holiday.'

'Well, that's fine. I can come and see your aunt.'

'No, it's all right,' said Nathan. 'They was broke already.'

'Are you *sure*?'

'Yeah, they was going to the menders today. It's all right, really.'

The woman looked very doubtful. 'Look,' she said, 'I'll give you my address. You show this to your aunt, and she can send the bill to me. I really must at least help to pay for them.'

'I think it's on the National Health anyway,' said Nathan,

who had never troubled himself about such matters before. 'I don't think nobody got to pay for them.'

'Oh, well – you give my address to your aunt in any case. Don't forget.'

She went, taking the two little boys with her.

Julia came out of the water. Her long, skinny figure was quite blurred to Nathan, until she got really close. He thought, rather unkindly, of a particularly stringy piece of seaweed.

'You look different without your glasses,' said Julia.

'They're broke,' said Nathan. 'I don't know what I'm going to do without them. I can't see properly. I can see near things, but far away things are all fuzzy.'

'You'll get used to it,' said Julia, callously. 'Brr–rr–rr— I'm *cold*. Wish I had a towel. . . . You do look different, Nathan.'

The afternoon was waning now. Julia dried herself on the old torn dress, but the sharpening breeze from the sea was chill on her bare body, clad only in the wet bikini. She pulled her anorak round her for warmth, and raised the subject which had so far been avoided. 'Where we going to sleep?'

Nathan looked around. 'I don't know,' he said peevishly. 'I can't see nothing. I can't *see* nowhere to sleep. It's all right for you. You don't need glasses.'

'There's a pier over there,' said Julia. 'We could sleep under that.'

Silence. Memories of last night's discomforts occupied the thoughts of each.

'At least there's the sea to wash in,' Julia said, brightening. 'At least I'm clean now. You ain't even clean yet, Nathan.'

Nathan scowled, and brooded. 'There's hotels by the sea,' he said at last. 'Couldn't we go to a hotel?'

'They'd never let us,' said Julia, doubtfully.

'Why not?'

'Well – I dunno. What could we say?'

'I dunno.'

The children sat in silence for a while, trying to think of a solution.

'We could say I was your big sister,' said Julia, remembering the make-up and the skirt with the slit. The make-up had mostly come off in the sea of course, but she could easily put it on again.

'Don't be silly,' said Nathan, with heavy scorn.

'It's not silly. Why's it silly?'

'I'm a different colour to you.'

'Oh yeah – I forgot.... I know, you can be my *adopted* brother.'

'Can I?'

'Yeah – white people adopt black babies sometimes. My mum knows somebody who done that.... Let's go to a hotel, Nathan, and have a proper bed.'

The thought was very tempting.

'What shall we say then?' said Nathan. 'Shall we say we come for a holiday?'

'That don't sound right,' she said. 'Why did we come without our mum?'

'Oh yeah – that's the trouble.'

'I know,' said Julia, 'Our mum's in hospital near here and we come to stay so we can visit her.'

'That's a excellent idea,' said Nathan, forgetting for the moment to sulk about his glasses.

'Might as well look for a hotel now then,' said Julia, pulling on her clothes over the wet bikini. She made up her face again, balancing the mirror on her knees, because Nathan was brooding again and wouldn't hold it for her.

They scrambled back over the pebbles, and climbed the steps to the promenade. They crossed the busy seafront road, because there were the buildings that looked like hotels.

'Here's one,' said Nathan.

'We can't go in there,' said Julia, scandalized.

'Why not?'

'That's not for us, that's for posh people.'

'Oh. Where is there one for us then?'

'In a *little* street, I expect. Let's try up here.'

They turned off the seafront and wandered back towards the town. They weren't quite sure which were hotels and which were private houses, because Nathan couldn't read the sign-boards without his glasses, and Julia couldn't read them anyway. They stopped in front of an establishment with a notice in the window. 'What does that say?' said Nathan, and Julia spelled out the letters for him.

'Va-can-cies,' said Nathan.

'That means there's rooms empty, don't it?'

'Course it does, you silly stupid fool.'

The house didn't look all that nice. The mustard-coloured paint was peeling off the window frames, and the net curtains inside were a bit dingy.

'Shall we try, then?' said Julia.

'Go on. See what happens.'

The woman who answered the doorbell looked about a hundred. She had sparse white hair, held together by a net, and a crumpled yellowish face. She was very thin, and she moved stiffly, as though her joints hurt her, but her tired eyes looked kind, and the smile she gave the children was something like a candle in a draughty room – shaky and uncertain, but still radiating light and warmth. 'Yes?' she said sweetly, looking from one to the other.

'Have you got a room?' said Julia, in what she hoped was a grown-up voice.

'I have, yes. For the two of you?'

'Me and my little brother,' said Julia, gaining confidence.

'I see.' The lady's expression said that she didn't, at that moment, *quite* see – but she was too well-mannered to ask personal questions. 'One room with two beds? Is that all right?'

'Oh yes, yes that's all right,' said Julia, trying to sound as if she did this sort of thing all the time.

'It's seven pounds each, bed and breakfast,' said the lady.

'Every day?' said Julia, amazed.

The lady laughed, and her laughter was like little cracked silvery bells. 'Bless my soul that's cheap,' she said. 'You won't find anywhere cheaper than here. Just the one night, is it?'

'No,' said Julia, 'lots of nights. Lots of nights I expect. I don't know really.' She stopped, not knowing what to say next.

'I see,' said the lady. 'Well – would you like to see the room?'

'Yes please,' said Julia, with relief.

They climbed some stairs, covered with an awful thread-bare carpet. The old lady panted and puffed as they went up. At the last step she grasped the bannister and heaved herself on to the landing. She laughed again, but she looked as though everything hurt. 'I can't get around as well as I used to,' she confided. 'Here you are, this room's free.'

She opened the door and showed them a very shabby room. It had one double bed, and a smaller bed by the window. 'Is it all right?' the old lady asked, anxiously.

It occurred to Julia that the lady really wanted very much that she and Nathan would take the room. Perhaps she needed the money badly. Perhaps she didn't get many people asking for rooms. 'It's all right,' she said, 'we'll stay here, won't we?'

This last was addressed to Nathan who was gazing in something like rapture at the ancient bedspreads. He was not actually seeing the bedspreads, however, he was seeing the two beds. For the first time in his life, Nathan was going to have a whole bed all to himself. 'It's great,' he said, meaning it. He could hardly wait for night to come.

The old lady looked worried, hesitated, opened her mouth as though to speak, changed her mind and closed it again. Then she took a deep breath. 'I'm afraid there's no television,' she said humbly.

'Television?' said Julia, puzzled.

'In the lounge. It's gone for repair. The man said it'll probably be back by the weekend.'

'Don't matter,' said Julia.

'You don't mind?'

'Nah – don't matter,' said Nathan, who was only interested in the sleeping arrangements, and the luxury of the single bed.

'Well, bless my soul,' said the old lady, greatly relieved, 'you're the first young people I've met who don't mind about not having the telly. Bathroom's along here, by the way. . . . I suppose you'll be going to get your luggage now.'

'Our luggage?' said Julia.

'Yes – your cases. I suppose you left them at the station. People often do that while they look for somewhere to stay.'

'O yes – yes, we did. We better go and get our luggage now, hadn't we Charlie? . . . *Charlie!*'

Nathan, who had gone back to admiring the beds, was being slow on the uptake. Julia prodded him with her toe.

'My name's Mrs Parsons,' said the old lady to Julia as they went down the stairs. 'I know this young man's Charlie. What's your name, dear?'

'It's Beverley,' said Julia. She had always wanted to be called Beverley.

'Well bless my soul,' said Mrs Parsons, beaming delight

all over her crumpled face. 'That's the very same name as my granddaughter. Oh – you won't be wanting an evening meal, will you?' Mrs Parsons was looking worried again.

'No, no,' said Julia, anxious to give all the right answers.

'That's good then. I used to do evening meals as well as breakfasts, but I can't manage them any more. It's too much work for me all on my own. Most of my guests get take-aways. You can bring them to your room if you like, I don't mind.'

It didn't look as though she was going to ask any awkward questions at all. Julia and Nathan walked sedately down the road, but as soon as they were round the corner they exploded into triumphant giggles, and Julia did a little pirouetting dance. She looked extremely silly doing it, but Nathan was too full of unaccustomed happiness to jeer. 'We got a *room*,' they crowed to each other.

They found a street of shops, and looked for somewhere to buy a couple of suitcases. The big shops were closed by now, but there was a large newsagent still open, which sold souvenirs and seaside things as well as newspapers. The children bought two beach bags with zips on them. It looked a bit peculiar to be packing clothes in beach bags, but it was the best they could do. They could not return to Mrs Parsons' without some sort of luggage. They stuffed the beach bags with crumpled newspaper to make them look full. Tomorrow though, Julia said firmly, Nathan really *must* buy himself some clean underwear, as he couldn't go on wearing the same stale things any longer.

They bought fish and chips, and took them back to their room, as Mrs Parsons had said they might.

'I'm having the big bed,' said Julia, before Nathan could claim it.

Nathan didn't mind. In any case he thought he might feel a bit lost all by himself in the big bed. The little one was the one he really wanted. He sat on his bed, eating fish and chips out of the newspaper, and looking forward to bedtime.

'You owe me some money,' Julia said, when they had finished eating. Though she had only a hazy idea about the total amount of money she had, her memory of small sums was pretty good, and she had kept account in her mind, more or less, of everything they had spent between them since leaving Euston that morning. She had worked out that Nathan owed her five pounds thirty-two pence. From now on, she decided, she would keep all her money in the shoulder bag they had bought in Victoria. 'You can go and wash your hands, Nathan, before you give me the money. I don't want a lot of greasy change in my new handbag.'

She was carrying the big sister act rather far, Nathan thought. He punched her in the back, quite spitefully, which hurt Julia's feelings as well as her back, because she thought it was for nothing – but really it was for carrying the big sister act too far. He had enough big sisters at home, always nagging him to wash.

'I wonder what they're doing at home,' said Nathan suddenly.

'I expect they've gone to the police,' said Julia. 'I expect they're looking, all over London. They won't find us here though, will they!'

'Will your mum be worried?'

'Nah – my mum don't like me. She don't care about me. Does your mum care about you, Nathan?'

Nathan had stopped thinking about his mum, but now he thought about her again, just for a minute. He supposed his mum *would* mind, a *bit*, that he had run away, but then again she was always so busy. 'I don't expect she'll miss me *really*,' he said. 'I expect she'll be glad there isn't so much work. . . . Is it bedtime yet, Julia?'

Julia thought bed was a good idea. She had slept little the

night before, and was tired out now with effort and excitement and the sea air. They had no night clothes, so Julia slept in her torn school frock, and Nathan slept in his clothes.

Julia fell asleep immediately. Nathan lay awake for a few minutes, thinking about his dream. The one about the ship. The waking dream carried him blissfully over tossing waves, green and blue and foam-topped and always warm, promising endless delights of rainbow-coloured adventure. The waking dream carried him into the sleeping dream, where the one merged into the other.

7

Discovered!

At breakfast time, Mrs Parsons was chatty. There was one other couple in the dining room, an elderly lady and gentleman of such nondescript appearance that Nathan said they should be called Mr and Mrs Nobody. They had little to say, either to each other or to Mrs Parsons, so Mrs Parsons addressed most of her chat to Julia and Nathan. She told them all about her daughter working in London, and her son in Australia, and her granddaughter Beverley, whom she had never actually seen. Then she asked about the children.

'You two planning to have a nice holiday then?' She wasn't being nosy, just conversational.

Julia took a deep breath. 'We aren't on holiday. We come to visit our mum.'

'Visit her? Don't you live with her?'

'Yes, but she's in hospital. Here.'

'Oh bless my soul, nothing serious I hope.'

'Yes it is a bit serious, she had to have an operation.' Julia thought she had better say that, in case they wanted to stay a long time.

'Which hospital is she in – Brighton General?'

'Yes, that's right.'

'Well, bless my soul, fancy them sending her all the way down here for an operation. There are so many hospitals in London. Fancy that!' She hurried away to fetch more toast, and was still exclaiming 'Fancy that,' and 'Bless my soul,' when she came back. Julia thought she might have made a mistake, saying her mother had come here for an operation, so she changed it.

'No, I mean, she didn't have the *operation* here, she come here for convalescent.'

'At Brighton General?'

'No, not Brighton General. That's not the name. I forget the name.'

'I suppose you're worried about your mother, dear. Don't worry, I'm sure she'll be all right. Is it one of those new convalescent homes out at Hove?'

'Yes, that's right.'

'Well, you go along and visit her now. I'm sure she'll feel much better when she sees the two of you. You can give her my best wishes. Tell her Mrs Parsons hopes she'll soon be quite well.'

'Thank you, I will.'

Julia was amazed at the way Mrs Parsons seemed to believe every word she uttered. Teachers and mothers weren't like that at all. They often thought you were lying, even when you were telling the strict and absolute truth. She began to feel just a little bit uncomfortable. It wasn't nice having to tell lies to someone you liked, someone who trusted you.

The children went back to the beach. The weather was lovely again, and Julia wanted to swim. Nathan didn't care about swimming, he wanted to look at ships. It was a nuisance not having his glasses, but if he practised without them, perhaps he would get used to it as Julia had said.

In spite of the warm weather, Nathan took his anorak, partly because he always took it, and partly because his money was still hidden in the lining. Julia's money had all been transferred into the new shoulder bag. She wore it like a satchel, with the strap across her chest, clutching it to her stomach all the time. 'In case somebody thiefs it,' she explained.

When she went swimming she had to trust Nathan, but she was beginning to feel he *could* be trusted. It was a good feeling. They were mates now, sort of, she supposed.

They spent the whole day at the beach. When they were tired of swimming and paddling they walked along the front, sampling the delights of the various little shops and amusement arcades. They bought sticky rock and ice cream. They drank Coke out of cans, and had two beef-burgers each for their lunch. They spent a whole hour working the slot machines, the sort where you rolled a coin down a shoot and waited to see if a moving arm would push a pile of other coins into a hole and out of the machine for you to keep. They didn't actually win anything, but it was fun, and there was always tomorrow.

There was a great bouncing thing, made of inflated rubber and shaped like a castle. Nathan had a go on that, and Julia was just going to have a go, when she remembered her sixteen-year-old image, and decided it wouldn't be suitable. She envied Nathan, still a child, bouncing about in the rubber castle, but of course you couldn't have everything.

On the way home, late that afternoon, they bought underwear for Nathan, and some toilet things for each of them. They also bought a spare tee-shirt for Nathan, and a change of blouse for Julia. There was a placard outside a newsagent with the headline 'MISSING CHILDREN' – but Julia could not read it, and Nathan could not see it properly because it was on the other side of the road, and too far away for him.

'How's your mother?' asked Mrs Parsons, meeting them on the stairs.

'A bit better,' said Julia, cautiously.

'That's good then. Bless my soul, you look well, dear. You look as though you've been in the sun.'

Indeed, Julia's face was glowing, her pale eyes bright from the happy day. 'We went on the beach,' she said.

'That's good. Did your mother come too?'

'Yes, she came. She said the sun done her good. She said she can do with weeks and weeks like this.'

Mrs Parsons laughed. 'We'll be lucky to get weeks and weeks of this weather,' she pointed out, honestly. 'Your brother doesn't say much, does he, Beverley.'

'He's shy,' said Julia.

Nathan scowled. Whatever else he was, he was *not* shy.

'I think it's because he's not really my brother,' Julia went on, 'He's my adopted brother. My mum adopted him when he was little.'

'I see,' said Mrs Parsons, smiling as though she was glad that particular mystery had been cleared up. 'But then it's the same, isn't it. He is really your brother now.'

Julia thought Mrs Parsons was probably the nicest lady she had ever met. She thought again what a shame it was that she had to tell lies to a nice lady like her.

That evening Julia washed out her dirty clothes and Nathan's, and hung them over the window sill to dry. She had to use toilet soap instead of proper washing soap, but at least now everything was clean and sweet-smelling. She was enjoying herself very much. At home she had to be nagged to do any of her own laundry but here, now she was in charge, it was fun.

The weather continued good, and the children spent the next two days on the beach. There was so much to do, they thought they would never get tired of it. Julia's skin was turning golden brown. She admired her deepening tan a hundred times a day. 'I'm nearly as brown as you now, Nathan,' she claimed, laying her arm alongside his.

When they arrived back at the boarding house on the Friday afternoon, Mrs Parsons had news for them 'The television's back,' she said, with a beaming smile. 'You'll be able to watch it in the lounge this evening.' They hadn't missed it all that much, but they were glad to hear the television was back. It would be quite a treat, after they had had their supper.

They watched *Murder She Wrote*, and then a comedy programme called *Home to Roost*. Nathan had to sit very close, to be able to see the screen without his glasses. Halfway through the comedy programme, the colourless old couple whom they had seen in the dining room joined them in the lounge, and came unexpectedly to life by asserting their right to have the nine o'clock news on BBC1. There was a film on Channel 4 which Nathan wanted to see, and he was rather disagreeable about having to miss it.

'What a rude little boy,' said Mr Nobody. 'Didn't you ever hear of having respect for older people? When I was your age I'd have had my ears boxed for as much as opening my mouth at the wrong time.'

'We got equal right as you,' said Nathan, glaring. 'We paid as much as you.'

'Shut up, Charlie,' said Julia. 'You mustn't speak to the gentleman like that – where's your manners?'

'Rat-bag—' Nathan began, turning on her furiously– but the retort on his lips was never finished for suddenly, incredibly, there was his picture on the televison screen! Julia's too. Nathan gazed, in horrified silence. He could feel Julia gazing, beside him, he could sense her fear.

'There is still no news of the missing children,' the newsreader was saying, 'and no definite witnesses as to their movements since Monday evening, though they are believed to have been traced as far as Euston. . . .'

'It's the fault of the schools,' Mr Nobody was complaining in a loud voice – not about what the newsreader was saying, but about Nathan's rudeness. 'I blame the teachers, and the parents. There's no discipline these days.' He spoke so loudly that his voice quite drowned out the next thing the newsreader said, which was that the police had reason to think the children might possibly have tried to get to Brighton.

'You're quite right, dear,' Mrs Nobody soothed her husband. 'Let's look at the news now though.'

'An appeal is being made to anyone who thinks they may have seen this girl and boy to come forward,' the newsreader was continuing. 'The parents of both are greatly distressed, the girl's mother in particular is said to be in a state of near collapse.'

'Naughty little girl!' expostulated Mr Nobody. 'I know what I'd do to her if she was mine!'

'They'll catch her,' Mrs Nobody promised. 'And the boy. Soon, I'm sure.'

'Another little perisher!' Mr Nobody ranted on. 'Upsetting his parents.' He turned to Nathan and addressed him directly. 'I hope you're listening to all this. Look what that boy's doing to his mother and father. No consideration, no consideration.'

'It ain't nothing to do with me,' said Nathan.

'I know it's nothing to do with you,' said Mr Nobody. 'It's just an example of how young people behave nowadays. Be quiet now, and let's listen to the rest of the news.'

Miraculously, they had not been recognized. Their pictures had been on telly, and Mr and Mrs Nobody had not recognized them at all. True, Julia's picture had been that of a pale eleven-year-old with plaits. Not very much like this suntanned young lady with the flowing locks and the pink lipstick. And Nathan's picture showed him with thick glasses, which distorted the shape of his eyes and made him

93

look quite different from the little boy sitting beside his 'sister' this evening.

Julia and Nathan went on sitting side by side. They knew they mustn't move too soon. Then Julia faked a loud yawn, and immediately clapped a hand over her mouth. 'Oh, manners!' she reproved herself. 'I must be tired – it's all this fresh air.' She yawned again. 'Are you tired Charlie? Shall we go to bed?' She hoped her voice sounded natural, after the fright.

'Hush!' said Mr Nobody, who was still watching the television.

'Sorry,' said Julia in a whisper. 'Come on, Charlie.'

In the safety of their bedroom they let the tensions go. They cheered and crowed and bounced up and down on their beds. Nathan stood on his head and managed to stay there for half a minute before he fell in a giggling heap, while Julia sang a little song she made up for the occasion. 'They don't kno-o-w us. They don't kno-o-w us.'

'They won't ca-a-tch us. They won't ca-a-tch us,' Nathan added to Julia's song.

Both children went to bed in high spirits.

Both children woke, in the early hours. Nathan heard Julia tossing and fidgeting in the big bed, and he thought he heard a sob.

'What's the matter, Ju?'

'Nothing.'

'What you making that noise for then?'

'Nothing. I can't get back to sleep.'

'Nor I can't get back to sleep neither. . . . Julia, I thought you said your mum don't care about you.'

'She don't.'

'So why is she collapsing?'

'She must be putting it on.'

'Yeah – so's my mum and dad putting it on.'

'Yeah – they just want us back so they can tell the police of us, don't they, Nathan.'

'Yeah – and put us away.'

'What else was it they was going to do to us, Nathan?'

'Oh you know – thingy.'

It was something very bad, wasn't it; and it was on the tip of his tongue, of course, but he couldn't *quite* remember what it was.

There was a long silence.

'Nathan.'

'What?'

'Shall we ring up our mums in the morning?'

'Yeah, if you like.'

'Just tell them we're all right.'

'If you like.'

Consciences appeased, Julia and Nathan slept soundly until morning.

They went out early, to use the public telephones.

'I just remembered,' said Nathan, 'we ain't on the phone no more.'

'How could you forget something like that?' said Julia.

How indeed? It was less than a week since they left London, but already home seemed shadowy, almost unreal. Nathan had to think really hard to remember ordinary details.

'I'll tell my mum to tell your mum,' offered Julia.

Julia's mother was still in bed when the phone went. Half asleep still, drugged with the pills the doctor had given her to soothe her nerves, she stumbled into the lounge to answer it. 'Hullo?' It might be the police. They might have some news.

'Hullo, Mum? It's me – Julia.'

'I don't believe it, oh I don't believe it. Julia! Where are you?'

'I'm not telling you where I am. I'm all right though. You don't have to worry about me. You don't have to collapse about me, Mum.'

'Julia – come back, come back, there's a good girl.'

'You don't want me. You got Vince.'

'I do want you. I'm missing you, and that's the gawd's truth.'

Julia wavered, just for a moment. 'I'm all right though. I'm having a good time.'

'Having a good time!' Mrs Winter's voice was suddenly shrill. 'You having a good time when we're all doing our nuts looking for you? The police is looking for you, do you know that? And that Nathan Browne – is he with you?'

'Yes he is. He's all right too.'

'You listen to me, Julia. You come right home this minute. You tell me where you are, and the police'll come and find you both. You hear what I say? . . . Julia? . . . You wait till I get my hands on you if you don't do what I say! . . . Julia? . . . You still there? . . .'

Julia put the phone down.

It was unfortunate that Julia could not see to the other end of the line. That she could not see her sharp-tongued mother in a paroxysm of real grief and self-reproach. She had been within reach of getting her child back, and she had made a mess of it. Again.

'Your mum angry?' said Nathan, unnecessarily.

Nathan was actually glad his parents were not on the phone. He wanted them to know he was all right, but he didn't want any scenes. He didn't want to hear, for instance, how they were all praying for him to come back. Because there was no way he was ever *going* back. He was not going back to whatever horrible fate they were saving up for him at home. Anyway, not for a very long time. And anyway, he'd made up his mind to run away, so he was going to stay running away. As long as he could.

The children sat on the pebbles, looking out to sea.

'Nathan,' said Julia, 'do you expect Mrs Henrey knows about us?'

'Course.'

'And Mr Barlowe?'

'Course – we been on telly, innit!'

'And all of Class 8. They all seen it. We're famous, ain't we! Fancy us famous. I never thought I would be famous, did you, Nathan?'

'I dunno. I might be extremely famous one day.'

'How?'

'I dunno. I might do something famous. I might write a book. Like *Treasure Island*.'

'You could write a book about us running away.'

'Nah – that's too ordinary. I mean Adventure on the High Seas, stuff like that.'

'Oh.'

Saturday afternoon lengthened into Saturday evening, and next day was Sunday, with the church bells ringing and the hordes arriving in their cars, and by coach and train. Being the weekend, of course the weather had turned blustery and squally. Julia felt silly with her school anorak over the sixteen-year-old outfit. The big clothing shops were closed, but she managed to get a smartish plastic mac in one of the little places on the seafront, and shivered in that. The sea was grey-green today, and choppy. A few hardy souls were bathing, but Julia didn't fancy it. Nathan was happy enough, watching for ships and playing the slot machines. But to Julia the day seemed somehow long, and without purpose. She was restless and irritable and hoping the sun would shine again tomorrow.

It didn't. On Monday morning Mrs Parsons asked Julia

would she like to settle the bill now, since she and Charlie had been there a week. She asked how their mother was, and Julia said not so well yesterday. She said that so it would look all right to stay another week perhaps, and Mrs Parsons said she was sorry to hear the news about Julia's mother, but she wasn't altogether surprised since she had noticed that Beverley had been looking a bit down in the dumps the last day or two. 'Cheer up, dear,' she added. 'Bless my soul, your mother will be as right as rain, you mark my words. These things take time, you know.'

They went to the seafront, and Julia stared glumly at the cold-looking waves, the colour of old roofs in London, breaking frothily on the pebbles. Dark threatening clouds piled up over the sea, and the first drops of rain splashed on to the promenade. Julia and Nathan sat in a little seafront café and drank Coca-Cola, waiting for the rain to finish.

Other holiday-makers had the same idea. They crowded into the little café, sheltering from the dismal weather, and soon Julia and Nathan found themselves sharing their table with a family of four, all enormously fat people, who proceeded to distend their already bulging stomachs with buns and milk shakes. There was a mother and father, a sticky baby with ice cream all over its face – and a boy about the same age as Julia and Nathan, who kept giving them funny looks. He stared quite rudely, first at Julia, then at Nathan, then back at Julia again. Finally he poked his father in the ribs and whispered something in his ear. The children could not hear what he said, because the sticky baby was bawling its head off by this time, with frustration at being cooped up in the café when it wanted to be crawling on the pebbles. The father jerked his head round sharply, to get a good look at Julia and Nathan.

'Don't talk stupid,' he said to the boy, his mouth full of bun.

'It's not stupid, it's *them*,' said the boy in a loud whisper.

'The girl's much too old,' hissed the father.

'But that boy wears glasses really, you can see the mark on his nose.'

'Keep your voice down, can't you!'

Julia went very red. Nathan fidgeted anxiously, and his heels drummed against the table leg. 'Let's go, let's go,' he muttered, under cover of the baby's continued squalls.

'Come on, Charlie,' said Julia. 'We better hurry now. Mum'll be waiting for us.'

They knew they ought to walk – show complete unconcern – but as soon as they were out of the café, panic took over, and they ran. Julia whipped off the spiky heels and held them in her hand as they both pelted along the seafront in the rain. A glance behind showed the fat boy running after them, a joyful expression on his pudgy face. But he soon stopped, out of breath. Julia saw him looking disappointed before she and Nathan rounded a corner and were out of sight.

'Let's go back to Mrs Parsons',' said Julia, who was quite shaken by the incident.

'Nah,' said Nathan, 'let's stay here. I ain't scared. It's boring at Mrs Parsons'.'

'We could watch telly.'

'I rather here.' Nathan had found himself near his beloved slot machines.

'That boy might find us again,' said Julia, fearfully.

'Don't matter, he can't run,' said Nathan spitting on to the pebbles in contempt. 'He runs slow as a tortoise.'

They played the machines, and Julia nearly won. Every time she dropped a penny down the chute, it *nearly* tipped over all the rest. Nathan thought he could do it better, but Julia wouldn't let him have a go. She wanted all the prize, and all the glory for herself. So Nathan watched, encouraging her. In this case, he didn't much care who won, as long as one of them did.

For both children, the fright in the café was totally forgotten. They were easily caught off their guard.

'How you doing, Nathan?' came a voice from nowhere – and Nathan fell right into the trap! Without thinking he raised his head, looked around to see who was calling him – and too late realized his mistake when he found himself looking right at the face of the fat boy, leering fuzzily a couple of metres away.

Julia was oblivious of all this. Her coin had tipped the pile and the mountain of pennies rattled into the receptacle below. 'I won, I won,' she shouted triumphantly, scooping out the money with her hands. 'Nathan – I won!'

'Shut up,' said Nathan.

But the damage was done. Julia had said his name. The fat boy, still leering, advanced on Nathan, who was still trying to collect his wits.

'I know you, Nathan Browne,' said the fat boy. 'I caught you now, didn't I!'

Julia stopped scooping out the money, and her mouth dropped open in bewilderment and dismay. As she watched, she saw Nathan dodge and try to run. But round the other side of the machine, barring his way, was the fat boy's father! Nathan dodged back, swung round Julia nearly toppling her over, and was blocked again by the fat boy.

Desperate now, Nathan lashed out with his fists. The fat boy was taller, and much heavier, but Nathan was wiry and agile. Unsportingly, Nathan punched him hard in the stomach, and as the fat boy howled and doubled up, Nathan sped through the arcade and on to the wide open seafront, leaving Julia to her fate.

'We've got you anyway, young lady,' said the fat man grimly, ignoring for the moment the bellows of pain coming from his son, and stretching out his hands to grab Julia.

At that moment, Julia found her feet. She started to run, but the spiky heels of the ridiculous little sandals impeded her. Her ankle turned over, and she lurched painfully against the machine. The fat man caught her easily, and gripped both her arms in a vice. 'Got you, got you,' he repeated.

Julia writhed and struggled. 'Let go, let go you're hurting me,' she screamed. She tried to stamp on his feet, and when that failed she bent her head to bite the hand that held her. She was frantic – beside herself with fear.

Everyone in the arcade was looking by now. Two tough-looking youths misunderstood the situation. 'Leave her, Dad,' one of them called.

'It's Julia Winter,' said the fat man, gasping with the exertions of having to hold Julia.

But the name meant nothing to the youths, who loped menacingly towards the struggling pair. In spite of the chill, they wore only tee-shirts and jeans, and there were lurid tattoos on their arms. The hair of both stood up in spikes. 'I said leave her, Dad,' the one with the voice growled again.

The fat man had no more breath with which to explain. His face was already turning an ominous purple, and when the two strong lads grabbed his arms one on each side, he gave up the unequal fight. Released, Julia charged at the exit, and disappeared into the rain outside.

The fat man sucked ruefully at his hand, where Julia's teeth marks clearly showed. 'She bit me,' he muttered.

'Serve you right,' said the youth with the voice, 'molesting young girls!'

'I wasn't molesting her, you moron,' gasped the fat man, angrily. 'I was catching her. That's Julia Winter, the kid who's run away from home. And the other one's Nathan Browne. They went off together, didn't they – it was on telly *and* in the papers. Now they've both got away, thanks to you. . . . Come on, Stuart,' he addressed his moaning son, 'he can't have hurt you that much. He's only a little runt!'

The two youths looked at each other, feeling silly. 'Better

get after them hadn't we?' said the silent one, speaking now for the first time.

'Ah leave it,' said the one with the voice. 'Let the Bill see to it. You want to tell the police, mate. They'll get 'em all right.'

'That's exactly what I'm going to do,' said the fat man. 'Now.'

Meanwhile Julia blundered, sobbing wretchedly, along the seafront. Nathan – where was Nathan? She didn't even know which way he'd gone. She felt horribly frightened and alone. She peered into various dives along the way, but Nathan didn't seem to be in any of them. She even peeped into the Gents' toilet, but he wasn't there. He had deserted her. Trembling, her knees still like jelly, she looked over her shoulder to see if the fat man was following – but there was only sheeting rain. Julia herself was getting very wet, she realized. The blouse and skirt were drenched all down the front, where the plastic mac flapped open.

She would go back to Mrs Parsons', she decided, and get dry. She would wait for Nathan there. Perhaps he was there already. Most likely he *was* there. Why hadn't she thought of that before? The fright had made her all muddled, so she couldn't think properly. She brushed the tears and the rain out of her eyes, and stumbled her way back to the boarding house.

Mrs Parsons hobbled from the kitchen, as Julia came through the front door.

'Beverley – bless my soul, how wet you are! You'll catch your death, dear.' She hesitated, because it was not really polite to mention that she could see Julia had been crying. 'Have you been to see your mother?'

Julia turned her head, too distraught still to trust herself to speak.

'Charlie's here,' said Mrs Parsons. 'He seemed a bit upset. It might help to talk about it.'

'She's *worse*,' said Julia. 'She's worse all the time.' She had an excuse now to let the tears flow.

'You poor child,' said Mrs Parsons, gently.

'I'm not a child,' Julia sobbed.

'I know, you young girls think you're very grown-up these days. But you know, Beverley, I daresay you won't like me saying this but really, with all that stuff off your face, you really don't look much more than eleven years old!'

8

On the run

'You took your time, man,' said Nathan, savagely. He was sitting on his bed, his knees hunched up to his chin, his eyes glaring fear. He was feeling bad about having abandoned Julia, so naturally he took it out on her.

'You left me alone,' wailed Julia. 'What did you leave me alone for?'

'I thought that man caught you, didn't I.'

'You still shouldn't have left me alone! You shouldn't have!'

'So? What you going on and on about it for? It's boring.'

Julia sat on the edge of the big bed, her feelings hurt, her back pointedly turned towards Nathan.

'What happened then?' said Nathan sullenly.

'What you want to know for?'

'All right, *be* like that.'

'I got away, didn't I.'

'Good,' said Nathan.

'Why good? You don't care.'

'Yes I do.'

'You don't. You left me all by myself.'

'Oh don't start that again. . . . We got to go, you know.'

'What do you mean? Go where?'

'Away. Away from Brighton.'

'What for?' said Julia. 'Oh yeah – that man. He's going to tell the police about us, isn't he.'

'They'll be looking all over. Probably looking now.'

'They won't know to come to this house though. We'll be all right if we just stay indoors. Can't we just stay indoors?'

'Don't be stupid, man. What's Mrs Parsons going to say?'

'Oh yeah – I forgot. . . . Let's stay though, Nathan. I don't want to leave this house, I like it here.'

'So do I, but we don't want to get caught, do we?'

'All right,' said Julia, sadly. 'What shall we tell Mrs Parsons?'

'Tell her we're going home. Tell her our mum's better.'

'I just this minute said she's worse.'

'Don't tell her nothing then – let's just go.'

'Not say goodbye?'

'Are you mad or something?'

'All right.'

The children found their beach bags and started to pack. When Julia came to the torn school dress, mended with Sellotape, she paused. A vacant look came over her face, and she sat down heavily on the bed, staring into space.

'Get on with it, Julia, don't waste time.'

'I'm thinking.'

'You can think on the train. If we don't hurry up, the police is going to be at the station, waiting to catch us.'

No answer.

'Come on, Ju.'

'Shut up. I told you, I'm thinking. . . . All right, listen. The police is going to catch us anyway if we go out looking the same.'

'Same as what?'

'Same as we look now. They know I got make-up now, and they know you don't wear glasses no more. We got to change ourself.'

'Oh yeah – we better do that.'

'See. You didn't think of that, did you, Nathan Browne!'

'How are we going to change ourselves though?'

There was a long pause.

'I could cut my hair,' said Julia. 'They think I got long hair, but I could cut it.'

'Oh yeah, you could.' Another idea struck Nathan, a strategy frequently used in books. 'You could cut it *really* short. You could be a *boy*,' he said.

'Oh Nathan – I never could!'

'Why couldn't you? You could cut your hair short and have jeans and a tee-shirt like me.'

'I'd look silly.'

'No you wouldn't. You wouldn't. Come on, Ju, that's a magnificent idea I had. You dress up like a boy. You'd make a brilliant boy!'

'I don't know though. . . .'

'We need some scissors.'

'We shall have to buy some,' said Julia. Her mind was a turmoil of new thoughts, but she struggled to bring out one more idea, before it should get lost and forgotten. 'Couldn't we change you as well? A bit?'

'How? I'm not going to be a *girl*.'

'I didn't mean that. I mean . . . they're going to be looking for a white kid and a black kid, right?'

'So?'

'And there's not all that many black people in Brighton anyway, not like at home, so you going to be easy to notice.'

'So?'

'But you ain't really *black*.'

'Yes I am.'

'I mean you ain't *very* black. I don't think it notice *much*, only for your hair.'

'I can't change my hair.'

'You could cover it over. You could get one of them seaside caps with the letters on it.'

'They'd still see I'm black though.'

'Yes, if they really *look* they'd see, but what I mean . . . what I mean . . . if they don't specially *look*. . . .'

'Oh I get it, I get it, you mean they won't go past me in the street and think, "There's a black boy, I wonder if he's Nathan Browne", they'll only just notice I'm a boy.'

'That's what I mean. Especially for when they see us together.'

'Let's go and get the things now then,' said Nathan.

'Yeah but – I think we didn't ought to both of us go out.'

'Why not?'

'We don't want the police to see us together before we change ourselves. In case the fat man told them about us already.'

Pause.

'I'll go,' said Nathan. 'I can run faster than you.'

'Yeah but – you got to get clothes for me, and you might not get them the right size.'

Nathan measured her up and down with his eye. 'I'll get them perfect,' he promised.

'I'll give you the money.'

'No, it's all right.'

'I will.'

'It's all right – I don't mind.'

It was the first time either of them had offered to buy anything for the other.

Nathan slipped out of the house without being seen.

Outside, the rain had stopped and a pale watery sun was trying to break through. There was little warmth in it, but the brightness was faintly cheering. Nathan splashed through the puddles, on his way to the shops.

The clothes were no trouble. Jeans and tee-shirts you could buy in lots of places, and no one bothered that they were not in Nathan's size. He just had to say they were for his brother. That was even true in a way, since Julia *was* going to be his sort of brother.

The scissors were more difficult. Nathan had no idea where you could buy scissors. He studied the fronts of all the shops, and finally spotted some curved nail-scissors in a chemist's window. He went inside and bought them, hoping they would be all right.

It was when he was coming out of the chemist's that he felt the first breath of danger. There was a policeman on the other side of the road, and the policeman was looking at him – hard.

Nathan tried to keep his head. The policeman might not be looking at him really. He might be looking into the chemist's shop. There might be a thief going to rob the chemist, and the policeman was looking to catch him. Nathan sauntered casually along the road, his purchases in the plastic bag they had given him in the shop where he bought the jeans.

The policeman kept pace with him, on the other side of the road, still looking.

Don't panic, Nathan told himself. Good job he came and not Julia. Julia would panic for certain. The policeman couldn't *know* it was him. He'd have given chase by now if he *knew*. Probably he'd been told to look out for *any* small black boys around. Probably he'd go away in a minute, when he saw Nathan wasn't worried.

The policeman began to cross the road and come towards him.

Nathan ran. Fortunately for him, a sudden spate of traffic in both directions held up the policeman's crossing. By the time the policeman had landed safely on the same pavement as Nathan, Nathan was already turning the corner into a side road. He heard the police whistle as he went.

He must hide. Wildly, as his feet pounded down the road, Nathan considered the possibilities. Shops and cafés were out of the question. Once inside, anyone could denounce him, and he would be trapped. He dodged around other users of the pavement and one or two told him to look where he was going. At any moment, one of them might grasp the fact that he was not just a small boy running, but a small boy running from the police.

He turned a corner, and another, and another. No one seemed to be following. Had he escaped? He was in a large square. His heart was pounding now, his breath coming in great gasps, and there was a stitch in his side. His knees were beginning to buckle – he knew he could not run much further. On the corner of the square was a telephone box. Not much cover, but he might just get away with it. The square seemed empty – not like the street with the cafés which was thronged with people. Nathan didn't think there was anyone to see. Weakly, he stumbled into the telephone box and curled up on the floor into a tight little ball. If anyone looked, they would just think someone had left an old coat in the box. He hoped no one would want to use the telephone.

Nathan did not know how long he lay curled in the telephone box. He could neither see nor hear anything of what was going on outside. Were the police in the square? Would they think of looking in the telephone box? Time went by, and Nathan felt safer with the passing of every minute, but he wasn't taking any chances. He wasn't coming out yet.

He thought Julia would wonder why he was taking so

long to do the shopping. He remembered that he hadn't bought that cap yet. Where could he get one of those caps, he wondered? There were plenty of places on the seafront, and this square must be near the seafront, since he had run downhill to it all the way. But the seafront was disaster. Fat boys and their fathers, and other nosy parkers no doubt, lurked there ready to point the finger and say, 'That's Nathan Browne, that's the boy who ran away. Catch him!'

After a bit, Nathan heard the rain once more, spattering on the telephone box. Lightly at first, and then lashing down in a fury. He was so cramped now, from crouching in one position, that he thought he could not bear the pain any longer. Surely it would be safe to come out. Surely even policemen would be sheltering from this weather.

Cautiously raising one arm, Nathan pushed open the door of the telephone box and crawled out into the square. His legs had gone to sleep so he could not stand up. He rubbed them, while the rain drenched him. He was soaked and shivering in a minute, but he didn't mind that. The rain gave him an excuse to wear the hood of his anorak, so his hair was covered, and his face hardly visible anyway. He was just any small boy, running to get out of the rain, carrying his shopping in a plastic bag.

Muffled up like this, Nathan felt it was even safe to go on to the seafront.

The seafront shops were crowded with holiday-makers sheltering from the dismal weather. Nathan pushed his way through a barrier of jostling bodies, mostly clad in dripping plastic macs. He found the little caps and chose one – any one. He offered his money at the counter, and the woman standing next to him, buying two sticks of rock, jammed her elbow into his eye.

'I was first,' she claimed, still waving her hand with the money in it.

'No you wasn't,' said Nathan, indignantly.

And then, to his horror, he saw who it was. It was the fat woman, wife of the fat man, and mother of the sticky baby!

Once more, Nathan ran. The cap and the plastic bag in one hand, the money for the cap still in the other, he clove through the press of wet bodies around him, ducking and squirming to get to the door.

'Hey, you haven't paid for that.' 'Stuart, Stuart, it's that boy again!' 'Little thief, stop him!' The cries sounded all around, but everything happened so quickly that Nathan was out of the shop before anyone could actually catch him. Two or three of the more athletic, lacking anything better to do, followed him along the seafront. At the first corner, Nathan plunged on to the beach, rolling over and over down the steep slope of pebbles. The cascading pebbles half buried him as he rolled. He dug his toes into the shifting mass, to stop himself sliding any further, and peered cautiously at the promenade above him. His pursuers lumbered mistily past, and Nathan dropped his head on to the smooth cold pebbles, heaving to regain his breath.

He hadn't meant to steal the cap. He wasn't really a thief, he wasn't! But he couldn't go back and pay for it now. Under shelter of the shelving pebbles, Nathan doubled back along the beach, then climbed back to the seafront walk, and from there up the steps to the promenade and the busy road with the traffic thundering past. He kept the anorak hood over his head, even though it wasn't raining any more. He went a long way round to Mrs Parsons', weaving and dodging just in case there might be someone following him.

By the time he got back it was late afternoon. Julia was frantic with worry. 'I thought you got caught, I thought you got caught,' she wailed. Nathan explained that he nearly did. In few words, but with relish and some embroidery, he

111

told his story. When he had finished, Julia had a picture of the world outside populated almost exclusively with threatening policemen and hawk-eyed members of the public. Nathan had forgotten to buy any food, but Julia practically had hysterics at the idea of his going out again to get some. They shared a bag of crisps left over from the day before, and drank water from the wash-basin in their room, and Nathan wished he'd been a bit more discreet. Another time, he'd be more careful what he told her.

After they had eaten, Julia examined the clothes Nathan had brought for her. They looked all right. She had rigged up a private dressing cubicle for herself in a corner of the room, using a spare blanket off the bed, and she retreated into this to change.

The tee-shirt and jeans were just right,. Julia's long, thin, flat-chested figure looked convincingly boyish inside them. Julia was less happy when she saw the curved nail scissors. 'I can't cut my hair with them,' she protested.

'Yes you can,' said Nathan. 'Go on – you can!'

Julia stood in front of the mirror, the little scissors in her hand. Now that the moment had come, she was fearful of beginning. She had always had long hair – well, as long as the meagre little rats' tails would grow. To cut it now to seemed an awfully big step. Besides, she'd got used to looking nice. It really hurt to have to spoil that.

Feeling slightly sick, Julia took a front strand in one hand, closed her eyes, and jabbed at it with the scissors. There was a ripping sound, as the blades went through the hair. Julia shuddered and opened her eyes. The deed was done, or as good as. There was no going back now.

Carefully, Julia worked round her head, hacking away with the little scissors. Nathan watched in silence, and increasing dismay. Julia's feelings, as she saw what she was doing to herself, were of sheer mounting horror. 'It looks awful,' she moaned, when it was finished.

It did. The long hair flowing round her face had softened it, distracting attention from the bony contours. Now these features were prominent again – even more so than they had been with the plaits. Worse still, the cut hair was jagged, shapeless.

'Let me do the back for you a bit,' said Nathan.

He snipped anxiously here and there, and made some marginal improvement, but it was soon clear that, if they worked at it all night, their combined efforts were in no way going to produce anything like a proper haircut.

Julia was too shattered to cry. She sat on the bed, pouting and shaking her head. 'I ain't going out like this. I ain't going out,' she kept repeating.

'But we got to go,' said Nathan. 'The police. Come on, Ju, it's not that bad.' He had a sudden inspiration. 'I know – you could wear my cap.'

He produced the cap, and Julia put it on. The cap covered most of the terrible haircut. Julia regarded herself doubtfully in the mirror. 'What do the letters say, Nathan?'

She meant the wording across the front of the cap. Nathan peered closely, to read the legend. He opened his mouth to tell Julia what it was, but changed his mind at the last moment. 'I can't see without my glasses,' he claimed.

'Liar,' said Julia.

She took the cap off and tried to read the words herself. They were not very long words. Julia tried very hard, sounding out the letters. 'KISS ME, it says KISS ME,' she announced. Triumph at having actually read something struggled with outrage at what she had read. 'I ain't wearing that,' she decided, throwing the cap on the floor. 'No way, I ain't wearing that.'

'Don't be silly,' said Nathan, 'it ain't that bad. Plenty of people wear caps that says that.'

'Not me,' said Julia.

113

'Come on, Ju,' said Nathan picking up the cap and trying to replace it on her clipped head. Julia pushed him away and then sat with her hands over her head, her mouth a stubborn line. She was being totally unreasonable, but nothing Nathan could say or do would shift her. 'I know,' he tried, 'wear your anorak hood.'

'My anorak hasn't got a hood. I lost it.'

'That plastic mac then. That's got a hood.'

'It's a girl's one. How can I wear a girl's mac if I'm supposed to be a boy?'

'Wear the cap then.'

'No.'

'What do you want to do then?'

'Stay here.'

'We can't.'

'We could stay one night. My hair might have growed a bit by tomorrow.'

'Not much though. You going to breakfast like that then? What's Mrs Parsons going to say when she sees you with your hair cut?'

Appalling thought. 'I won't go to breakfast, I'll stay here.'

'And then we'll go. Eh Ju? We'll go then, eh?'

In the cruel light of day? With the morning sun on her poor shorn head?

'No,' said Julia.

'What you mean, no?'

'I ain't going out, not till my hair's growed.'

Nathan lost his patience. 'You're stupid!'

'No I ain't.'

'Yes you are, you're a silly stupid Rat-bag.'

'I hate you, Nathan Browne.'

'So do I hate you.'

'I wish I never run away with you.'

'Good.'

'I want to go ho–o–o–ome,' Julia wailed, in sudden anguish.

'You can't.'

Why couldn't she? There had been a reason, but from this distance, and in her misery, she couldn't remember what it was.

'Yes I can, you can't stop me.'

'Go on then.'

'I'm going now.'

'Go on then, I said.'

'It's all your fault. You made me come. I'm going to tell of you, when I get home.'

'Who cares!'

'You made me cut my hair too.'

'You didn't have to. Silly stupid Rat-bag! . . . Can't read! . . . Silly stupid dunce!'

Julia turned her face to the wall, and retreated into wounded silence. Nathan, angry and frustrated, kicked at his bed-post, then at Julia's bed-post. Then he went to the window and drew patterns on the pane with his finger, humming a bit to show how little he cared about the quarrel. He was at his wits' end, though, to know what to do next.

Suddenly he stiffened. 'Ju – there's a police car coming up the road!'

No answer.

'They stopping. They stopping outside. Ju – the police is coming to the door!'

She looked round then, her pale eyes tragic with fear. 'Are they coming for us?'

'They must be.'

'Oh don't let them get me! Lock the door, Nathan, don't let them come in!'

'That's no good.'

'What is then? What shall we do?'

'We could climb out the window.'

'It's high up. I'm scared to.'

'I could do it.'

'But I'm scared.'

The sound of the doorbell vibrated through the house. The children looked at each other in dismay.

'We'll climb out the window when the police is inside. Come on, Ju. I'll help you.'

'No I'm scared, I'm scared.'

Nathan's thoughts were a turmoil. He didn't want to desert her but. . . . 'Let's see when they come in the hall,' he said. 'We could run down the stairs perhaps. We *could*. If they ain't standing in the doorway, we could get out then. Perhaps.'

He opened the bedroom door and tiptoed on to the landing, leaning over the bannisters to see what was going on in the hall below. He saw Mrs Parsons moving stiffly to answer the bell, and caught the gist of the conversation on the doorstep. A moment later he was back in the bedroom, grinning broadly.

'It's all right, it's not about us.'

'What's it about then?'

'It's about a house was burglared, next door.'

'Are you sure?'

'Yes, it's not about us at all.'

'We ain't caught then?'

'No.'

'Oh, I was *scared*.'

'I thought you wanted to go home though. You said you wanted to go home.'

'I changed my mind.'

'Shall we escape then? When the police is gone?'

Julia did not commit herself. She stood at some distance from the window with Nathan, watching until the police came out of the house and drove away in their car.

116

'Shall we go now?' said Nathan.

'No.'

'Why not?'

'My hair.'

They were back to that.

'How can we go anyway? The police is going to be watching the station, you said so,' said Julia.

'We can go by bus.'

'How do you know they ain't watching the buses?'

Actually, she could be right. Nathan was silent, considering the problem. Buses, trains – what other means of transport were there? 'We could stow away on a lorry.' he said, with sudden inspiration.

'You're mad,' said Julia.

'No I'm not, they do it in stories.'

'That's in stories!'

'Well *we* could do it. It's better than the train.'

'Where will we go to though?'

'Wherever the lorry goes. A long way. We'll get one of them long-distance lorries that travels all night.'

'Where we going to sleep though?'

'In the lorry.'

'But after? Where we going to sleep after? I'm not sleeping in no more building sites. That was horrible!'

'You won't have to sleep in a building site. We can sleep in the lorry tonight and then – I know, I know, we'll have a tent!'

'I ain't going in no tent with you, Nathan Browne, I don't like you,' said Julia, remembering recent insults.

'All right, we'll have *two* tents. One each.'

That was an even better idea, Nathan thought. A tent all to himself! Almost as good as a house. Julia also liked the idea of a tent. She began to cheer up, thinking about it, and even half-heartedly fiddled with her packing.

'You coming then?'

'I suppose so.'

'I'll help you pack,' said Nathan, thinking that the sooner they got out of the house the better. Before she changed her mind again. 'What about your money? How you going to carry that now?'

'In my shoulder bag of course, like I always do.'

'But you're a boy now, boys don't have shoulder bags like that.'

'Oh no, I forgot.'

'Why don't you put it in your anorak, like me?'

'There's no hole in my pocket.'

'Make one then, cut one.'

But Julia was scandalized by the idea of such an act of deliberate destruction. She would put the money round her waist like before, she said. She fussed around looking for a suitable plastic bag, and Nathan was getting very impatient, because it was well into evening by now and he thought all the long-distance lorries would have started their night journeys, and he and Julia would be too late to find one. Then Julia needed something to fasten the bag with, and there was no string, and in the end she took the elastic out of a pair of knickers and used that.

'Shall we go now then?' said Nathan.

They might have made it but unfortunately, just as she was picking up her beach bag, Julia caught a glimpse of the terrible haircut in the wardrobe mirror – and sat down heavily on the bed again.

'What's the matter now?' said Nathan.

'My hair.'

'Oh forget your silly hair! It's going to be dark soon, anyway. They won't see.'

No answer.

'Come on!'

Julia sniffed and pouted, and tossed back the plaits that weren't there.

'Come on, Rat-bag, the police might really come for us next time. They might be here now. Any minute, they might be at the door!'

No answer.

Nathan kicked Julia, quite hard, on the ankle.

'Don't you kick me, Nathan Browne!'

'Shall if I want to.'

He kicked her again, harder. Julia began to wail.

'Shut up, stupid Rat-bag!'

Julia's wails rose to a shriek.

'Shut *up*,' said Nathan, frantically. 'Someone's going to hear. Mrs Parsons is going to come!'

'You hurt me!'

'Serve you right. You're stupid, innit!'

He did not kick her again, though he would have liked to. Instead, he lay down on his bed – it was almost bedtime anyway. It looked as though they were stuck for the night, and what after that? Perhaps they were stuck here for ever. Perhaps he would never persuade Julia to leave the sanctuary of their room. Perhaps, perhaps . . . *he would have to go by himself.*

Nathan curled up with his face to the wall, and tried to go to sleep. It might be all right in the morning. By the morning the problem might have gone away.

But he was too upset to sleep. He fidgeted and turned the other way and saw that Julia was still sitting there on her bed, shoulders hunched forward, fingers pulling hopelessly at what was left of her hair, as though she were trying to force it to grow again. Angry as he was, Nathan felt a pity for her which really hurt. He fell into an uneasy sleep at last, and when he woke he saw by the moonlight streaming through the bedroom window that Julia was also sleeping, after a fashion, sprawled across the bed with her feet still on the floor.

Long before dawn both children were wide awake,

exhausted with sleeplessness, wretched with anxiety.

'We could go before Mrs Parsons gets up,' said Nathan, pretending the quarrel had not happened.

Julia looked quickly in the mirror, and quickly away again.

'Shall we go then?'

'My hair hasn't growed.'

'Well it won't, will it. It'll take weeks. Anyway you supposed to be a boy.'

'I ain't coming out like this.'

'All right,' said Nathan, regretfully. He got off the bed, and picked up his beach bag. 'Bye then, Julia.'

'You're not going without me!'

'I'm not staying here to get caught.'

'Don't leave me!'

'Come on then.'

'No.'

Nathan walked to the bedroom door and opened it. Would she change her mind and follow? He looked over his shoulder and saw that she was still sitting on the bed, her face a mask of total despair.

Nathan crept down the stairs in the dark. The front door was locked and chained and Nathan was very much afraid that Mrs Parsons or someone would hear him unfastening it. But all the house was sleeping soundly, and in a moment Nathan was safely in the street.

He felt very lonely, plodding along by himself. Running away on your own was quite a different matter from running away with somebody else. He didn't quite know how he was going to manage alone; he couldn't quite see it.

He had turned the corner, and was halfway up the next street before Julia caught up with him.

9

Stowaways

'Shall we go in a lorry then?' said Nathan.

Julia did not answer. She was coming out of desperation, not enthusiasm. Nathan thought he must treat her carefully, or she might change her mind again. She slouched along at his heels, her long face drawn with tiredness. Nathan turned a couple of times, to give her an encouraging grin, but she wouldn't look at him.

They were vulnerable, and conspicuous – two children alone in the deserted early morning streets. Nathan was terribly afraid they might meet a policeman. There seemed to be an extraordinary dearth of lorries in Brighton today. They wandered from street to street, searching, while the sun came up and the town came to life.

Nathan was seeking a lorry with such single-mindedness that his mind didn't register the caravan till they were way past it. He stopped suddenly.

'Let's go back a bit.'

'What for?' They were the first words Julia had uttered since leaving the house.

'Have a little rest. Here, on the pavement.'

She followed him apathetically and they squatted side by side. The caravan was parked on the opposite side of the road, where a man with a bald head and a woman with crimped grey hair were fussing around, making last-minute preparations for their holiday. The caravan was big, with orange curtains, and it was hitched to a shiny, new-looking car. The man and the woman kept going into their house, and bringing out more odds and ends which they packed into the car or the caravan.

'See that caravan,' said Nathan, cautiously.

'What about it?'

'Would you like to ride in it? Instead of a lorry?'

'You're mad.'

'But if we get in when they aren't looking.'

'You're mad.'

'But if we *could*.'

'Where's it going?' asked Julia.

'I dunno, do I. Somewhere. Probably another seaside.'

'We can't anyway; they'll see us.'

The woman got into the car and sat in the passenger seat. 'The rug, dear,' she called to her husband. 'You forgot the rug. Oh – and my blue coat. I left it upstairs, I think. On the end of the bed.'

The man went into the house, and the woman began to study a large map. She was using a magnifying glass, and peering at the map very intently.

'What's she doing?' said Nathan.

'She's reading,' said Julia, without much interest.

'We could do it now,' said Nathan. 'Quick, before he comes back.'

Julia said nothing.

'Come on, Ju. Come on, let's.' It was too bad – the opportunity was there, and it was being missed.

Julia was cold, in spite of the early morning sunshine. She

had had no breakfast and little to eat the day before, so she was also hungry. But above all, she was tired. The caravan did seem to offer, if nothing else, shelter and rest.

'Come on, Ju. Let's . . . eh?'

'All right.'

'Brilliant!' Nathan seized Julia's hand, and dragged her with him across the road. The woman in the car was still studying the map. The caravan door was unlocked. Nathan scrambled up and turned to help Julia, hauling her inside. He closed the door carefully – it hardly made a sound. He looked around for a hiding place. There was a table at one end, with blue upholstered seats on either side. Nathan dived under the table.

'Come on, Julia, hurry!'

With maddening slowness, she crawled after him. There were footsteps outside. The caravan door opened, and for one heart-stopping moment it looked as though the man was going to get in. But he only threw a rug and a couple of coats on to the seat by the entrance. 'And let's hope her ladyship doesn't think of anything *else*,' he muttered. He slammed the caravan door, and the children heard a key being turned.

'He's locked us in,' said Julia, not caring very much.

'I know,' said Nathan, dismayed.

'How we going to get out, then?'

'I dunno. Out the window perhaps.'

'How do they open?'

Julia climbed out of her uncomfortable hiding place to look at the window fastenings.

'Keep your head down, stupid!'

'Don't call me that.'

'No, you're not stupid, you're not stupid, but keep your head down. We don't want nobody to see us before we even started.'

Julia lost interest in the window. She crawled along the

123

floor, so Nathan wouldn't shout at her again, and stretched herself along the seat at the back, taking the best bed as a matter of course. She covered herself with the red tartan rug which the owner of the caravan had so obligingly provided, and almost immediately delicious waves of sleep began to wash over her. A little jolt, as the caravan moved off, jerked her momentarily awake – and then she sank, down, down into warm and blissful slumber.

Nathan sat on the floor for a while, afraid to move in case his shifting weight should make the caravan tip. His eyes were on the man's warm-looking coat, and at last he dared to crawl, slowly and carefully, towards it. The caravan went on riding smoothly, and Nathan dragged the coat back to where the table was. Then he curled up on one of the short seats with the man's coat over him, and soon he too was fast asleep.

It was the lack of motion that woke them, hours later. Nathan raised himself cautiously, to peep out of the window from behind the orange curtain.

'Where are we?' said Julia, still half dazed with sleep.

'I dunno. Oh yes – we're in a car park. There's a sort of caff over there. It's all right, it's all right, our man and lady's going in. I expect they're going to eat something. Good job they didn't come in here to have their lunch. That's good, innit. Eh?'

Nathan scanned Julia's face anxiously. She'd been very boring since last night. Perhaps, now that she had slept, she would be better.

'I want to go to the toilet,' said Julia.

Now she mentioned it, Nathan was aware of the same need. That was awkward, seeing they were locked in. He began opening cupboard doors, looking for some means of improvisation – and was amazed to find a perfect little toilet unit, complete with fitted shower, in a corner of the caravan.

'Look, Julia, that's neat, innit. That's really convenient.' He was delighted with what he had found – surely Julia must be equally pleased. 'This is a good caravan, isn't it, Julia. It's really comfortable.'

'I'm hungry,' said Julia.

'There's sure to be food,' said Nathan. 'They sure to have packed some food.'

They had. The cupboard under the fitted sink was crammed with tins and packets of biscuits.

'What shall we have?' said Julia, beginning to sound interested.

'You choose,' said Nathan to keep her happy.

'Isn't it stealing?' said Julia, anxiously.

'We could leave some money to pay for it,' said Nathan.

Julia chose a tin of sardines and a tin of corned beef. They couldn't find any crisps, which was a disappointment, but there were some cheesy biscuits which were almost as good. There was no Coca-Cola, so they had to make do with a can of beer each. They found some plastic plates to put the food on, and some forks to eat it with. They didn't like the taste of the beer much, and it made them sleepy, so after they had eaten they settled down on their couches once more.

'This is a nice caravan,' said Nathan, who was feeling very mellow and content. 'I wish we had a caravan like this, don't you, Ju? I know – why don't we buy one with our money, and live in it?'

'We haven't got no car to drive it,' said Julia.

'Oh no – I forgot.'

'Shush,' said Julia. 'They're coming back now.'

There was the slamming of doors, and the sound of the car engine starting.

'I wonder where we're going,' Nathan whispered.

'I hope it's somewhere nice,' said Julia drowsily. . . .

When she woke again, a couple of hours later, she was

feeling much more herself. The unfamiliar lack of weight in the region of her head troubled her for a moment, and she put her hand up to feel her shorn hair. 'Nathan – you awake?'

'Yeah – what?'

'It's funny being a boy. I'm glad I'm not one really. I much rather be a girl. . . . Nathan?'

'What?'

'How we going to get out of this caravan when it stops?'

It was a question to which Nathan did not know the answer, and which he had avoided thinking about. He brooded. 'I know what they do on the telly,' he said at last. 'But I don't know if *we* can.'

'What's that?' said Julia.

'We rush them,' said Nathan. 'Soon as they open the door we push past and rush out. They're so surprised to see us they don't even think to run after us till it's too late.'

'Where do we run to?' said Julia.

'We find a place to hide, and then see.'

'All right.'

'We have to be quick though.'

'All right.'

'You have to run really fast, Julia.'

'All right, I said.'

'Follow me then.' If he went on about it too much she'd take the huff again. 'Keep as close behind me as you can, and keep your head down so they don't see your face. I know – you can put on your plastic mac. Don't matter if they think you're a girl, you can be a boy again after. And I'll have my anorak hood up. Are you scared?'

'Course I'm scared.'

'I'm not,' said Nathan, untruthfully. 'Nothing to be scared about. You'll see.'

At last the caravan began to bump over uneven ground.

126

Nathan sat up to look out of the window. 'Julia – we're there. We're in a camping place. There's all trees and bushes. Plenty of place to hide. Get your plastic mac, quick.'

Julia found the mac and put it on. Then she started fussing with the money bag at her waist.

'Quick, get behind me,' said Nathan at the door. 'Hurry up, what you doing?'

'The money for the food,' said Julia.

'We going to get *caught*,' said Nathan frantically.

'All right, I'm ready.'

Actually they had plenty of time. There was a long wait while the caravan was shunted backwards and forwards, and swung this way and that. Then the key was turned in the lock, and the children were poised with dry mouths and beating hearts, ready to spring.

The caravan door swung open.

'Now!' said Nathan.

He plunged to the ground and began to run downhill, away from the road, to where the trees and bushes were thickest. Astonished, the owner of the caravan stood open-mouthed, watching Nathan run. As Julia plunged out too, the man took an ineffectual step forward – but too late to grab her.

'What's happening, dear?' his wife asked, getting out of the car.

'Blessed if I know,' said the man, scratching his bald head. 'Looks like we had stowaways. See – there they go!'

'Good heavens! Get after them, quick!'

'At my age? You want me to have a heart attack?'

'Well get the police. Get one of the other campers. There's a young man over there. He could catch them for us.'

The man with the bald head shrugged. 'Oh leave it.

They'll be gone to ground. Let's just see what damage they've done.'

Nathan and Julia had long since reached the cover of the bushes. By some miracle, Julia had not crashed into a tree, or twisted her ankle, or tripped over a stone, or broken anything. She had arrived in one piece, reasonably close behind Nathan, though totally winded by the effort. She lay now, wedged between the roots of two shrubs, panting and heaving, each breath like an engine whistle.

'Breathe quieter,' said Nathan.

'I can't,' said Julia.

'Come on then,' said Nathan. 'Let's get further away.'

'I can't,' Julia whimpered. 'Wait for me, Nathan.'

She couldn't see him. Only a rustling from the bushes beyond told her where he had gone. Panicking now, Julia pressed towards the rustling. A sharp twig scratched her face and there was a nasty ripping sound as one pocket was torn from the plastic mac.

The ground seemed very steep all of a sudden. Charging ahead nevertheless, Julia's feet began to slip. She slid a short way, taking loose earth and stones with her, then thumped on to her bottom, and continued on that. As she slid she gathered speed. She grabbed wildly at passing bushes and clumps of turf, trying to stop herself. It was all very painful—the seat of her jeans must surely catch fire, she thought. She wanted to scream but she didn't; at least she had that much presence of mind.

The slope eased off, and with it Julia's descent. She had stopped falling, she had a chance to look around her. She was sprawled on a little tussock of grass, and Nathan was up against a bush, a short way to her right. In front of her was an uninterrupted expanse of grey-brown: grey-brown stones, grey-brown mud, grey-brown water.

'Nathan,' Julia whispered, 'look, we're by the sea again.'

10

A dangerous moment

'It's not a very *nice* sea, is it,' said Julia, disappointed.

'Don't matter,' said Nathan. 'Come on, let's get away from that camping place. You still got your bag?'

She had lost it, of course. It had fallen out of her hand when she slipped, when she was only thinking of saving herself from crashing down the cliff to possible death. The children looked up the way they had come, but neither could see the bag.

'Never mind,' said Nathan, 'it's only got your girl's things in it. You're a boy now.'

'What about my clean underclothes?'

'You can buy more. You might as well take off that silly mac thing now. We don't want nobody to see you in that. Hide it in the bushes.'

'It's not very warm here,' said Julia, shivering. There was a fresh wind blowing off the beach, and her tee-shirt had no sleeves. 'I think I better find the bag, Nathan. It's got my anorak in it.'

'No, come on, they might be looking for us,' said Nathan. 'Let's walk along the beach. We bound to come to some shops soon, then we can buy you another coat. A better one, Ju, with a hood.'

Cheered and encouraged by the prospect of an anorak with a hood, Julia scrambled awkwardly down the rest of the cliff face after Nathan. She regretted the loss of the grown-up blouses and the skirt with the slit in it. They represented a brief, but on the whole very happy interlude in her life. She did not like being a boy, in jeans and tee-shirt. She remembered again about her awful hair.

'Nathan,' she said sheepishly, as they stood together on the beach, 'I don't mind if I wear that cap?'

'You sure?'

'I don't mind.' She felt now that she had been silly before, and unreasonable about the cap.

Nathan gave it to her, and she put it on. 'Do I look like a boy now?' she asked, willing to do her best.

'You look fine,' he said, not feeling too certain.

They stumbled along the beach, which compared with Brighton was almost deserted. There were only a few scattered groups from the camp-site above, and none of them took the slightest notice of Nathan and Julia. Two kids scrambling down a cliff was a perfectly normal occurrence, and no one knew who was staying at the camp at any one time. People were coming and going every day.

It was hard travelling. The loose stones were uneven, and there were great rocks to be climbed here and there. Nathan lagged behind on purpose, to watch Julia picking her way over the obstacles. He was feeling increasingly unhappy about her disguise. 'Julia,' he said, catching up with her, 'why don't you walk a bit more like me?'

'What for?'

'So you look more like a boy.'

'Oh, that.' She was silent for a few minutes. 'Do I actually *have* to be a boy?' she said, at last.

'What you mean?'

130

'Couldn't I just be a girl who wears this sort of clothes?'

'Oh all right, if you like.'

'It'll be easier anyway. I shan't have to keep remembering.'

'All right.' It was a pity his idea hadn't worked, but never mind.

They battled on, over the rocks and the stones. Now they were the only ones on the beach, the only ones in a desolate sunless world, all grey, except for the reddish cliffs beside them.

'I don't like this seaside,' said Julia, for about the tenth time. 'There's no sea.'

Indeed, the tide did seem to be a very long way out – a cold looking, slate-coloured strip on the far horizon, past the mud and the rock pools.

'Never mind,' said Nathan. 'We sure to come to the shops soon, and the fish and chip places and the machines.'

But there was no sign of such civilized comforts yet, and Julia's legs were beginning to be very tired.

'Nathan, where we going to sleep tonight?'

'You slept already – in the caravan.'

'I know I *slept*, but we still got to have somewhere to stay tonight.'

'Shall we go to another hotel?'

'*Course* we can't go to a hotel! *Course* we can't!'

'Why not?'

'They'll wonder why we came without our mum.'

'Couldn't we say our mum's in hospital, like before?'

'You're silly, Nathan, you're really silly. Course we can't say that now!'

'Why not?'

'I don't look grown-up now, do I?'

'Oh yeah – I forgot. You could say you're thirteen.'

'That's still not old enough.'

'You could get some more make-up.'

Julia shook her head. 'My hair's wrong now. I wish I hadn't of cut my hair.'

'It'll grow again.'

'Where we going to stay tonight though? ... You said about a tent.'

'Oh yeah. I don't think we can get a tent tonight though,' said Nathan, unhappily. 'It must be getting late.'

'Why – what time is it?'

'I dunno, do I. Must be five o'clock I should think. We'll be lucky to find a shop open to buy your coat.'

'I can't stay all night without a coat, I'll freeze!'

'We might come to a shop though. Let's hurry.'

'You should have let me find my bag,' said Julia, beginning to whimper. 'You should have let me. Now I'm going to freeze to death.'

'We could stay in that cave if we have to.' Nathan had almost stumbled over its narrow entrance, and now peered in shortsightedly, glad to have found a solution to the problem.

Julia regarded the 'cave' without enthusiasm. It was not much more than a crevice in the rock.

'Not without my coat. I'm going back for my coat.'

'No – Ju, no, please. The caravan man's back there. He might be on the beach. He might see us, or the lady might. He might have told the other people to look for us. He might have told the *police*.'

'I'm going anyway.'

'*You can have my coat!*'

It was an enormous sacrifice. Julia looked at Nathan in disbelief. 'Can I really?'

'Yeah. Only tonight, I mean. In case we're too late to buy one.'

They trudged on. Presently they came to some huge boulders that had to be climbed over. By now they had almost given up hope of finding any signs of human habitation. They seemed to be at the back of beyond. Suddenly Julia gave a cheer. 'Hooray. Look, Nathan!'

'What?'

'Are you blind? Oh yes, of course, you are! Look though – houses, on top of the cliffs! And steps.'

They stumbled towards the steps and climbed them. Here, at last, would be the shops and the amusement arcades. At last they had arrived at a proper seaside.

But it was not like that at all. Only a quaint old street with little olde worlde cottages. There was a fish and chip shop though, and another place with a big map in the window, on the opposite side of the road. The children began to limp down the hill. Their legs ached, their feet were sore from walking so far on the stones, and they didn't think much of the place they had come to, so far. But ahead of them was a sort of promenade, and what looked like a harbour only they hadn't time to investigate because, oh joy, to their right was a miniature High Street, with all sorts of shops in it.

The shops seemed to be open, so it wasn't too late after all. They found a place which sold anoraks, and Julia tried one on. The warm feel of it was heaven, after the chill wind on her bare arms. 'I'll have it,' she said. 'My other one was stolen.'

'That's a pity,' said the woman in the shop. 'Have 'ee told the police?'

'No,' said Julia. 'It was only a old one.'

While they were about it, the children bought themselves a warm pullover each, and Julia bought some underwear and a spare tee-shirt. They put Julia's things in Nathan's beach bag, since Julia had lost hers.

'I see your mum trust 'ee to buy your own things then,' said the lady in the shop. But she was only making conversation. She didn't seem suspicious at all.

'Our mum ain't very well,' said Julia. 'We have to do all the shopping for her.'

'Oh what a shame. Never mind – I can see you'm good children to your mum. You on holiday yur then?'

'Yeah.'

'Not vurry nice weather today. Better tomorrow I expect.'

The children left the shop and went to buy fish and chips at the place they'd seen in the other street.

'They talk funny in this country,' said Julia. 'Not like they talk in England.'

'Don't be stupid, Ju, this *is* England.'

'How do you know? Might not be.'

'Must be. We haven't gone across any sea.'

'Might be Scotland.'

'Nah, can't be Scotland. There's nobody wearing kilts.'

They took their fish and chips and cans of Coke and sat on a seat by the harbour to enjoy them.

'Shall we get our tents tomorrow then, Nathan?'

'Yeah – tomorrow.'

They'd faced enough problems for one day. Just now they could relax, warm in their new pullovers in spite of the cold wind. The cave would do for tonight. It was a bleak and stony prospect, but it was only for a few hours. Tomorrow everything would come good again. Probably. Tomorrow was another day.

The tide was still out, and the little harbour banked with unpleasant-looking thick grey mud. There was a big ship right ahead of them – well, big compared with the little sailing vessels scattered around. An old man, who looked like a local, plonked himself on the seat beside Nathan, and said 'Evening,' very pleasantly, so Nathan asked him where the big ship was going to. 'That'n? Norway I reckon,' said the old man. And the fantasy Nathan had toyed with all through the long sunny days in Brighton came a step nearer reality. It was still a very private thing though, not to be shared with Julia, not to be shared with anyone. Nathan put his fantasy away for another time.

There were very few people on the promenade now. The evening was chilly and closing in. Black rain clouds loomed threateningly. Everyone was indoors, the children thought, in their homes or their boarding-houses or their caravans. Watching television, most likely. Warm and protected anyway.

'We better go back to that cave, I suppose,' said Nathan, reluctantly.

'Yeah, we better be quick an' all. They'll think it's funny if they see us going on the beach when it's raining.'

Back to the stony beach and the rocks. The cave offered scant comfort. There were sharp edges, and it dripped a bit –but at least it was out of the wind and if rain came, as looked probable, they would be reasonably dry. There was not another soul on the beach. Julia and Nathan sat huddled side by side, watching the sea at last creep nearer, as the grey light faded into darkness.

Sleep was unlikely. It was really a matter of waiting out the night, until the shops would be open and they could buy their tents. 'It'll still be cold though, inside the tent, won't it,' Julia speculated, shivering now in the damp night air.

'We'll have sleeping bags,' said Nathan who knew about such things from his reading.

'Will we? That'll be good. What else will we have?'

'I dunno. Yes I do, we'll have a little cooking stove and a pan to go on it.'

'A real cooking stove? In a tent?'

'A little tiny one. You have some special stuff to burn in them.'

'Fancy our own cooking stove!' Julia was enchanted by the idea, she could hardly wait. 'What else will we have, Nathan?'

'Well – we'll have some tins of food, to warm up on the cooking stove.'

'And a light for when it gets dark. Shall we buy a big torch, with a battery in it?'

'That's right. I forgot about the light. It's going to be fun, isn't it, Ju?'

'I wish it was morning now.'

They slept a bit towards dawn, and woke stiff and cramped, chilled to the bone once more. In the murky light they saw that the tide was again retreating over the rocks and the seaweed.

'I'm hungry,' said Julia.

'The shops won't be open yet. We better hide a bit longer anyway. We don't want people to see us out too early.'

Even so, the streets were still deserted when they climbed the steps from the beach, and emerged on to the road with the quaint little houses. They dawdled, knowing there would be nowhere yet to buy food. This time Nathan took more notice of his surroundings. He was getting used to being without his glasses. He could even read the signs on things now, if they were near enough and the letters were big. He noticed that lots of places seemed to be called 'Lorna Doone' something, and the name reminded him of a story he'd read last winter. Well anyway, he'd read a *bit* of it. Actually, he wouldn't have read even that bit, only the lady in the library said she thought the book would be too hard for him, so he took it anyway, to show her up.

In fact she was right, the book *was* too hard for him. He did like one part, in the beginning. Something about a river, with fast dark water and great boulders in it, and a boy wading against the stream, and finding a little girl who'd been captured by robbers. Nathan read that bit over and over. He tried to get past it, and kept getting stuck, so he took the book back to the library and told the lady he'd read all of it, because of course it would be too much shame to admit he hadn't.

136

Nathan thought a lot of people in this town must have read that story.

On their way towards the shopping street, the children passed the shop window with the map in it. A thought struck Nathan and he frowned, turned back, and pressed his nose against the glass, trying to read the names on the map.

'What you looking at that stupid map for?' said Julia.

'It's not stupid. I think it's a map about where we are. Come here, Ju, come and tell me what it says.'

Julia scuffled reluctantly back. She would not be able to read the words on the map, of course. 'Where?' she asked, ungraciously.

'There – just tell me the letters. I can't quite see them.'

Julia concentrated. The word he was pointing at did not look too long. She would *not* endure the shame of having to tell Nathan the letters, she would read the word. She *would*. 'Ex – ex – m–m–m– *moor*. *Exmoor*,' she pronounced, triumphantly.

'*Exmoor*, are you sure?'

'Yes, that's what it says.' Julia glowed with pride. She had actually read a new word, all by herself.

Nathan squatted on the pavement, frowning and thumping his head.

'What are you doing that for?'

'I'm thinking.'

'Do you know where we are, then?'

'I know where we are a *bit*. I know what Exmoor is. I saw a programme about it on the telly, and it was about a story – *Lorna Doone*. There was some robbers on this moor. It's all wild up there, Ju, and hardly any people.'

'Is this Exmoor then?'

'Nah, can't be, can it? But it must be somewhere near. Be

good to camp up there. Shall we get our tents, and go to Exmoor?'

'All right. How are we going to know where it is though?'

'I dunno. We'll have to ask somebody.'

'Let's get some breakfast first.'

In the little shopping street, the children found a small shop which had just opened. They bought milk, and two packets of biscuits, and Nathan asked if there was a shop where they could buy a tent. The counter assistant, a young man with red hair and a long nose, looked rather surprised.

'A tent? Did 'ee say a tent?'

'Yes – you know, for camping.'

'Well . . . not yur, I don't think. Not that I know of. Not in Watchet.'

'Where, then?'

'Well . . . Taunton I suppose.'

'Where's that?'

'You know Taunton. You must know Taunton.'

'Well I don't,' said Nathan.

'We're on holiday here,' Julia explained. 'We don't know the names of all the places.'

The young man looked puzzled. 'Should have thought you'd know Taunton though. Everybody knows Taunton. Wur you staying then?'

'Oh – in the caravans. Up there.' Julia waved a hand vaguely, and the young man nodded.

'I see,' he said, doubtfully.

'That's why we want a tent,' Julia improvised. 'There ain't much room in the caravan, with our mum and dad as well, so we want a tent for us. Actually, we want two tents.'

The suspicious frown faded from the young man's face. 'Oh, I see. You'd better go to Taunton then.'

'How do we get there?'

'Had'n your dad got a car?'

'Yes, but he's busy.'

The frown came back. 'You better go on the bus then.'

'Where do we get the bus from?'

'Top of the road, you'll see.'

'Come on,' said Julia, to Nathan. She was beginning to feel uneasy. The young man was staring very hard – she could sense his gaze boring into her back as they left the shop. 'I think he suspects something,' she said, as they walked in single file along the narrow pavement.

They sat on the seat at the bus stop, Nathan's beach bag between them, drinking their milk and eating their biscuits. The early morning breeze was chilly, but the day promised to be fine.

'I wish there was somewhere to wash,' said Julia.

'When we get our tents, we'll put them by a river,' said Nathan. That was what people did in books. It was the country here, so there were sure to be plenty of rivers about.

'I wish the bus would come,' said Julia.

So did Nathan. Accustomed to the city, where buses arrived every few minutes, he had naturally expected to be out of Watchet in no time. But the milk and biscuits were finished, and they'd played a game of I-Spy, and still the bus had not come. A few early shoppers joined the children on the bus stop seat, and at last the green bus was in sight, sedately approaching them down the hill.

'Here it is,' said Julia, joyfully.

'No it isn't,' said Nathan, screwing up his eyes, peering as the bus came really close. 'It don't say Taunton on the front, it says Minehead.'

They sat down again, frustrated and disappointed.

'They have funny names here, don't they, Nathan?' said Julia. '*Minehead*, that's a funny name. And *Watchet*. Watch it,

139

Nathan!' She giggled at her joke, but stopped giggling when Nathan nudged her sharply, and pointed across the road. Coming towards them was a woman with a gleam in her eye, and an unmistakable purpose. Someone was intending to ask them questions.

From the way she was dressed, she was a summer visitor rather than a resident. She wore pink trousers which were much too tight for her, and a pink tee-shirt which was similarly inappropriate. Her several chins quivered as she spoke, and you could somehow tell she was a nosy sort of person. She advanced on the children, showing all her false teeth in an insincere smile.

'Come on bus,' muttered Nathan.

Puffing a bit, from the effort of heaving herself up the hill, the woman sat down beside them and began a sort of conversation.

'What's your name then, my dear?'

'Beverley,' said Julia, coldly. She wanted to say 'None of your business,' but thought that might be a bit too rude.

'Are you sure it's not Julia?' said the woman in the pink trousers, peering keenly at both children.

'Of course,' said Julia. 'I told you, it's Beverley.' She gave the woman a look which she hoped said 'Why are you asking me these mad questions?' She was keeping her head, but the panic was beginning inside.

'And what about you, young man? Let me guess. I bet your name's Nathan. There – aren't I right?'

'I don't know what you're talking about,' said Nathan.

'Well – you do seem to be on your own, don't you.'

'We're staying with our mum and dad,' said Nathan. 'In the caravans.'

From the corner of his eye he had seen another bus coming down the hill. Surely this must be the right one. Another few moments and they would be out of the clutches of this horrible, dangerous woman.

'Oh – which caravan site is that?' The woman was really

140

excited now. Her voice was actually trembling with the excitement of catching Nathan out, asking him a question he couldn't answer.

Nathan glared at her, hating her. 'You know, that one, that one up there,' he floundered. '*The Lorna Doone Caravan Site*,' he tried, in sudden inspiration.

The woman's face fell. 'Oh I know it,' she admitted, looking quite disappointed, 'up West Street. Here's your bus then. Bye-bye.'

Nathan gave Julia a triumphant thump, as they climbed on to the bus. There really *was* a Lorna Doone Caravan Site then! He might have known there would be.

Back in Brighton the police, acting on information received, were searching the town for the missing children. Now they were interviewing seaside landladies, and a very unhappy Mrs Parsons was talking to a kind young constable in her private sitting-room.

'She seemed such a *nice* girl,' said Mrs Parsons, for the fourteenth time. 'Bless my soul, who'd have thought it? The boy was a bit surly I thought, but the girl! So worried about her mother, and so sensible. All those stories, and none of them true! Bless my soul, who'd have thought it?'

Mrs Parsons was very upset. She was not good at knowing when people were telling lies, and she had been dreadfully hurt and puzzled when the children's room had been found empty yesterday morning. She had half thought of going to the police herself, but since she was not good at making decisions either, she had dithered and put it off. And now this nice policeman had come to her house, and it really did seem as though Beverley and Charlie were, after all, Julia and Nathan – the two children from London who had run away from home. The ones whose pictures had been in the paper. And she, Mrs Parsons, had never suspected it for a moment.

'So now – tell me about their appearance,' said the policeman. 'The boy wasn't wearing glasses, you say.'

'No, but when I come to think about it . . . of course he *ought* to have been. He was going round peering at everything, closely, as though he were very short-sighted. Bless my soul, I *ought* to have suspected, oughtn't I!'

'No, no,' said the policeman, soothingly. 'You mustn't blame yourself. You're not a trained detective, after all. And the girl? Dressed to look older, I understand – with her hair long, loose round her face.'

'Oh no,' said Mrs Parsons.

'No? The man who caught her down on the front described her like that.'

'Oh no, didn't I tell you? She cut her hair off. It was all over the floor. You'll be looking for a girl with hair cropped really short. She left if all over the floor. All over the floor, poor child, for me to sweep up.'

'Thank you, Mrs Parsons,' said the policeman, and he wrote it down in his notebook.

11

A nasty accident

'Did you see how that lady wobbled?' said Nathan,
maliciously. 'Like a jelly. A great, big, fat, pink wobbly jelly.
Strawberry jelly!'

He giggled, and Julia giggled too. They held their
stomachs and laughed with relief, the exploding giggles
bursting out of them in mad little spurts. 'Wobble, wobble,'
said Nathan, to set them off again.

They sat together near the front of the bus and watched
the sunlight move in patches over the endless rolling
green.

'Nathan,' said Julia, suddenly, 'how are we going to *carry*
the tents?'

'What you mean?'

'You know, Nathan. They'll be heavy and big – and sleeping bags and all the other things. How we going to carry
them?'

Nathan was suddenly resentful. Everything was going so
well, and now she had to spoil it by making difficulties
about little details like how they were going to carry the
camping things. 'I dunno,' he said, crossly. 'You think. It's

your turn to think. I thought of the tents, you think of a idea how to carry them.'

Julia was silent. Nathan was probably right, it was her turn. She gazed out of the window, waiting for inspiration to strike. Inspiration was a long time coming, and when it came it was via two cyclists on the other side of the road. Two cyclists with packs on their backs and heavily laden machines.

'I know,' said Julia to Nathan, 'We'll have bicycles.'

'That's brilliant,' said Nathan admiringly. 'Can you ride a bike though?'

'Used to have one, but it broke. Can you?'

'Of course.' He was not going to admit that he was a bit unsteady, having only ever practised on one belonging to his cousin, who lived the other side of London. No doubt he would soon get the hang of it though. That was a terrific idea of Julia's. She was a good mate, Julia.

It was a pretty ride. The bus was taking a long time, meandering round the villages, but Nathan and Julia didn't care if the journey took for ever. They had never seen country like this, all those green and purple hills, sparkling this morning in the rain-washed air.

At one stop, a young mother with a little girl of about five got on and sat in the seat behind Julia and Nathan. The little girl had a nasty cough, and she whined and grizzled a great deal to begin with, but when she noticed Nathan in the seat ahead of her, she seemed to cheer up. Tentatively, she reached out of her own seat and stretched one hand round the back of Nathan's, to touch his springy hair. Nathan jumped when he felt her hand on his head and the little girl drew back into her own seat, sniffing and coughing again. But a few minutes later she was back, this time stroking his bare arm. Embarrassed, Nathan tried to hitch away.

'Leave the little boy alone, Cheryl,' said the mother sharply. 'He doesn't want you touching him.'

'That's right, I don't,' said Nathan.

At the sound of his voice, Cheryl was apparently quite enraptured. She slipped out of her seat altogether now and squatted in the aisle, gazing adoringly into Nathan's face. And presumably because she was less trouble like that, her mother left her there. The unwelcome attentions of Cheryl rather spoiled the rest of the journey for Nathan, and there was even worse to come, for when the bus finally reached its destination, and the child's mother tried to drag her away, Cheryl managed to plant a great wet parting kiss on Nathan's cheek.

'Ugh!' said Nathan, wiping off the kiss with the back of his hand.

'She had spots too,' said Julia. 'Coming out all over her face, didn't you see? I think she had measles?'

'Which shall we get first?' said Nathan as they climbed out of the bus, 'the bicycles or the tents?'

'Another cap first,' said Julia, 'to cover your hair.'

Black people were really conspicuous, it seemed, in this country place. Apart from Nathan himself, they hadn't seen any so far.

They bought a cap in Marks and Spencer's, then they found a cycle shop without much difficulty, and spent a happy half hour making their choice. When he saw they were serious, and they really had the money to spend, the owner of the shop was most attentive. They had both had birthdays, they said, and Julia said they lived in Taunton because it would perhaps seem odd to be buying bicycles in a place where they were only on holiday. She was cunning enough to have judged that Taunton was quite a big town, so that shop man would not be surprised that he had never seen them before, even if they did live there.

When they emerged once more into the sunlight, Julia and Nathan were each proudly wheeling a shiny new cycle, complete with front and rear carriers, chains and padlocks for locking the bikes against thieves, and panniers for carrying extra luggage. Julia explained that they belonged to a club for going camping. She had thought that one up on the bus, and had the story ready. It would do for the tent shop as well, she thought. In an uneasy moment she reflected that she had never told so many lies in her life. When she was grown up, she decided, she would tell the truth all the time, to make up for it.

The children could not wait to try their new bikes. Nathan jumped on his first, and pedalled inexpertly along the road, wobbling and swerving as he went. The traffic in the shopping street was quite heavy, and several cars hooted Nathan as they passed. Julia was alarmed. She pedalled quickly to catch up, and shouted a warning at Nathan. 'Keep in to the pavement –you going to have a accident!'

Nathan was annoyed at the criticism. 'All right, all right,' he called back, and pedalled harder to show off. Julia followed anxiously. Nathan was going at great speed now; Julia had a job to keep up with him. Unfortunately, a car with a bad driver in it was going even faster. The car passed really close to Nathan, hooting as it went. Startled by the loud horn, and the feel of the car whooshing past him, Nathan swerved. His front wheel touched the car's retreating bumper, and Nathan, with the bicycle on top of him, crashed to the ground. Julia, sick with dismay, pedalled as fast as she could to where Nathan lay under the bicycle, a crowd already beginning to gather.

'You all right, son?' someone asked.

Nathan lay silent, raging inwardly. There was a sharp pain somewhere, but he was mostly angry. The indignity of it! To fall off his bicycle– him, not Julia! Julia was supposed to be the clumsy one, not him. Julia was the one who had accidents all the time.

'I reckon he's really hurt. Better get an ambulance.' This

146

was a kind-looking man in the crowd.

'Yes, better phone.'

Hands were lifting the bicycle off Nathan, and Nathan was registering what the voices were saying. An ambulance? Hospital? Questions? No! A vicious pain stabbed through his wrist as he sat up, but Nathan stifled the yell he wanted to make. 'I'm all right,' he said. 'I don't want no ambulance.'

'Are you sure?' asked the kind man. 'That was a nasty fall you had, there might be something broken.'

'No, I'm all right,' said Nathan, struggling to his feet to prove it, and biting his lips to keep from wincing as the searing pain tore through his wrist again.

'Yes he is, he is, he is all right,' claimed Julia, coming out of a shocked stupor and stepping forward to grasp Nathan's arm. She was half afraid Nathan would fall down again, and the kind man would fetch the ambulance after all.

'He's hurt his arm though, hasn't he?' the kind man persisted.

'No he ain't,' said Julia, emphatically. 'You ain't hurt your arm have you, N— have you, Charlie?'

'No, it's all right,' Nathan repeated, wishing they'd all just go away, so he could suffer the excruciating agony of his wrist in peace.

'Can you move it?' said the kind man.

'Yes, I can move it easy.' For the benefit of the little crowd, Nathan flexed his injured arm at all the joints, and words would never tell how much it cost him to do so.

'Well . . . ,' said the kind man, doubtfully, 'if you were my boy I'd want it X-rayed. Just to make sure there's nothing broken.'

'Oh no,' said Julia, 'there's nothing *broke*. Is there, Charlie?'

'Well, I don't know what you'd know about it,' said the kind man, regarding Julia with some coolness. But he went, anyway, and so did the rest of the crowd.

'Does it really hurt?' asked Julia, anxiously.

'Course it hurts,' said Nathan.

'Let me see.'

'Nah – it's all right.'

'You're very brave,' said Julia.

'I'm stupid, innit. I fell off.'

'Never mind that. Can you still ride?'

'Don't know.'

Nathan was actually quite shaken, and the last thing he wanted to have to do was to get back on that bicycle. 'I think I'll just push it for a bit.'

'Let's find a caff and have a cup of tea.'

'Tea?'

'Yeah, with lots of sugar. That's what they give people when they've had a shock.'

To Nathan's surprise, the thought of hot sweet tea was quite attractive, though in the normal way he would have chosen Coke every time. His wrist hurt badly, and it was beginning to swell, but he could manage to use it just enough to steady the bicycle, while taking the weight with the other hand. The children fastened their bicycles with the new padlocks, and went into a small café for tea. They filled up with beefburgers and sticky cakes while they were about it, and when they had finished, Nathan was feeling a little bit better. His wrist still ached and throbbed, but he was getting used to the pain, it was getting to be part of him. 'Let's go and get the tents now,' he said.

The third passer-by they stopped was able to direct them to a camping shop. It was quite a way to walk, pushing their bicycles along the pavement, but a real Aladdin's cave when they reached it.

'Look at this, Ju,' Nathan marvelled. 'Shall we have one like this?'

He was looking at a large frame tent, big as a house, with

an arrangement of separate compartments inside.

'Don't be silly,' said Julia. 'How we going to get something like that on our bikes?'

They settled in the end, on the shopkeeper's advice, for two tiny one-person tents, complete with groundsheets, and two featherweight sleeping bags which rolled up into nothing at all. There were other things they needed, like backpacks and a mallet to knock the tent pegs in – besides the camping stove, run on a special gas cylinder, the pan to go on it, the torch for when it got dark, and the plastic plates and cutlery, and the tin opener. Most wonderful of all, in Nathan's eyes, was an all-purpose scout knife, the sort you were not, on any account, allowed to bring to school. He would have enjoyed the knife a great deal more if his arm had not, at that point, started violently throbbing and aching again. The pain made him feel angry and irritable.

'How far is it to Exmoor?' Nathan asked the shopkeeper.

'Exmoor? Oh – twenty mile, I reckon. Yeah, a good twenty mile for certain.'

Twenty miles! Nathan knew he could not push that bicycle twenty miles. He glared at the shopkeeper, as though it was his fault that Exmoor was so far away.

They would have to find somewhere nearer to put up their tents. First though, they had to load everything on the cycles. Julia had to do most of the work, of course, and Nathan watched her sullenly, criticizing every mistake, although in his heart he had to acknowledge that she wasn't doing too badly. For someone with such clumsy feet, she was really surprisingly good with her hands. She was really making a passably neat and sensible job of packing everything and stacking it into place. But because the pain was making him so irritable and short-tempered, Nathan could only find fault.

'That's no good. . . . What you put it there for, stupid? . . . Do it like this!'

'What are you so grumpy for?' said Julia, at last. 'I'm doing my best.'

'My arm hurts.'

'I know it hurts. It ain't my fault you fell off your bike.'

'It was your idea to have bikes.'

'So?'

'If we didn't have bikes I couldn't have fallen off, could I? Come on.'

Nathan took his loaded bicycle and began to wheel it with his good arm. Puzzled and hurt, Julia trailed behind.

In a gloomy silence, the children proceeded in single file through the streets of Taunton. Neither had any idea where they were going. When it looked as though the town with its supplies was about to be left behind, Julia stopped at a small grocer's shop to buy tins of baked beans with sausages in them, and some bread. She called out to Nathan that she was going to do so, but he was so far ahead he didn't hear her. She saw his small surly figure stumping on, the feet dragging a bit now, and she thought, serve him right if he thinks he's lost me. He wouldn't get very far with that arm, not very fast anyway. There was no danger of *her* losing *him*.

When she came out of the shop, however, there was no sign of Nathan in the road ahead. Julia stowed her groceries in one of the bicycle's panniers, then climbed on and pedalled. It was good to be riding, instead of all that wearisome pushing. She found Nathan sitting on a grass verge at the side of what was now a country road, the bicycle beside him, a picture of abject misery.

'I thought you was gone,' he greeted her.

His brown eyes were full of misery, like those of an injured dog, and Julia, who had been feeling resentful at his treatment of her, relented and forgave.

'Is it your arm?'

150

'Course, what do you think?'

'Let me see.'

He held it out gingerly, for inspection. The wrist was very swollen now, and there was a puffy blue-black bruise. The skin was not broken, though.

'It needs a bandage,' said Julia.

'How do you know?'

Julia shrugged. She didn't know how she knew, she just instinctively felt that the wrist needed strapping up.

'Anyway,' said Nathan, bleakly, 'we haven't got a bandage.'

'I could cycle back and get one,' said Julia. 'Won't take me long. I'll find a chemist.'

Nathan watched her as she rode off, ungainly on the bicycle but a competent rider, and felt sorry that he had been mean, and rude and unfair. She returned before long, with a bandage, some cotton wool and a can of lemonade. 'You owe me one pound thirty-eight,' she said.

'Let's have a drink then, I'm thirsty.'

'The lemonade ain't to drink, it's to put on the cotton wool to make it cold. Because we haven't got no water. The chemist said to put something cold on your arm. The lemonade's been in the fridge, so it's icy.'

The lemonade cold compress made Nathan's wrist feel better immediately, and the support of the bandage took away some of the throbbing. He thought Julia might have strapped it just a little too tightly, but he wasn't complaining. For someone with no experience of first aid, she really hadn't made a bad job of the bandaging at all. She had some idea that the arm ought to be in a sling, and wanted to improvise one out of Nathan's spare tee-shirt. But Nathan said no, his arm was feeling so much better with just the bandage, he thought he could manage to cycle a bit as long as he had the use of both hands.

Progress was much faster now. If only they knew where

they were going! Nathan hoped they were heading towards Exmoor, but there didn't seem to be anyone to ask, and in any case it was out of the question to cycle twenty miles today. What they wanted was a nice field, any field, with a river in it for washing. And no houses. No one to spy on two runaway children putting up their tents.

They were passing fields now, but there were still houses in sight, and no rivers visible. Besides, the road they were on was busy, with a lot of fast traffic, and the children needed all their concentration to keep well in to the left, out of any further trouble.

Presently they came to a crossroads. Straight on was to somewhere called Barnstaple. Nathan and Julia read the word together. The road to the right was signposted Minehead, and Nathan thought they should take that one, but only because it was going to a place he had heard of, and the familiar sound of the name was somehow a bit comforting.

After a bit, Julia declared she was sure they were on the same road the bus had taken them that morning. She recognized one particularly pretty pink cottage, she said, with a thatched roof and a mass of flowers in the garden. Nathan said they didn't want to go back to Watchet, did they, and Julia said they must be still miles and miles from Watchet, but in any case they were clearly on a main road, and wouldn't it be better to turn down a side road next time they came to one, and really start looking for a field with a river in it?

They took the next turning to the left, a narrow winding road between high ragged hedges, and now they were really in deep country. It was fields all the way, and hardly any houses. They peered over every gate they came to, but there were no rivers. They pressed on, hoping each time that the next gate would be the right one.

The sun was hot and the hills were very steep. Even in low

gear it was impossible to cycle up some of them. The children had to keep getting off their bikes to push and it was hard work. They were getting hungry too, and very thirsty, and there was nothing to drink.

'You should have got some lemonade to drink, as well as put on my arm,' Nathan complained.

'All right,' said Julia, sharply, 'You can't expect me to think of everything.'

'Not *everything*, but you could have thought of *that*.' Nathan's wrist was nagging him again. He was exhausted and in pain, and he didn't think he could go much further.

'Oh shut up,' said Julia, whose own legs were now aching unbearably.

And then they saw it. Through the bars of a gate they saw a bright meadow, speckled with buttercups and daisies. The meadow was like a sea, flowing in great waves down to a tiny stream, far below. The stream snaked between trees, gleaming darkly. Beyond it the ground rose steeply again, and on that further hillside was a wood, a dense screen that might have been put there just for Nathan and Julia – a fortress of green, to keep them safe from prying eyes. It was perfect.

The children pushed open the gate, and wheeled their bicycles into the field. They ran with their bicycles down the undulating slope, and although every step jarred poor Nathan's arm, his spirits were rising with Julia's. They dropped the bicycles on the grass, and threw themselves full length on their stomachs to drink from the little stream. At least, Julia threw herself – Nathan's lowering was more cautious, and accompanied by several grunts and sharp intakes of breath. But the result was the same for both, they drank until they could drink no more.

'You can hear the water sloshing about in my tummy,'

said Julia, bumping up and down on her bottom to illustrate the point.

'I wonder if it's really *clean* enough to drink,' said Nathan, too late.

'We'll boil it next time,' said Julia, who had heard somewhere that that was what you did with water of doubtful purity. 'It looks clean though, you can see every little stone on the bottom.'

They lay on their backs, and the warm sun's rays soothed their aching bodies.

'I'm too lazy to put up the tents,' said Julia.

'Is there anything to eat?' said Nathan.

'Only bread, until we get out the cooking stove,' said Julia.

They ate dry bread, and it had never tasted so good.

'My arm hurts,' said Nathan. So Julia put another cold compress on it, using water from the stream this time. It wasn't as cold as the lemonade had been, but it helped. 'That's better,' said Nathan. 'Let's put the tents up now. Where shall we put them?'

Julia considered. 'Further along,' she said. 'Over there by those trees, where they can't see us from the gate.'

Neither child had ever erected a tent before, so it took quite a while to work out the procedure, and matters were not helped by the fact that Nathan had effectively only one hand. But eventually the tents were up, after a fashion, end to end along the bank. They sagged a bit, and some of the pegs kept coming out, but Julia did not think they would actually fall down. She crept into hers and lay on top of the sleeping bag. The space inside was tiny, and as the sides had not been properly stretched, they collapsed inwards so that they almost touched her where she lay. Furthermore, the ground was sloping, so Julia had to brace herself not to roll over and crash against the walls of the tent. It was not going

154

to be a very comfortable night.

'They don't look like they did in the shop,' said Nathan.

'That's because we haven't had no practice,' said Julia, crawling out. 'Let's try the stove now.'

At home, Julia hated cooking. Her mother's complaint to Mr Barlowe about her had been quite justified. She never lifted a finger to help in the kitchen, or everywhere else in the house unless she was made to. But this was different. This was her very own cooking stove, part of her very own adventure. Julia could not wait to try it out.

The stove was easy enough to light, but in the open air it seemed an interminable time before the sausages and baked beans were hot. They made a good supper though, the most delicious supper in the world, and Nathan said so too.

Julia washed the plates and cooking utensils in the stream, and thoroughly enjoyed a chore she would have had to be nagged and bullied into doing at home. She would have done these things for Mrs Henrey, of course, but that was different too, that was a privilege. She washed her own face and hands and feet, and made Nathan do the same. The stream was not private enough for bathing properly, but Julia thought she could organize that another day.

Then she supposed Nathan's arm should be attended to once more, and Nathan thought that was a good idea, because really the cold compresses were making his arm feel a lot better. So Julia undid the bandage, and did it up again, quite expertly now – she was getting more dextrous all the time.

'You're a good nurse, Ju,' said Nathan.

Julia flushed with pleasure. 'That's what I want to be,' she said, the idea just then occurring to her. 'When I grow up.

That's what I'd like to be.'

Nathan was silent for a moment. 'Actually, Ju, I don't think you could be that,' he said. He didn't want to hurt her feelings, but facts were facts.

'Why not? You said I was a good nurse.'

'You're a excellent nurse, you're a fantastic nurse. . . . But you can't read.'

'What's that got to do with it?'

'You have to pass exams to be a nurse.' Nathan knew that because one of his aunts was a midwife, back in London.

'Oh,' said Julia, crestfallen. She pondered the situation, then spoke again. 'I can read a *little* bit.'

'Not enough for the exams though.'

'I could learn. I read a hard word today. All by myself.'

'Yeah but – we aren't going to school any more, are we.'

Julia pondered again.

'Couldn't *you* learn me, Nathan?' she said at last. The words came out with great effort, she was intensely embarrassed by what she was asking.

'We haven't got no books.'

'We could buy some. We could buy some tomorrow. Please, Nathan. Please.'

She waited for his answer, and Nathan considered carefully. He was cautious about committing himself. It would be really boring trying to teach this dunce. On the other hand, she had supported him today when he needed it. She was a good old Rat-bag really. 'All right,' he said.

'You really will?'

'All right, I said. Don't you understand English? I'm going in my tent to sleep now. See you in the morning.'

'See you,' said Julia, happily. She undressed and crawled into her own sleeping bag and closed her eyes, although it

156

was still daylight outside. It had been a long and exhausting day, with practically no sleep the night before. She was not sorry to say goodbye to today, but tomorrow, tomorrow was going to begin a whole new chapter of her life. The best one yet.

12

Elizabeth

It was a hideous night for Julia. First, there were sounds, the swishing and rustlings of country things, moving beyond the flimsy walls of the tent. Then there was the hardness and bumpiness of the ground, which got harder and bumpier as the hours dragged on. And the fact, of course, that she couldn't relax properly because if she did she would just slide, or roll, down the slope towards the stream. For all she knew her weight would drag the tent pegs right out if she did that, pitching her into the cold black water below. So Julia held on, ramming her knees as hard as she could against one lump protruding through the ground-sheet, and grasping another lump with an outstretched hand.

Of course, it was impossible to sleep well like that, and Julia found her night a succession of wild dreams – mostly about toppling over cliffs, or dangling out of third-floor windows –punctuated by wakeful periods, filled with the heavy rubbery smell of the tent, and the increasing damp cold which seemed to seep through everything, even the quilted sleeping bag. Somehow, Julia had thought being in a tent would be much the same as being indoors, but it wasn't at all. Tomorrow night, she thought regretfully, she would have to sleep in all her clothes.

The dawn chorus began. One little twitter followed by another, the twitters joining and swelling until the whole field was wracked with the din. Julia had never realized the country could be so *noisy*. She wriggled miserably out of the tent, sleeping bag and all, on to the dew-soaked grass.

'You awake, Nathan?'

'Yeah.'

'Did you sleep?'

'Nah.'

'Does your arm still hurt?'

'Yeah.'

'You want me to bandage it for you?'

'If you like.'

Julia peeped into Nathan's tent and saw him curled in his sleeping bag, holding on as she had, to stop from rolling down the bank. He was wearing his anorak, that much she could see, and probably all the rest of his clothes as well, she presumed. So at least he would be warmer than she had been.

Julia crawled back and shuffled round in her own tent, awkwardly pulling on her jeans and tee-shirt. She put on the silly cap from Brighton, because it covered her unsightly haircut. She felt happier when no one, including Nathan, could see that. Even the cap, now she had got used to it, was better than the haircut.

'You'll have to come out,' she called to Nathan. 'I can't do your arm with you in there.'

'It's cold,' he complained, emerging into the damp chill of the morning.

His face was drawn with pain and he looked particularly ill-tempered. He scowled at Julia as she unwrapped the bandage, and winced when she made a clumsy move. 'Careful, stupid. That hurts.'

159

Julia's spirits, already low, sank still further. If Nathan was going to be grumpy, that was going to make discomfort even more miserable.

'You said I was a good nurse yesterday.'

'Yeah, well – that was yesterday, wasn't it.'

Julia made no answer. The wrist though still puffy, looked if anything less swollen this morning. She took a fresh pad of cotton wool, and made for the stream to dampen it; but she forgot the guy ropes of the tent, and as her foot caught in one, she lost her balance and fell painfully on to her hip. There was no great damage, except to her feelings when she heard Nathan's unkind jeers. But on her way back from the stream, she forgot the guy ropes and tripped over them again.

'Look where you're going, you fool,' said Nathan, quite unpleasantly.

The sudden tears ached in Julia's throat, and stung her eyes. She swallowed and blinked, and the tears ran down her cheeks nevertheless. She was humiliated to be crying in front of Nathan, but she could not help herself. She bent her head over the task of dressing his arm, knowing the tears could still clearly be seen trickling down her nose, and waited for his jibes. They did not come. There was silence for a few moments and then, 'Sorry, Julia.'

Sniff, sob. 'What did you say?'

'I said sorry. I'm sorry I was a pig to you.'

'It's all right,' said Julia, astonished. Nathan *apologizing*? Wonders would never cease.

'Stop crying then.'

'It's all right, I have.' She blurted out a further admission, testing the sincerity of his repentance. 'There's nothing for breakfast. I didn't think to buy nothing for breakfast yesterday. Only bread.'

'It's all right.'

'Just bread then – and boiled water.'

160

'Great.'

'We'll get some tea today as soon as we find a shop, and some milk and all sorts of things.'

'Good. Boiled water's all right for now though.'

It was soon after they had finished these meagre refreshments that the next crisis was upon them. 'Look!' said Nathan in dismay, pointing up the slope of the meadow towards where the gate leading to the road was. Coming from that point, plodding relentlessly in their direction, was first one four-legged animal, and then another, and another, and another. . . .

'Bulls!' screamed Julia, horrified. She wanted to run, but her legs were paralysed with fright.

'Cows, cows I think,' said Nathan. But to a town boy, even cows were frightening. Especially when there were so many of them. Mesmerized, the children watched them coming. Nearer and nearer the army of young cows advanced.

'They're going to kill us,' Julia wailed, her eyes wide and staring with fear. 'Run, Nathan, we going to be killed!' She found the use of her legs and scrambled shakily to her feet, knees wobbling and heart pounding sickly. At the sight of her movement the young cows halted in their tracks and stood snorting and pawing the ground.

Nathan jumped to his feet as well and began waving his arms and shouting. The cows in synchronized movement shuffled a few steps back. Nathan stamped and ran towards them. 'Get back, get back!' His arms flailed the air, and the cows turned tail, stampeding in alarm up the steep slope.

'Look, Ju, they're scared of us!' said Nathan, grinning.

The children giggled together, their fright fading, and Julia took the breakfast things to wash them in the stream. When she scrambled back to the tents she found that the cows had once more advanced on the camp, and were now standing in a circle, wide-eyed with curiosity and snorting now and again.

'Make them go away,' said Julia, nervously.

'They won't hurt you,' said Nathan. 'They're only look-ing. They're nosy, that's what.'

'I don't like them,' said Julia.

She crawled into her tent to straighten her sleeping bag, and was startled at the feel of a thick warm nose, pushing itself against her face through the wall of the tent. She screamed, and the pounding hooves on the ground outside told her that her screams had driven the animals away again.

'They aren't going to leave us alone,' said Nathan.

'Let's go,' said Julia. 'Let's go somewhere else. Let's go now. Come on, Nathan.'

'All right.'

'I don't like this place anyway; it's too slopy. Let's find a flat place to put our tents.'

'All right.'

It took a surprisingly long time to strike camp, and they had to keep stopping to drive away the cows. The sun came out as they were packing up, flooding the meadow with golden light. The children waved tent poles at the cows, and the fun lifted their spirits. Julia forgot to be afraid of the cows, and Nathan almost forgot the pain in his wrist. At last, the long morning shadows already shortening at their feet, the children wheeled their bicycles back to the road, and set off on their travels.

Along the country lanes again, and now the going was all steep hills. No sooner had they finished grunting and straining their way upwards, on foot, than the glorious vista of a downward run would lie before them. Going downhill, they sped as though their bicycles had sprouted wings – fast, faster, with the breeze in their faces and the warm sun bathing their heads. 'Yippee!' yelled Nathan, and Julia echoed him.

In a tiny village, so pretty it could hardly be real, they found a tiny shop. There they bought tea bags and milk, cans of Coke and biscuits, crisps, and more tins of food to warm up on their stove. Julia remembered she wanted a book to learn to read out of, but the only books in the shop were some paperback romances that looked as though they had been there, collecting dust, for years. Each book had a picture on the front of a woodenly handsome young man, and a swooning young woman. They were different stories, but they all seemed to have pictures of the same two people on the front. Nathan didn't think the books looked at all interesting, but Julia was so keen about learning to read she bought all three of them.

Nathan asked the woman in the shop how far they were from Exmoor, and was disappointed when she said she thought about twenty miles. They didn't seem to be getting any nearer.

They sat in a gateway by the side of the road and had a picnic lunch, and Julia fell asleep in the sun because she was so tired after two bad nights. Nathan did not actually sleep, but he felt very relaxed and contented, and he suddenly realized that was because his arm didn't hurt any more. What a good feeling it was, not to have a pain.

When Julia finally awoke, it was mid-afternoon, and Nathan thought they should start looking for a place to camp straight away. Their requirements were not going to be easy to meet. Now they wanted flat ground *and* water, and in this hilly country it might well take them the rest of the day to find somewhere. They didn't want to be stuck with darkness falling, and nowhere to put the tents.

They cycled round all the tiny twisty lanes, but everywhere they went it seemed there were streams and no flat fields, flattish fields and no streams. 'There's water down there,' said Nathan, for the third time.

'But the ground's all slopy,' Julia objected. 'We'll be falling over all night again. . . . I know, Nathan, what about that wood over there?'

'There's no water.'

'We could carry the water.'

'Where from?'

'From the river we just saw.'

'All that way?'

'It's not very far.'

'What will we carry it in?'

Julia considered. The need for a water carrier had somehow been overlooked when they were in the camping shop.
'There's the pan for the stove, but it ain't very big. I know,
what about the plastic bag the shop lady put our grocery
things in?'

Julia was certainly full of practical ideas.

They were now drawing level with the wood, which was
not very far off the road. The ground there appeared to be
level, at least for a little distance, before the inevitable
plunge down into yet another valley. The children found a
gate and wheeled their bicycles across a field towards the
trees. The grass in the field had been cut for hay, which was
lying in ridges to be dried in the sun. It smelled delicious,
summery and sweet. Inside the wood the ground was hard
and dry, and covered with sharp little twigs. 'Be careful,'
Julia warned. 'We don't want to have punctures in our
tyres.'

They found a suitable clearing, and began to unpack the
camping things. Putting up the tents was easier this time, in
spite of the hardness of the ground, which made driving the
tent pegs in somewhat difficult. They had swept the site
clear of twigs, but Julia thought it was still going to be a bit
hard for sleeping on, so she went to the field outside and
came back with armfuls of half-dried grass, which she
stuffed under her groundsheet.

Afterwards, she fetched some grass for Nathan's bed
as well.

It was a longish trek to the water, further than it had

seemed to be when they were sailing along the road. Julia thought she had better go by herself, since one of them ought to stay behind to guard the camp and the bicycles. Nathan said he would get the stove going, and warm up a tin of stewed steak for their supper. Julia was not enthusiastic about Nathan using the stove, which she regarded as exclusively hers, but she was beginning to feel hungry again, so she let him do it.

The plastic bag held the water quite well, but it was not easy staggering up the slope without spilling it. Julia was glad to smell the stewed steak which Nathan was cooking – she really was *very* hungry now. Nathan put the steak on the plates when he saw her coming, and Julia rinsed out the cooking pot and filled it with clean water for tea. True, most of the water did get spilled in the course of this operation, but Julia felt quite satisfied with her efforts on the whole. She enjoyed the supper very much, and so did Nathan.

After supper Julia trekked down to the water again, to rinse the plates. It was nice and private by the stream, so she took off all her clothes and had a bath. She was a bit nervous in case anyone should come, but no one did. Next time, she thought, she must remember to bring the soap with her. She filled the plastic bag with water again, to take back with her, and this time she decided to hang it on a tree near the tents, so it wouldn't spill.

Then she dug out her three novels. 'You said,' she reminded Nathan. 'You did say.'

'All right, all right.' It was true, he had promised. 'Come on, then. Let me see first,' He held the book close, to read the title. 'Now you.'

With some difficulty, and a fair amount of prompting, Julia puzzled out the words – THE EMPTY HEART. 'What does that mean, Nathan? "The empty heart"?'

'*I* dunno. Come on, what does it say next?'

It said,

Madeleine lay full length on the grass. Summer was in the air, and summer was in Madeleine's heart because she was in love. This time yesterday, she had been still an unawakened girl. But now she was alive as never before, and the world had taken on new meaning.

It took a long time for Julia to struggle through this much, and Nathan was not very patient. 'It's a rubbish story,' he complained.

'Perhaps the others are better. I did all right though, didn't I? I did read it, Some of it.'

'You did great. Let's leave it for now though. I think I'll go down and have a wash now, like you did.'

'You're trying to get out of it.'

'You want me to be clean, don't you?'

'All right.' Julia's eyes went back to the page, reading the same passage determinedly over and over again. *Madeleine lay full length on the grass. . . .*

Both children slept well that night. Julia wore her jeans and tee-shirt, and spread her new anorak over the sleeping bag. Nathan slept in all his clothes anyway.

Dawn came, and Nathan was up first. He had a half-formed idea of suggesting they move on this morning, get closer to Exmoor. But when he noticed the flat tyre on the front wheel of his bicycle, he changed his mind. The flat tyre was a problem, and he didn't feel like facing problems that day. He covered the evidence of the puncture with a few well positioned loose branches, so that Julia would not see it. Then he lit the camping stove and took Julia a cup of tea in bed, which pleased her enormously. Both children were surprised at how fond of tea they were getting, now there was the fun of making it on their own stove.

Nathan said he thought they should stay here, at any rate for today. For several days, perhaps. It was nice here, and anyway his arm wasn't entirely well yet, he thought he should rest it for a bit. What did Julia think? 'There's ants in my tent,' said Julia.

Apart from the circumstance of the ants, she was happy enough to be staying. It was going to be another fine day, she could sit in the sun, down by the stream perhaps, and practise her reading. She didn't think about what Nathan was going to do.

Nathan, in fact, found he was very happy just wandering. The children took it in turns to guard the camp, and when it was Julia's turn to stay behind, Nathan meandered through the wood and down to the stream. Since the day was hot, he did not wear his anorak, but knotted it round his waist by the sleeves. He spent an hour trying to catch the tiny fish which he could see darting about when he bent really close, and when he tired of that he paddled a long way, his shoes in his hand, treading carefully on the pebbles, and making up stories in his head. He pretended to be John Ridd in that story *Lorna Doone* —though he knew this wasn't the right river. And when he tired of being John Ridd, Nathan climbed out of the water and wandered over the grass instead, and this time he went back to thinking about *Treasure Island*, and made up a story in his head about pirates. He wondered vaguely if he would ever get the chance to finish reading *Treasure Island*.

Although it was clearly farmland they were on, there was no farmhouse in sight, and the children met no one all day.

Julia worked hard at her reading. Nathan helped her for half an hour in the morning, but she was so slow, and the story so boring, that he soon made an excuse to drift off. Julia persisted on her own, going over and over the bits she had done with Nathan until she was word perfect, then trying to tackle the next bit by herself.

In the late afternoon, a farm hand appeared in the next

field to round up the cows for milking, and the children hid in the wood until he had gone.

Later, after supper, Julia went down to the stream with the plastic bag, to fill it with water once before they went to bed. Left alone, and sitting on a tree stump, Nathan's thoughts drifted back to the punctured bicycle tyre. All day long he had succeeded in *not* thinking about it. Would the problem have to be faced tomorrow? Not necessarily. They could stay here another day. Several days, in fact. For ever, perhaps, if it came to that. Someone would have to go for more supplies tomorrow, of course, as they were running out of food. Well, Julia could go. Julia's bicycle was all right.

Nathan found the beautiful scout knife, and began to carve a ship out of a lump of wood. As he worked, he was suddenly aware of being watched. Not that he had heard anything. At least, he was not aware of having heard anything. He just felt, unmistakably, that strange eyes were being focused on the back of his head. He turned, apprehensively – and there, framed between two trees, was a girl. A girl older than he was, he guessed, about twelve or thirteen, with piercing blue eyes, chestnut hair, and a million freckles. Nathan could not read her expression. She was neither smiling nor unsmiling – just very cool, he thought, and sure of herself.

'Who are you, then?' said Nathan, scowling at the intruder.

'Who are *you*?' said the girl.

'This is our camp,' said Nathan, discouragingly.

'This is my father's wood,' said the girl. 'He doesn't like trespassers, In fact, if he finds you, he'll probably shoot you.'

'Who cares about your father?' said Nathan, not believing her.

'Please yourself,' said the girl, without rancour.

168

Her gaze wandered over the scene, taking in the tents, the bicycles, and the cooking arrangements. 'Who sleeps in the other tent?' she asked.

'My friend – I mean, my sister. What's it got to do with you?'

'Don't be like that. I won't tell on you.'

'There's nothing to tell.'

'You're trespassing.'

'Oh well, yes – that.'

'What else could there be?'

'Nothing.'

'What's the matter with your hand?'

'Nothing. I fell off my bike and hurt it.'

'Who put that bandage on – your friend, or your sister?'

'My sister.'

'You ought to go to the doctor. It might be broken.'

'It's all right. It don't hurt now.'

'Let me see. I know a lot about injuries and things. I'm going to be a doctor when I leave school. Can you move it?'

'Course I can move it. Why don't you go away?'

'It's not broken then. Is this your sister coming now?'

'Yes it is.' Thank goodness Julia was back. Two of them ought to be able to get rid of this inquisitive nuisance.

'That's not your sister, she's the wrong colour.'

'I'm adopted.'

'Where are your mother and father?'

'I'm not going to tell you.'

'Hullo. Are you his sister?'

'Yes,' said Julia warily. She was not pleased to find they had a visitor.

'What's your name?'

'Ju – Beverley. What's yours?'

'Oh, I'm Elizabeth. I live here. On this farm.'

'Is it all right for us to stay here?' asked Julia, anxiously.

'Well *I* don't mind. My father wouldn't let you, but he hardly ever comes this way. This is where I come. This is my special place.'

'I had a special place in London,' said Nathan, in spite of himself. 'It was a empty house.'

'Is that where you live then? London?'

Nathan was silent. He had opened his mouth when he shouldn't have.

'Are your parents in London, then? Have they let you come all this way by yourself?'

'Our mum and dad's in Watchet,' said Julia.

'In the Lorna Doone Caravan Site,' said Nathan. 'We just come on our own for a few days.'

Elizabeth was silent. She seemed to be enjoying a private joke. 'I don't believe you,' she said at last.

'Don't then,' said Nathan, sourly.

'I think you've run away.'

'No we haven't, said Nathan. 'We haven't run away. It wasn't us on telly, it was two other kids.'

'Oh, have you been on telly? I don't see much telly. I'm at boarding school and we have to do horrible prep in the evenings. It's the holidays now, thank goodness.'

'*Boarding* school?' said Julia, faintly. 'Did you do something wrong then?'

'Something wrong? No, of course not. Oh, I know what you're thinking of – no, not that sort of boarding school. You *have* run away, haven't you! You can tell me. You can trust me, actually. I'm always running away myself. I've run away about five hundred times altogether.'

'As many as that?' said Julia, amazed.

'Well, five times. Three times from home, and twice from school. How long have you been out?'

Useless to resist. Trying to fight this barrage of questions was like trying to push water uphill. Julia looked at Nathan.

He shrugged his unwilling agreement, but his face was like thunder.

'I forget,' said Julia. 'A long time.' Looking back, it seemed for ever. 'A week and a half, I think.'

'Really? You're doing very well then,' said Elizabeth. 'The longest I ever stayed out for was six days. They'll find you in the end, you know. Or you'll go back by yourself.'

'I'm not going back,' said Nathan. 'We're never going back, are we, Ju. We like it here.' He did not want to talk about the future. One day at a time was enough. 'What do you run away for then?'

'Oh this and that,' said Elizabeth, airily. 'When I quarrel with my sister, or they give me a detention for nothing at school. What about you?'

'What you mean?'

'You know what I mean. Why did you run away?'

'Nothing. We just wanted to.'

'What about money? How are you managing for money?'

'We got money.'

'Did you pinch it?'

'No.'

'How did you get it then?'

'I'm not telling you,' said Nathan.

'All right . . . These your bikes? They're new, aren't they?' Elizabeth walked over to where the bicycles were propped, each padlocked to its own tree. 'M-m-m – nice, very nice. Oh look – this one's got a puncture.'

'I know, I know,' said Nathan, furiously. 'Why don't you mind your own business?'

'A puncture?' said Julia. 'You didn't tell me!'

'Do you know how to mend it?' said Elizabeth.

'No,' said Nathan.

'What are we going to do?' wailed Julia.

'I'll mend it for you,' said Elizabeth.

'Will you?' said Nathan, not daring to believe she meant it.

'Oh thank you,' said Julia.

'I know a lot about machines. I'm good with machines. I'm probably going to be an engineer when I leave school.'

'When will you do it?' said Nathan, still not trusting her.

'Well, not this evening. Unless you've got a puncture outfit here. Have you?'

'No.'

'I'll have to bring mine then. I'll come over in the morning. I'll come over after breakfast. All right?'

'You won't tell no one we're here,' implored Julia.

'Certainly not. We runaways have got to stick together. See you in the morning.'

'What do you think of her?' said Nathan, when Elizabeth was barely out of sight.

'S-s-sh,' said Julia. 'She'll hear you.'

'So what? What you think then?'

'I like her,' said Julia. 'She's going to help us, isn't she. She's going to mend your bike.'

'*If* she does. *If* she comes back. *If* she don't tell her father and her mother and her sister and the police. . . .'

'I don't think she's going to tell,' said Julia. 'I just *feel* she won't tell nobody. I just *feel* it. She *said*.'

'Huh!'

Nathan spent an uneasy night. The little world of secrecy in which he and Julia had been living had suddenly been invaded. A sort of trust had been growing between the two of them, a bubble shutting out everybody else, so that only they two, inside it, were quite real. Now Elizabeth was inside the bubble as well, and Nathan didn't like it. He didn't trust Elizabeth. He didn't trust anybody except Julia.

Actually Nathan need not have worried, Elizabeth was as good as her word. She appeared in the wood at about ten o'clock next morning, with the puncture kit in one hand and a plastic bag in the other. She gave the plastic bag to Julia, since Julia was clearly the friendly one of the two. Inside the bag were apples, pears, and a large slice of ham and egg pie.

'Oh thank you,' said Julia, quite touched.

Elizabeth set about mending the puncture, and a very capable job she made of it too. Julia, anxious to be hospitable, lit the stove to make a cup of tea for Elizabeth. Nathan sat on a tree-stump, glaring at Elizabeth as she worked.

'Are you putting the Evil Eye on me?' she asked, conversationally.

'What's that?'

'A curse, like a spell. You do it with your eyes. Curses do work sometimes, it's a well-known fact. Is that what you're doing, looking at me like that?'

'No. I don't know what you're on about.'

'I only asked. Actually it might be quite good experience for me if you were. I need to know about these things because I'm going to be an anthropologist when I leave school.'

In between being a doctor, and an engineer, presumably. 'I think she's mad,' Nathan whispered to Julia.

Mad or not, Elizabeth finished mending the punctured tyre in less time that it took Julia to make the tea.

'What's it like in boarding school?' asked Julia, while she waited for the water to boil. 'Is it awful? Is it terrible?'

'It's all right, quite fun really.'

'I know *I* wouldn't like it,' said Julia with a shudder.

'You get used to it. Oh, thanks, Beverley, or Ju, or whatever your name is. Lovely tea. . . . Where are you going next, now the bicycle's mended?'

'Must we go?' said Julia.

'Well – I shall miss you, of course. It's been fun knowing

173

you. But it's better for you to keep moving. Less chance of getting caught.'

'How do we get to Exmoor?' Nathan asked, thinking he might as well make use of her while she was here.

Elizabeth considered. 'The way I know you go to Porlock,' she said.

'How do you get there?'

She gave them a few directions and then said, 'Keep straight on that road, straight, straight and follow the signs for Watchet. When you come out on the main road you'll see the signs for Minehead. Follow that, and when you get to Minehead you'll see signs for Porlock. You can't miss it, but it's quite a long way.'

'What happens when we get to Porlock?'

Elizabeth frowned. 'Well, that's where it gets a bit difficult.'

'Why?'

'You have to go up Porlock Hill. It's the steepest hill in the country, I think. You'll have a job to get the bikes up there. There aren't any shops on the moor either. Well – there are some, but only very little ones. You can't use them if you don't want people to know you're on the moor, because they'll remember you. You'll have to get all your supplies in Porlock. You could hole up on the moor of course, it's a good place for that, but you will have problems.'

'We won't go there then,' said Nathan. 'We'll go somewhere else.'

'But you *wanted* to go to Exmoor,' said Julia, surprised to think he would give up so easily. 'You been talking about it all the time.'

'It's too steep,' said Nathan. He tried to wink at Julia, but she didn't seem to notice. 'Elizabeth said it's too steep. We'll go somewhere flat. Tell us somewhere flat to go, Elizabeth.'

'All right . . . you could go to Sedgemoor. That's *really* flat. Good for cycling.'

174

'How do we get there?'

'Turn right at the main road, and follow the signs for Bridgewater.'

'That's where we'll go, then. That's settled, isn't it, Julia ... Julia? Innit settled we're going to – where was it? – Sedgemoor.'

'All right,' said Julia, who was fairly indifferent about where they went.

'I think I know a place you could camp.' said Elizabeth, 'but I'm not sure how to direct you. .... Oh! I've just had an idea! Why don't I come with you?'

'No!' said Nathan.

'Why not? I'd be useful. I'd be *very* useful.'

'You haven't got a bike.'

'Yes I have, I've got a super bike.'

'You haven't got a tent then.'

'I could share with Julia.'

Julia thought that would be a bit of a squeeze, but she didn't like to say so.

'How about it, then?' said Elizabeth. 'Can I come?'

'NO!' said Nathan, bluntly. 'We don't want you. Me and Ju don't want you.'

'I know lots of interesting places round that way,' said Elizabeth, trying to win him. 'Glastonbury Tor for instance. You can climb right to the top and there's a marvellous view. And there's the legends of King Arthur – you know, the Round Table – he's supposed to be buried at Glastonbury. I could tell you all about it if I came.'

'Who cares about King Arthur?' said Nathan. 'King Arthur's rubbish.'

'*I* like King Arthur,' said Julia, ashamed of Nathan's rudeness, and wanting to make up for it.

Nathan got up and began to kick his tree-stump. 'What do you know about King Arthur?' he snarled at Julia. 'What do you know about anything?'

He began to shuffle away, through the wood, kicking at

175

tree-trunks as he went. About twenty metres further on he turned, and shouted venomously at Elizabeth. 'Anyway you ain't coming with us! No way you ain't coming with us.' Then he sat down on the ground, sulking, with his back to the girls.

'Pity he's like that,' said Elizabeth.

'He does get the hump sometimes,' said Julia with a sigh.

'He must be the grouchiest person in the world,' said Elizabeth. 'He should go in the *Guinness Book of Records*.'

'He is my friend though,' said Julia.

'I know, poor you! Why don't you ditch him?'

'What do you mean?'

'Leave him. Come with me. That grumpy misery can't be much company. Now *I'd* be *very* good company.'

'Do you mean you want to run away again?'

'Absolutely.'

'What for though?' said Julia, mystified.

'For fun, of course.'

'What!'

'Well– you know how it is. The holidays are super at first, but they do get to be a bit of a drag. I haven't any friends around here.'

'You've got your sister.'

'Oh, *her*. Let me tell you, my sister is an utter, utter bore. She has the intelligence of a pea, and she never wants to do anything *exciting*.'

Julia was quite overcome by the implication that Elizabeth's sister was a poor companion, but she, Julia, was a desirable one.

'How about it then? What do you say? Shall you and I team up?'

Julia hesitated. She was tremendously flattered that Elizabeth had asked her. This older girl, with the posh voice and the confident manner – fancy someone like that wanting *her*.

'Come on,' Elizabeth urged her. 'Say yes, say yes.'

'Shall I?' said Julia, uncertainly.

'Yes of course. We'll have a marvellous time. You won't regret it, I promise you.'

'I'll have to think about it,' said Julia.

'Go on then. Think.'

Julia had never been so dazzled by anyone in her life. She thought it would be wonderful to go with Elizabeth. The glittering prospect was just too tempting, and Julia opened her mouth to say yes – but just then her eyes focused on Nathan, still sitting sulking in the middle of the wood. He looked lonely and abandoned – though he was the one who had stumped off – and Julia wondered how he would manage without her. And then she thought suddenly that what she was nearly going to do wasn't right. When you ran away with someone, you couldn't leave them halfway through and go off with someone else.

'No,' said Julia.

'You mean, no, you won't come with me?'

'I have to go with Nathan,' said Julia, simply.

'You won't get another chance like this,' said Elizabeth. 'Going with me would be really something.'

'I know,' said Julia, 'but I have to go with Nathan.'

'Oh well,' said Elizabeth, 'perhaps you're right. As you say, he is your friend.'

'I'm sorry,' said Julia.

'Not to worry. Obviously it just wasn't Meant to Be.'

'Come on, Nathan,' Julia called, but he refused to answer or even turn round, so she had to go right up to him and repeat herself. 'Come on, we're going now.'

'Just us two?' he growled, without looking up.

'Yeah.'

'You sure? You sure *she* ain't still trying to push in?'

'She's not coming, honestly she's not. It's just us.'

'Good, then.'

He dragged his feet back to the camp, not fully convinced,

and glaring suspiciously at both girls.

Elizabeth bore the two of them no grudge for rejecting her. She helped them pack up, working with a will. Nathan, still profoundly mistrustful, gave her a few sideways looks as they pulled the tents down, but his scowls seemed only to amuse her.

As they rode off, Nathan delivered his parting shot. 'I was only joking what I said about Evil Eye spells.'

'Oh really?'

'Yeah – actually I do a lot of Evil Eye spells. I was putting an Evil Eye spell on you just now, while you were talking to Julia.'

'Oh, how interesting! What was the spell about?'

'If you tell anybody about Julia and me, about us camping here, and going to Sedgemoor and all that, you—'

'Yes?'

'You going to get really sick; you probably going to die!'

Elizabeth broke into peals of laughter, and cheerfully waved them out of sight.

13

A terrible hill

'I wonder what it will be like at Sedgemoor,' said Julia, when they stopped by the roadside for a rest.

'Don't matter what it's like, because we're not going there,' said Nathan.

'I thought you said.'

'That was just for Elizabeth. In case she tells anybody. We're *really* going to Exmoor.'

'I see. What about the steep hill?'

'What about it?'

'Shall we be able to push the bikes up?'

'Can't be that bad. We been up lots of steep hills. That Porlock Hill can't be much worse.'

'Wonder what Elizabeth's doing now.'

'Long as she ain't grassing,' said Nathan, grimly.

Julia was sure that Elizabeth would not give them away. Show-off and know-all she might be, but she was no sneak. Julia did not tell Nathan that Elizabeth had asked her to leave him. That was her secret, there was no need for him to know.

They came to a crossroads, and the sign showed that the

road to Watchet was straight ahead, with Minehead to the left. Julia read the signs, all by herself, and told Nathan what they said. He went close to check she was right, and she was. 'You're coming on, Ju,' he said, quite surprised.

Julia was quite surprised too. After all, she had only been working at the reading for two days. She dimly perceived that it was largely a matter of really wanting to learn, and having confidence. Nothing succeeds like success, and success was really coming to her now. In all sorts of ways. At last.

They rode steadily along the road to Minehead. They were on a main road now, and although there were ups and downs, the going was much less hilly than before. With no steep slopes to climb on foot, the children were able to make much faster progress. It felt good, bowling along in the summer weather – so good that Nathan found himself breaking into song, a thing that he did not remember ever doing before. He sang 'We all live in a Yellow Submarine', which he had learned in school, and he had a voice which sounded surprisingly sweet in his own ears.

'You sing good, Nathan,' shouted Julia, coming up behind him.

Nathan was pleased that Julia had praised his singing, and in a sudden burst of generosity and goodwill, he offered to change caps with her. She could have the plain one which they had bought in Marks and Spencer's, and he would wear the one with the hated KISS ME on it.

Julia accepted joyfully, and they stopped to make the exchange.

'I think your hair's growing a bit,' said Nathan to encourage her, as she stood bareheaded for a moment. Julia put her hand up to feel. She didn't think there was really any difference yet, but it was kind of Nathan to say there was. The children mounted their bicycles again, and pedalled on.

Every time they came to a signpost, Julia practised reading the names. Washford, Billbrook, Carhampton, Dunster. She couldn't manage them all by herself, but Nathan helped her.

On the outskirts of Minehead, the smell from a fish and chip shop reminded them that it was lunch time and they were hungry. They bought chips and a piece of fried chicken each, and because it didn't seem quite right to sit on the pavement in a town they rode on, following the signs for Porlock until they were in open country once more, and there was a comfortable grass verge where they could rest and eat their meal.

'I'm *starving*,' said Julia.

'I'm *ravenous*,' said Nathan, showing off that he knew the word.

It was the first freshly cooked food they had had in days. Fun though it was to use their stove, it had to be admitted that stuff warmed up out of tins just wasn't the same.

'We forgot to buy something to drink,' said Julia, suddenly feeling thirsty.

Nathan was feeling thirsty too. He had put rather a lot of salt on his chips, and with no Coke to wash them down, he was rather wishing he hadn't. 'Let's ride on a bit,' he said. 'There's sure to be another shop soon.' He screwed the paper that had wrapped his chicken and chips into a rough ball, and threw the ball into the hedge.

'You didn't ought to do that,' Julia scolded him 'It's dirty to throw litter about.'

Nathan scowled. He didn't like being criticized. The children rode on, but somehow the happy mood of the morning was clouded over. They were thirsty, and beginning to feel stiff and tired. Pushing the pedals was more effort than pleasure, and there were no shops anywhere along this road.

'You should have remembered the Cokes,' Nathan accused Julia, unfairly. 'There was plenty of places in Minehead. You're always forgetting the drinks.'

'What's wrong with you remembering?' said Julia. 'You was too greedy for your food.'

'So was you greedy.'

'I don't care.'

'Neither I don't care. I don't care what you say.'

'We bound to come to Porlock soon,' said Julia, tiring of this pointless exchange.

But it was a long hard ride. The beauty of the wooded hills to their right was lost on Nathan and Julia, as they slogged ahead, silent now, conscious only of increasing physical discomfort. At last there was a turning to the left and a steep, steep drop down. The bicycles gathered speed and Julia shouted in triumph as she read the sign by the road. '*Porlock*, we're here!'

'Hooray,' said Nathan, cheering up.

There was a long narrow street, with pretty cottages and lots of little shops. The chidren bought two cans of Coke each, and drank them sitting on the pavement even though it *was* a town they were in. Then they had an ice cream each and Nathan had a second ice cream, and thought about having a third but changed his mind because he was already beginning to feel slightly sick from the two he had eaten already.

'Nathan,' said Julia suddenly, 'I think that's the hill.'

'What hill?'

'You know – the big hill up to Exmoor. The one Elizabeth said we have to go up.'

Absorbed in other matters, they had almost forgotten why they had come to Porlock. They had forgotten all about the Hill. But now they realized they were looking straight at the horrid thing.

182

'I can't,' said Nathan. 'Not today. My legs won't go.'

Julia's legs would not go either. 'What shall we do then, Nathan?'

'I dunno. Put the tents up somewhere I suppose. Go up the hill tomorrow, when we had a rest.'

'Where can we put the tents though? Shall we go back the way we come, and look for a field?'

Nathan groaned. 'Ju – remember! *That* was a steep hill too. We'd have to push the bikes *up* it if we go back. Let's go on. Get it over with. See where this road goes to.'

'All right. I hope we find somewhere soon though. I'm *tired*, Nathan.'

'I'm more than tired,' said Nathan, 'I'm exhausted. I'm completely and absolutely exhausted. I don't know if I can even ride out of this town. I shall probably fall off my bike and break my other arm . . . not *really*, you fool.'

Fortunately, the onward road out of Porlock was fairly flat, and the pedalling was easy on the children's legs. There was nowhere to put the tents though, nowhere hidden, nowhere with water. They passed a sign which said CAMPING, and Nathan asked Julia what she thought though he knew the answer already.

'*Course* we can't go to a proper camping place, *course* we can't. They'll ask questions. They'll want to know where our mum and dad is.'

It was very frustrating. They had the money for a camp-site – for a hotel if it came to that – but they couldn't use it because people would ask questions, and they'd be caught.

They rode on, hoping for the problem to solve itself. Suddenly Julia gave a joyful yell. 'The sea, the sea!' They were coming to a place called Porlock Weir. Not a town this time, just a collection of picturesque cottages and little tearooms. But – yes, you could call it the sea. There was a strip of blue-grey on the far horizon which was undoubtedly water, and a vast stony beach in between.

'It's horrible seasides here,' said Julia, disappointed, 'Not a bit like Brighton. I much rather Brighton, wouldn't you, Nathan?'

'Yeah – what we going to do now though, Ju? There's no more road.'

It was true. The road ended here, in this tiny village. There was only the beach on one side of them, and steep wooded slopes on the other. And in front of them a little harbour, empty of water naturally, since the tide seemed to be permanently out in this part of the world, but full of colourful little boats. Sailing boats, rowing boats, motor boats.

'I'm hungry again,' said Julia. 'Do you think it's supper time?'

'Probably,' said Nathan. 'Let's have something to eat, then think what we're going to do.'

They bought more chips, and some hot pies to go with them, and a huge bottle of cherryade to wash it down. They bought chocolate bars for after, and sat on the hard pebbles to enjoy their feast, taking their time to make it last.

'There ain't even a cave,' said Julia despondently, gazing round the desolate scene.

By now the sun had disappeared entirely behind the high slopes, and a chilly wind had begun to blow. When they had first arrived, there had been a few people on the beach still, and on a sort of causeway on the other side of the harbour. But now the scene was empty of humans – there were only seagulls and, rather incongruously, a black cat with round wary eyes, picking its way delicately over the stones on the beach. Nathan called to the cat, and it came at once, rubbing its head against his stroking hand and purring. Cats liked Nathan. He thought of his cats in London, the ones in

184

the empty house, and wondered how they were managing for food, now he wasn't there to look after them. He felt a sudden and unexpected stab of homesickness, which he immediately and very firmly drove away. Just because they were a bit tired and miserable this evening, that was no reason to start thinking about home, and cats and stuff. Nathan stopped stroking the cat, and pushed its behind gently with his foot.

'Go away, puss, go on home.'

Offended, the cat stalked off, waving its tail stiffly in the air.

'Suppose we'll have to stay here,' said Nathan, since someone had to say it first.

'On the beach?'

'Where else?'

'Somebody might see.'

'We could cover ourselves with the tents.'

'They still might see – and the bikes. We'll get caught, Nathan.'

'But there isn't nobody here, Ju. There isn't nobody to see us. They're all in their houses having supper and watching telly.'

'I wish *I* was indoors watching telly.'

'No you don't. Not *really*. You don't *really* wish that, do you, Ju? Only 'cause it ain't very good tonight. It'll be better in the morning. It will!'

'Yeah . . . perhaps.'

'Come on, Ju, cheer up, cheer up – eh?'

'I know,' said Julia suddenly. 'I know what we can do. We can build a shelter with the stones.' She looked around. 'Over there, down that slope. If we go down there they won't see us doing it, even if they look out of their windows. I don't *think* they'll see us. Shall we do that, Nathan?'

'All right. That's a good idea, Ju. You do have good ideas.'

Now that there was purposeful activity, the adventure

was fun again. Tiredness forgotten, the children worked in the gathering dark to make a hollow in the stones big enough to hold themselves and their bicycles. They stretched the tents over the top, weighting the edges with pebbles to stop them blowing away. Then they crawled inside, to lie in their sleeping bags. It was hard and uncomfortable, but quite warm, and waves of drowsiness began to wash over them immediately.

'Night, Nathan,' Julia murmured, sleepily.

'Night, Ju. See you in the morning.'

'Yeah.'

'It's going to be good tomorrow.'

'*Yeah.*'

They slept.

It was just beginning to get light when they awoke, and Julia thought they should get moving straight away, before anyone in the village was up to see them coming off the beach. There were some biscuits and the remains of the cherryade for breakfast, and although it was not exactly what they were used to at home, it went down well enough. They were getting used to strange sorts of meals by now.

The tide was actually coming up the beach, so the children washed their hands and faces in sea water. Then they packed up, lugged the bicycles over the stones, and set off along the road they had travelled yesterday evening, back towards Porlock, and the dreaded Porlock Hill. Not that they were dreading it this morning. This morning they were full of bounce and confidence. The sun was peeping from behind early clouds, striking heartening warmth, and the birds sang madly in the hedges, encouraging them on their way. They could tackle *anything*.

'We'll have to wait for the shops to open,' said Julia, when they reached Porlock.

'What for?' said Nathan, who was hopping with impatience to get on the moor.

'Elizabeth said there's no shops.'

'Oh yeah, I forgot. We got to load up with stores.'

'We best take as much as we can. As much as the bikes will carry.'

The children waited, sitting on the pavement, until their shadows had shortened somewhat and a few other early risers appeared in the street. No one took any notice of Nathan and Julia. This was summer time and a holiday area, and strange faces and campers with bicycles were a common sight.

As soon as one grocery shop opened, the children made their purchases. Since it was Sunday, and the country, they were lucky to find a shop open at all.

They bought a few tins of meat, and some powdered milk for the tea, but mostly they bought crisps and biscuits, since Julia said those things would be lighter for carrying on the bicycles. Lighter perhaps, but still bulky. Every spare bit of space in the backpacks, carriers and panniers was stuffed with food, and still it would not all go in – so they hung plastic bags from the handlebars, and hoped the bags would not swing against their legs too much when they were pedalling.

It was not easy to ride the loaded bicycles. They wobbled from the weight, and wanted to topple over even along the flat ground. To ride them up Porlock Hill was out of the question of course. The children dismounted and began to push – knees bent and arms aching from the strain before they had gone more than a hundred metres.

They passed a ruddy-faced local, almost sitting in the hedge, who called out a genial greeting. 'You got a job on there, ab'm'ee?'

'Yeah,' said Nathan though he hadn't much spare breath to say it with.

'Better use they brakes when you gets to the steep part.'

What did he mean by the steep part? Wasn't this part

steep enough? Nathan grunted acknowledgement of the warning and plugged on. Julia managed a wan smile, but her legs were already buckling a bit, her breath coming in short gasps.

Unbelievably, with every step, the road in front of them seemed to rise more sharply. The children went on struggling to force the over-loaded bicycles up, and up, but the effort was untold agony. Soon the bicycles were starting to roll back, dragged by their own weight, and dragging the children with them. They tightened the brakes, and that helped a bit, but it wasn't enough.

At last they came to a horrendous bit – a sharp twist to the left, and what seemed like a vertical incline – and here it was that Julia's strength gave out. 'Nathan, I can't!'

'Yes you can,' Nathan insisted, but turning round to look he saw she meant it. White-faced, her chest heaving, she slumped over her bicycle, holding it still, but with her feet beginning to slide ominously backwards. 'Help me!'

'Hold on!'

In another moment Julia would lose her grip completely. The bicycle would hurtle backwards down the hill, knocking Julia to the ground, and getting itself smashed, possibly beyond repair, as it crashed. Nathan thrust his own bicycle into the hedge, ramming it between two roots to stop it from sliding. In almost the same movement, he grabbed Julia's handlebars and twisted them sharply to the left. She let go as he did so, and her knees sagged under her. She sat on the ground, sobbing and trembling. Nathan secured Julia's bicycle as he had secured his own, then tried to make her get up.

But Julia's nerve had gone, and she was beyond reason. In her mind she saw herself bowling head over heels down that dreadful hill, the bicycle bouncing on top of her, smashing her bones to powder. She shuddered, and pushed Nathan away.

'Leave me!'

Just at that moment, a car appeared. It was on the other side of the road, and going downhill, slowly in first gear because of the steep drop, and the woman driver called out to the children. 'You all right?'

'Yeah, fine,' said Nathan.

'Is she ill, do you need help?'

'No, she ain't ill. She's fine.'

'Are you *sure*?'

How many times did this stupid woman have to be told? 'We're fine. We're just having a rest.' Nathan forced his lips into a grin, and waved jauntily, to show that all was well.

There was danger everywhere. The danger of the hill, of the traffic, of people noticing them, just when they wanted to be particularly invisible. And on top of it all, Julia had to be difficult.

'Ju, come on,' said Nathan, losing his patience. 'Come on, you're not hurt. Come on, we're nearly there.' He didn't know if they were, of course, but there was no harm in saying it. 'Come on, Ju, we'll have a rest now. Against the hedge though. Come on, don't sit in the middle of the road. The next car might stop. They might start asking questions.'

But Julia ignored him. She just sat in an exhausted heap, weeping uncontrollably.

'*Julia!*'

'I wish we never come up this hill,' she sobbed.

'Come on, get up.' Nathan grabbed Julia's arm, and this time she let him drag her to her feet. They leaned against the bank, and Nathan searched his mind for an answer to their problem. The road ahead, he could see, was no less steep. Julia was too weak to push her bicycle any further. Even after a rest, he doubted she could do it. He doubted he could push his own. Not the way he'd been pushing it before.

Suddenly an idea occurred to him. 'I know, I know how

189

we can do it, Ju!' He seized the handles of his bicycle to show her his idea. 'Look, like this – we *wiggle* the bicycles. See? Side to side, like this. Keep twisting the wheel. See? Zig-zag, like this!'

It was certainly better that way. Still hard to push, of course, but the angled front wheel did prevent the bicycle from slipping backwards. 'Come on, Ju,' said Nathan. 'You try it.'

'No,' said Julia.

'After you rested then.'

'No,' said Julia, stubbornly, 'I ain't going no further.'

'What you want to do then?'

'Don't know.'

She was in one of her moods. Like in the bedroom, back in Brighton. There would be no shifting her.

'All right,' said Nathan. I'll push mine to the top, then I'll come back and push yours. You can just walk. You can do that, can't you?'

'Don't leave me alone,' wailed Julia, in sudden panic.

'I'm going anyway,' said Nathan, hardening his heart.

Well, what else could he do? She'd get over it. Ignoring Julia's lamentations, Nathan pushed off with his bicycle.

In a caravan site not far from Watchet, an elderly man with a bald head was having a cup of tea and trying to resist the nagging of his wife.

'Well, I say we ought to go to the police,' she persisted.

'Oh mother leave it alone. It's nearly a week ago now.'

'Yes, and we ought to have gone when it happened, straight away.'

'Well we didn't. How were we to know?'

'We knew they stowed away in our caravan. We knew they came all the way from Brighton. We *saw* it was two kids when they ran off into the trees.'

'We're on holiday. We can't be responsible for other people's kids.'

'But suppose it *was* those two children from London They're still missing, it says in the paper. We could have helped the police find them.'

'It can't be them. It's too much of a coincidence.'

'*Why* is it too much of a coincidence? They've got to be *somewhere*. In *someone's* town, or street, or back garden. I say we should go to the police. Today.'

'All right, all right, anything for a quiet life. We'll take the car and go into Minehead. There's sure to be a police station there. Come on, get your coat, we'll go now, and get it over.'

14

On the moor

Pushing the bicycle, Nathan's head was well down, his field of vision restricted to the road beneath him, with brief glimpses of the banks on either side. When he felt the ground levelling out, he looked up. But *this* was not the moor, *this* was not what he had seen on telly. Before he went back for Julia, Nathan wanted to get to the real moor.

There was a sort of metal grid in the road. Nathan clattered over that and looked up again. Still hedges on either side – *this* was not the moor. He pushed on, almost running with the bicycle now. Just a bit further, just a little bit further. Stupid Julia would be fretting, but she could wait.

And at last, there it was. And it was better than in the book, the one about Lorna Doone, better than the programme on the telly, better than anything Nathan had ever seen in his life, except perhaps the sea at Brighton. Bitterly, Nathan regretted the loss of the glasses that would have allowed him to see it better. Never mind, he could see, he could see!

He could see a great undulating carpet of green and

purple, spread all around him, away and away into the misty distance. He could see the sea, far below. 'Look at that!' he said aloud. 'What about that!' And he dropped his bicycle and did a little dance, tired as he was, all by himself on the moor, where there was no one to see him, and think he was mad.

Wait till Julia sees this, he marvelled. Wait till the old Ratbag sees where we're going to camp. Then she won't say she's sorry we came up the hill. Nathan laid the bicycle in the heather, and started to make his way down on foot. When he first caught sight of Julia, he saw that she was watching, with great interest, something going on in the hedge beside the road. As she saw him coming, she dropped her head and made herself look tragic and abandoned again, but she was clearly putting it on now.

'It's a bird, learning how to fly,' said Nathan, spotting what it was she had been looking at.

'Is it?' Julia tried to sound indifferent, but really she was so glad to see him, the remains of her mood melted into the air.

'Yeah – it's a young one.'

'I thought it might be hurt.'

'Nah – it's all right. Jul, it's terrific up there. Just you wait till you see it. It's *terrific*.'

Nathan grabbed Julia's bicycle and started to weave it up the hill. It seemed easier now he knew what was at the top. Julia followed him quite happily. At the top she gazed around her 'Gawd!' she exclaimed (her mother's favourite expression), 'it's pretty ain't it.'

'It's more than *pretty*, Ju.'

'What's that purple stuff?'

'It's called heather.'

Julia touched it with her hand. 'It's all springy. It'll be nice to put under the beds.'

Trust Julia, to think of something practical.

The children mounted their bicycles and began to ride, cautiously at first, still conscious of the hampering weight, but with increasing confidence. It was still quite early in the morning and there were no other humans in sight, only clusters of white sheep with their half-grown lambs, some of which raised their heads to glance warily at Nathan and Julia. But most of the sheep were not interested, just went on quietly munching their breakfasts, or elevenses, or lunches, or whatever meal it was they were supposed to be having.

The sun was on the children's faces as they rode, and the moorland air was clean in their city-bred lungs. The loneliness was awesome in a way – all that vast expanse of rounded hills, and tumbling valleys, and no one in it but them. But the solitude was comforting too, because there was nobody to question them, or look at them with suspicious eyes. The children felt safe.

They came to a fork in the road, and took the turning to the left, not because *Exford* had any meaning for them, but because that way seemed to be going deeper into the moor, further away from people. They were looking for a river, or a stream, but so far they hadn't seen one. Nathan was sure they must come to one soon though. He knew there was at least one river on Exmoor – the Bagworthy, dark and menacing, with great boulders in it. Not dark on a day like this though, surely. On a day like this it would be bright, sparkling, with little yellow lights from the sun.

When they were tired, the children sat in the heather and ate their lunch. They ate crisps and biscuits and little triangles of cheese out of a box. There was one can of Coke each, but Julia hoped it wouldn't be too long before they found a river, because after that there would be nothing left to drink. Besides, she didn't think she could ride much further today.

They mounted their bicycles once more and rode on. By

now they were no longer alone on the moor. Cars full of trippers were passing them all the time, and a boy in one leaned out of the window to wave to them. He was only being friendly, but Nathan didn't like to be attracting attention. On Exmoor, he had thought, they would be really hidden. When they set off again, they took another turning to the right, one that didn't seem to be interesting the passing cars.

And still they had seen no river.

They began to worry. Not out loud, but each silently, wondering what was to become of them if they could find nowhere suitable to camp. But they had not come so far for nothing. It was Julia who spotted it, of course. Nathan's eyes could not have seen so far, and even Julia almost missed it, because at the angle of the road they were travelling, it was almost hidden between two great hills. 'Look,' she shouted, braking quickly and slipping off her bicycle.

'Where?' said Nathan, shading his eyes and peering.

It was just a flash of silver, a long way down, below the heather and the bracken and the little clumps of woodland.

'There!' said Julia. 'I wonder if we can get the bikes down.'

It was not easy, dragging the bicycles over the rough ground, but there was no particular hurry, now they had found a place to go. Down in the valley the tiny brilliant stream danced over clean pebbles.

'Can they see us from the road?' said Nathan, anxiously.

'We can't put the tents just here anyway,' said Julia. 'It's too slopy. We'll have to go further on.'

They followed the stream, searching for ground flat enough to make camp. 'I don't mind if it's a *bit* slopy,' said Nathan, who was suddenly feeling very tired. After all, he had worked harder than Julia, that day.

'Might as well find a really good place while we're about it,' said Julia, who seemed to have found an extra spurt of energy from somewhere. 'Come on, lazybones!'

Who was she calling lazybones! Who did she think she was – after letting him push her bicycle half way up Porlock Hill? Nathan was going to say something nasty, but changed his mind. Julia was pulling her weight now all right, and he knew, without needing to be told, that when the camp was made she would take charge of the cooking and the laundry. She would make sure that the tents were tidy, and the rubbish cleared away, and he wouldn't have to bother with any of that. He would be free to dream the days away for ever, or at least as far as he could see. The outlook was good enough.

'There!' said Julia suddenly in triumph. 'Look!'

Nathan couldn't quite see it yet, but Julia was clearly delighted. And, getting nearer, Nathan too was glad he'd made the effort because there, right beside the stream, was a flat space covered with sandy earth, just big enough for one small tent. And beyond a clump of bracken, round a little corner, was another level patch for the second tent to go. 'Terrific!' said Nathan, dropping his bicycle and smiling a real smile.

'Are you tired?' said Julia, unnecessarily.

'What do you think?'

'All right,' said Julia, kindly. 'You did push my bicycle, didn't you. I'll have a little rest with you, and then I'll put up both the tents.'

'You don't have to,' said Nathan, not protesting very hard.

'I don't mind,' said Julia. 'I like it here. I think this is going to be our sort of home.'

A police car had arrived from Minehead, and a man and a woman in uniform were searching the bushes on the sloping cliff that ran down to the sea, below the caravan site not far from Watchet. They did not know what they were looking for, but the bald man and his wife had said that was where the stowaways had run, and it was always possible they might have dropped *something*.

It did not take them long to find Julia's beach bag. Inside were two grown-up blouses, the slit skirt, the high-heeled shoes, the torn school dress mended with Sellotape and – an anorak. Inside the collar, written on a tape in indelible ink as the school required, were the faint and smudged letters of a name, J. WINTER.

'It's her all right,' said the policewoman. 'They were here.'

'Six days ago,' said her colleague. 'Who knows where they are now.'

'Well, *we* weren't to know,' said the bald man, defensively, when he heard what the police had found.

'I told you,' said his wife.

'Oh leave it mother,' said the bald man. 'Everybody makes mistakes sometimes.'

15

A bad storm

The police had found the young man in the grocery shop, the one with the long nose and the red hair, who had directed the children to Taunton to buy their tents.

'I *knew* there was something funny,' he said. 'Two kids on their own going off to buy camping stuff. *And* they didn't seem to know where they were. Never heard of Taunton even. Well, I said to Mrs Nosy Parker—'

'Mrs Nosy Parker?'

'Don't know her name. We all calls her Mrs Nosy Parker—you can guess why. Well anyway, *she* reckoned it was they kids from London. She went after them, up to the bus stop. She came back after, though. Wasn't they London kids at all, she said. They were caravanners with their mum and dad. Staying up the Lorna Doone, she said. Well, *she* seemed satisfied.'

'Any idea where we can find this Mrs Nosy Parker?'

'Naw, she ab'm been in the shop good few days now. She id'n local – holiday-maker. Probably gone back where she came from. I can tell'ee for certain the kids went to Taunton though. Mrs Nosy Parker saw them get on the bus.'

'Well, that's a help. It's a lead, anyway.'
'Hope you track 'em down, poor little devils.'
'We will, we will.'

The next few days were the happiest either child had ever known. The weather was perfect, the grown-up world far away. With no pressures they relaxed, and blossomed.

Most of the time they went their separate ways. Nathan wandered over the moors, gathering heather and bracken for the beds and dreaming fantastic stories, which he might write down one day if he ever got his glasses back. Julia kept house, and practised her reading.

On the evening of the third day they saw three deer, silhouetted against the skyline. Nathan told Julia that people hunted the Exmoor deer, in packs, with horses and dogs. Julia didn't believe him at first, she thought he was making it up. No one could possibly be so cruel. Nathan told her there were wild ponies on the moor as well as deer, but they hadn't seen any of those yet.

On the fourth day, the spare cylinder of gas, which fuelled their cooking stove, ran out. Their supply of matches ran out at the same time.

'I could make a real fire,' said Julia, 'if we had some matches.'

'You can make a fire with the sun,' said Nathan, 'if you got a magnifying glass. Have you got a magnifying glass, Julia?'

'Don't be silly. . . . We shall have to eat our food cold. And drink water. Don't matter, eh?'

'Nah. It's all right here, isn't it, Julia. It's good. It don't matter having cold food.'

'Yeah, it's nice. . . . We ain't got caught yet, have we, Nathan. Elizabeth said we'd get caught.'

'We're probably cleverer than her.'

'Are we going to be running away for always though, Nathan?'

'I don't see why not. We got plenty money still.' Actually, the wads of money were shrinking fast. It didn't look as though there was going to be any left over for Nathan's house, after all. Never mind, there was still the tent. No need to think about the money running out just now. 'Anyway – pretty soon I expect we can get jobs.'

'What sort of jobs?' said Julia doubtfully, looking at the wilderness around them.

'I dunno. Something. Or . . . I know, we could grow things. Dig up the ground and grow our food. How about that, Ju? Isn't that a good idea?'

'Yes but – don't it take a long time for things to grow?'

'Probably. I dunno really. Anyway, we still got the money. We can go on buying stuff.'

Julia was silent, pondering for a good minute. 'Nathan,' she said at last, in a different sort of voice, 'is it really our money?'

'Course, I told you. We found it.'

'I hope it *is* our money. I don't want to be a thief.'

'Well you aren't – we didn't steal nothing.' But Nathan too was suddenly less sure than he had been.

'Grown-ups say finding's the same thing as stealing,' said Julia, pursuing the theme. 'What do they say that for?'

'Well, they have to say it, haven't they. So you'll give it back. It's not stealing though. It's *not*.'

On the fifth day, an unwelcome state of affairs had at last to be faced. 'There's no crisps,' said Julia, 'and only one more tin.'

'How about if I catch some fish from the river and we eat that?'

'You been trying to catch fish ever since we been here,

and you haven't caught none yet. Anyway, we couldn't eat them raw.'

'We'll have to go shopping, then.'

'Not down that hill. I couldn't!'

'We'll have to, Ju. We can't starve.'

'What about your Lorna Doone place, isn't there a shop there?'

'I dunno. I dunno where it is from here, and anyway it's only small.'

'A small shop would do. We could just buy whatever they got.'

'I know but – we don't want people to notice us, and a small place they would. You know what Elizabeth said.'

'They can notice us in Porlock.'

'They won't know we got a camp on the moor though.'

'They will; they can see us going up the hill.'

'Not the shop lady though,' said Nathan. 'The shop lady won't see where we go. Anyway, there's lots of different shops in Porlock. We can go to a different one than last time. As long as the shop ladies don't see where we go, that's the most important thing. . . . I rather Porlock, Ju.'

'But that *hill.*'

'I know.'

'Is there another way?'

'How should I know. Anyway, we might get lost.'

'I ain't going down that hill again, Nathan, no way!' Julia's mouth was pursing into a pout. She was all ready to go into one of her moods.

'I could go by myself.'

'Not and leave me alone!'

'We have to have some food.'

Julia lapsed into gloom. 'I don't like it here any more,' she said, petulantly.

'Yes you do.'

'All right, I do but – I don't like it so much.'

'It'll be all right, Ju. I'll go by myself. I won't take long, I'll go tomorrow morning. I don't mind the hill. That hill ain't nothing to me. Anyway, it won't be so bad without the tents and stuff. You stay here and look after the tents, eh? Eh, Ju?'

'All right,' said Julia, suddenly.

'You won't mind?'

'All right, I said.' It had occurred to her, out of the blue, that it was babyish to make a fuss. The shopping had to be done, so she wouldn't be difficult about it. She would say goodbye to Nathan in the morning, and smile and wave, and he would be really pleased at how difficult she was not being. The day woud pass quickly enough. She would give both tents a good tidy out, and practise her reading.

'Don't forget the matches,' she reminded him, when the morning came. She helped him haul the bicycle up the hill and on to the road. 'Sure you remember the way?'

'Yeah, it's easy. Left and right and down the hill.'

'Bring a nice lot, bring as much as you can.'

'I will.'

Nathan rode off, and Julia went back to the camp. It felt really strange, being alone in the middle of the moor. When Nathan was off wandering she hadn't minded, she'd known he wasn't far. But now she could picture him pedalling along the road, every moment taking him further away from her. The silence closed round her like a blanket, bringing panic, and a sense of suffocation. Julia found her paperback novel and began to read, with great determination. *Madeleine, like a bird fluttering to its nest, flew into her lover's embrace. His strong arms held her. Madeleine was home at last.*

There, that was the first story finished. She had hardly understood what it was all about, and she had cheated and skipped rather a lot, but with Nathan's help she had read a good many of the words, and that was the main thing.

Julia opened the last tin of stewed steak and ate it, cold, for her lunch. It was too much, really, for her to manage all by herself, but she forced herself because she didn't want to waste it, and she thought it would not keep very well, in the heat. It really was a *very* hot day. Sticky hot. The sweat kept collecting on Julia's forehead and trickling down her nose. She took off her school shoes (there was a big hole on the bottom of one, she noticed – they weren't going to last much longer), and paddled in the stream to cool herself off. Then she thought, since there was no one around, she might as well cool the whole of herself. So she took off all her clothes, and left them in a heap on the bank. Even though there was no one to see, she was careful to put the plastic bag with the money at the bottom of the pile.

While she was in the water, Julia had an idea about the plastic bag with the money in it. She splashed about a bit longer, thinking over her idea, then she dried herself in the sun and dressed (because you never knew, *someone* might come along and see her), and began looking around for something to dig with.

A flat stone served the purpose. Julia pulled out some of the pegs, and lifted the tent with its sewn-in groundsheet. Then she began to dig. She remembered digging in the park, at home, the day they found the money, and all that seemed very far away, unreal. She finished her task, and smoothed over the sandy soil, and replaced the ground-sheet and the bedding inside. No one, now, could guess that there were several hundred pounds buried under Julia's tent.

While she was digging, Julia noticed that the earth inside the hole was quite cool, and that gave her another idea. She took the stone and began digging again, outside the tent this time, down by the stream. When she had finished, there was an improvised larder. She packed the few remaining stores into a plastic bag. Thank goodness almost everything they bought seemed to come packed in a plastic bag – there seemed an endless supply, from their shopping, for every purpose. Julia put the bag into the new hole, with ferns over the top for shade.

Just as that was done, a shadow came over the sun, and Julia saw how the clouds had been gathering while she worked. A thick, inky mass of them, covering half the sky. On the far hills the sun was still shining, a last blaze of gold in the path of the approaching storm. Here, in their valley, the first big drops were beginning to fall.

Julia was not over-concerned. The rain would cool things down, and it would be fun to sit inside the tent, snug and dry, and watch it coming down. She crouched on her sleeping bag, knees drawn up to her chin, while the mottled blue-black canopy slithered across the sky, extinguishing the last bright rays of sunlight streaming over the edge of it.

At that moment, the thunder began.

Normally, Julia was not very much afraid of thunder. At home in London, safe within four walls, and with other human beings nearby, it was easy to be brave. But here, all alone in the middle of a moor, and with only one thin layer of fabric between her and the fury outside, she began to feel first apprehensive, then moderately frightened, and finally quite terrified.

The rain by now was sheeting down. It drummed on the tent roof, just by Julia's head. Like bullets, it struck the ground in front of her, bouncing back on her legs and her face, and striking through the open tent flap when she retreated further into the tent to escape it. Clumsily, and much too late, she struggled to fasten the opening. The end of her sleeping bag was soaking wet, and everywhere her head knocked against the canvas as she blundered about in the small space, the rain came through in great dripping pools.

Meanwhile, the lightning outside was tearing up the sky. Each flash lit the tent for a moment, then relinquished it to unnatural mid-afternoon darkness and a terrible, deafening cannon-roar of sound. Julia curled into a ball, her hands over her ears, her face buried in the sleeping bag, shutting out sight and hearing until the storm should be over.

At last, sensing stillness, she sat up and looked around to assess the damage. Nothing much after all that. Apart from the end of her sleeping bag, the bedding had only a few wet patches which would soon dry out, she hoped. Her pile of spare clothes neatly folded in one corner, had fortunately been covered with her anorak. The anorak was wet, but the clothes underneath were dry. Julia was still quite distraught with loneliness and fear. 'Nathan, come back!' she implored him out loud, though of course he could not possibly hear.

Suddenly Julia remembered Nathan's tent. She had tidied his clothes for him that morning, but there was nothing to cover them with because of course he had taken his anorak, with the money in the lining, tied round his waist by the sleeves as usual. The tent flap, she knew, was wide open. She had left it like that to air, so it would be nice and fresh for him when he got back.

She undid her own tent and peered out. The sky was still dark, the thunder rumbling round the distant hills threatening to circle and return. But for the moment the rain had almost stopped. Julia crept out and ran to Nathan's tent. She fastened it quickly, not waiting to inspect the contents. If they were wet they were wet – there was nothing to be done about it until the sun came out again, and that was not likely to happen today.

The thunder-claps were nearer; the storm *was* coming

back. Julia scuttled to her tent, moaning and sobbing and feeling very sorry for herself. Where was Nathan? Why was he taking so long? He ought to know she was all alone and frightened. He ought to hurry, knowing she was all alone in the storm.

It was only when the rain began again in earnest, and she heard through all the other noises the sound of the little stream rushing in full flood, that the thought occurred to her at last. Of course— *Nathan* will be drenched. He's out on the bicycle, in all that awful weather. Poor Nathan, he'll be soaked through! She thought that for about two minutes, and then the world crashed about her ears once more.

It was early evening when Nathan returned. The rain had finally stopped, and Julia had climbed to the top of the hill, so that she could watch for him, coming along the road. At first sight of him her heart gave a lurch of joy and relief. She ran to meet him, and almost threw her arms round him as he dismounted from his bicycle. She didn't though – Nathan would not have cared for that at all, and anyway he was much too wet to hug.

He was like a drowned rat, his clothes sticking to him, his shoes squelching water as he walked. But he was home, and that was the main thing, and he had brought enough provisions for a fortnight, Julia thought. How he had managed to push the bicycle up Porlock Hill with all that weight she would never know. She was full of admiration and gratitude; she helped him down the hill with the bicycle; she couldn't do enough for him. She lent him her anorak and her spare tee-shirt, and she would have lent him jeans as well, but she only had one pair. It was a thousand pities she couldn't make him a hot meal, not even a cup of tea. He had brought the matches, but everything was so wet after the rain. There was no hope of getting a fire started that day.

Exhausted and chilled though Nathan was, he did not

forget to ask Julia for her share of the cost of the groceries – and she fetched it straight away, as was only right and proper. She showed him, with pride, the hole she had dug under the tent, but he was too tired to be much interested in that.

Next morning the sun shone again. Not as hot now, fresher after the storm and altogether more pleasant. It should have been a happy day, but somehow it wasn't. Somehow Nathan wasn't himself; not the self he had recently become, that was. More like the surly, bad-tempered boy who was so unpopular in Class 8. He snapped and snarled at Julia, and she couldn't do anything right. In the end, his unpleasantness reduced her to tears.

'What's the matter with you, Nathan Browne?'

'Don't feel well.' Nathan coughed as he spoke, and it dawned on Julia that he had in fact been coughing a bit all day.

'Have you got a cold?'

'Yeah – getting wet yesterday, innit. My eyes are sore too.'

'Shall I try to make a fire now? Make us a hot drink?'

'Yeah, you try.' He sounded listless though, not really interested.

There was a little wood halfway up the hill above the camp. There might be some sticks in there that might be dry enough. Julia collected a bundle, and arranged them in a stack, down by the stream. It took her a long time to get the fire going, and she used a large number of matches, but she was happy to be doing something positive. 'I did it, I did it,' she shouted at last, as the flames spurted and crackled. She filled the little saucepan with water from the stream and later – actually a considerable time later – the two children sat side by side on the damp bracken, sipping cups of smoky tea.

Nathan shivered. 'I feel cold,' he complained.

207

'But it's warm, the sun's lovely and warm. You *can't* feel cold.'

'Well I do.' He wrapped his anorak round his shoulders, and shivered inside that.

'It's not properly dry,' Julia warned him. 'It won't do your cold no good. Here, you can have mine again.'

Nathan hugged himself inside Julia's anorak, but half an hour later he had thrown it off, and his shirt too. 'I'm *boiling*,' he fretted.

Julia regarded him with some concern. Something must be wrong. He must have a very bad cold to be going hot and cold like that. Perhaps he would be better after a good night's sleep. 'You'll be better in the morning,' she told him.

But in the morning he was worse. He was coughing more, and complaining that his throat was sore, and the light hurt his eyes. He stayed in his tent all morning, and didn't want anything to eat, though he drank all the tea Julia brought him. In the afternoon he seemed a little better. He sat by the stream, and carved a little boat out of a piece of wood. He made a sail for it out of a large leaf, and set it on the water. It capsized against a stone, and Nathan lost interest.

Next day, Nathan was really ill.

When Julia called to him, from outside his tent, he didn't answer her, though she knew he was awake because she could hear him thrashing about. When she crouched down, and pulled aside the flap to peep at him, he stared at her with glittering eyes that didn't seem to know her.

'Do you want a cup of tea, Nathan?' Julia tried to make her voice sound ordinary, but really she was beginning to feel quite frightened.

Nathan coughed, and struggled to push down the sleeping bag. 'Hot,' he said. 'I'm hot, I'm hot.'

Julia went to help him and, touching his skin, realized that he was indeed burning with fever. 'A cup of tea?' she repeated. It was all she could think of.

Nathan moaned, and threshed about some more. 'It hurts,' Julia heard him say.

'What hurts? Where does it hurt?'

'Everything. Head, throat, eyes.'

'You stay there, and I'll make a cup of tea.'

In the early morning damp, it took a long time to get the smoky fire going. Julia's fingers were not quite steady anyway. She was really afraid now. What should she do? It must be more than a cold that Nathan had. Perhaps it was something terrible. She took the tea to him at last. 'Do you want some breakfast?' she asked hopefully.

Nathan muttered something that sounded like, 'Yo ho ho and a bottle of rum' but of course it couldn't have been that. Julia waited while he drank half the tea, then he pushed the cup fretfully away. 'Shut the tent, Ju. The light's hurting my eyes.'

'Shall I wash you?' Julia had a vague idea that that was one of the things you did for people who were ill.

'NO! . . . Leave me.'

Deeply troubled, Julia went back to the fire to drink her own tea. She thought about getting some breakfast, but decided she wasn't hungry. To give herself something to do, and to take her mind off the crisis, Julia went back to the wood to get more fuel for the fire. She came back with an armful, and got a really nice blaze going. She did not think the smoke would be visible from the road, but in any case she was really past caring much about that. All she wanted was for Nathan to be better.

She went to listen outside his tent, hoping he would be sleeping. But he was still restless, and now and again talking rubbish. Julia heard the bit about the bottle of rum again, and there was a lot about the police coming to get him. Julia made up her mind. Kneeling on all fours, she pushed her head through the tent flap and called to Nathan in his delirium. 'Nathan, I'm going to get the doctor.'

He heard that all right. 'No, Ju – no!'

'But I must. You're sick.'

'Not the doctor, not the doctor! The police is going to come if you get the doctor.'

'But you're ill, Nathan. You know you're ill.'

'Only a cold . . . it's only a cold from the rain. . . . I don't want no doctor.'

Julia hesitated. How would she get a doctor anyway? Cycle into Porlock, all by herself? But Nathan was ill, and if she had to she would do it. 'All right, but if you ain't better by tonight I'm going. I mean it.'

She stood up, half blinded by tears – and tripped over a small stone as she went to walk away. It was a ridiculous thing to have done, and just her luck, and she had twisted her ankle – not badly, but it *did* hurt.

'What was that? What you done?' Nathan called from inside the tent.

'Nothing,' said Julia, bravely. But she was not sure about walking on the hurt ankle, let alone cycling to get the doctor. She limped down to the stream and bathed her foot in the cold water, and sobbed freely and loudly now that she was safely out of Nathan's hearing. What *was* going to become of them?

By evening, Nathan was no longer delirious, but lying still on his back, eyes gazing blankly at the roof of the tent. Julia peeped in at him, for about the tenth time.

'Do you want anything?'

No answer.

'Some tea?'

No answer.

'*Nathan* – don't you want nothing?'

The blank eyes swivelled briefly in her direction, then wandered indifferently away. Clearly the worst was about to happen. Clearly he was fading fast.

'Oh, Nathan,' Julia burst out, in uncontrollable anguish, 'I don't want you to *die*!'

'Die? . . . I ain't going to die, you stupid Rat-bag!'

'Nathan!' said Julia, joyfully, 'you're better!'

'If you really want to do something useful,' said Nathan, irritably, 'you can make a cup of tea.'

Gladly, Julia hobbled to make it. The sound of Nathan's rasping cough followed her as she went, and while she waited for the pan to boil, she searched her mind for a memory. Where had she heard a cough like that before? Recently?

Suddenly she remembered. A bus journey, and an annoying little girl with spots. Julia went back to Nathan's tent, and threw the flap wide open.

'My eyes,' he complained. 'Ju, I told you – the light!'

'I want to look at your face,' Julia insisted.

She examined it carefully, touching the cheeks with her fingertips to make sure, while Nathan wriggled unco-operatively, and tried to push her hand away. On Nathan's dark skin the rash was not noticeable to the casual glance, but it was there all the same. Julia smiled a big radiant smile that lit up her plain face and made it, for one moment, quite beautiful.

'I know what's wrong with you,' she announced, triumphantly. 'You've got measles!'

16

Disaster in Porlock

Now they knew it was only measles, the children expected Nathan to get well quite quickly, so he did. It was fortunate, probably, that they did *not* know that measles can be quite a serious illness. To them it was a joke, something to be made fun of in comics and on picture postcards.

'You must have catch it from that little girl on the bus,' said Julia.

'Will you catch it from me then?'

'Nah – I had it already. You can't only have it once.'

For several days Nathan continued to feel poorly. He pecked at his food, and was cross with Julia, and she bore it all with admirable patience. When he turned his nose up at something she had just cooked, she took the food away without comment, and offered to cook him something else. She was so glad Nathan was not going to die that nothing was too much trouble. Even walking on her hurt foot was not too much trouble, because Nathan was getting better, and she was doing it for him.

'Wish I could read,' Nathan grumbled, one afternoon.

'Shall I read to you?' Julia offered.

'What, for instance?'

'I could read *The Empty Heart*.'

'Do me a favour!'

'I started a new one now – it's called *The Dawn of Love*.'

Nathan groaned. 'Sounds worse than the other. Wish I brought *Treasure Island*. You couldn't read that one yet though, Ju, it's got a lot of hard words in it.'

'I'm getting on though, aren't I, Nathan.'

'All right. Not bad.'

'Mrs Henrey would be pleased with me, wouldn't she? All of Class 8 would be surprised at me, wouldn't they? That I can read.'

'I suppose so. . . . Did you think, Ju, there isn't no Class 8 any more?'

'Isn't there? Oh no, that's right. It must be the holidays now.'

'And after the holidays—'

'We're all going to our new schools. . . . I mean, they're all going to their new schools. . . . I mean – Nathan, ain't we *ever* going to our secondary schools?'

'What you want to go to school for? You can read now, nearly.'

'I dunno. . . . I wonder if they'd like me in my new school.'

'Don't matter though, 'cause you ain't going.'

'Nobody ever liked me,' said Julia, pursuing her theme. She thought for a moment of Elizabeth, and Mrs Parsons, but those encounters had been so brief they hardly counted. 'My mum don't like me even,' she added.

'Well *I* like you.'

'Do you really?' said Julia, flushing with pleasure.

'Yes I do. Actually – you're different than you used to be. When we was in Class 8, I didn't like you then.'

'Nor I didn't like you neither. You're different, too.' She didn't count him being cross with the measles. Anyone was allowed to be cross when they weren't well.

There was a long pause.

'Nathan.'

'What?'

'Do you think our mums are really missing us?'

'Nah – probably forgot all about us by now.' All of a sudden though, Nathan felt an uncomfortable stab of con science. He thought of his father, and the leather belt that came off too easily. But he also thought of the look his father had given him in Mr Barlowe's office – the look of deep troubled hurt, when he thought his son had been stealing. At the time, that look had seemed a threat. It occurred to Nathan now though, that perhaps it was more like sorrow. He thought of his mum as well, and that thought was too painful to be borne, so he squashed it down and trampled on it, and told himself his mum had all the others so she couldn't be minding too much about him. She *couldn't. Could she?*

There was another long pause.

'Nathan – do you think my mum would like me now?'

'I should think so. I should think *anyone* would like you now.'

'Even with my hair like this?'

'*I* like you even with your hair like this.'

'Oh yeah – so you do. . . . Nathan – why did we run away?'

'*You* know.'

'No but – why did we?'

'They was going to take our money away.'

'Our money's going to get used up anyway. . . . What else did we run away for?'

'They was going to do bad things to us.'

'What things though?'

214

'I forget,' Nathan admitted. 'I know what, they was going to put us away.'

Julia pondered. 'I don't think they'd *really* do that though, not *really*. . . . I don't think they'd do anything *really* bad to us, if we say we're sorry and we won't do it again.'

'You don't want to go back though, do you?'

Julia was silent, poking at the ground with her foot. 'I might,' she confessed at last. 'If my mum would like me I might.'

For a moment Nathan also toyed with the idea. He could go back, and go to his new school, and work hard and pass all sorts of hard exams. He could make his mum and dad proud, and make it up to them for what he did.

But he wasn't going to go back, was he! He was running away, wasn't he, and having a great time, him and Julia.

'Julia,' he said in sudden anxiety, 'you wouldn't go home and leave me on my own, would you?'

'Nah – I'm staying with you, Nathan.'

'Good. That's good. Good old Rat-bag. . . . How's the stores going?'

'All right. Wait till you see my larder I made.'

'How many days' food we got enough for?'

'Plenty.' She went to count. 'About four. It does use up quick Nathan.'

'I'll go back to Porlock and get some more soon.'

'You ain't well enough.'

'Yes I am. Nearly. Few more days I will be.'

'You're catching,' said Julia, doubtfully. 'You suppose to be in quarrelling.'

'*Quarantine*, Ju. Yeah, I know. I won't go near nobody. I won't go near no kids anyway.'

'Well mind you don't.'

Julia was not happy to see Nathan go off on the bicycle three days later, but she accepted that it was necessary if they were to eat. He was certainly better. The rash was gone and he had been proving how strong he was all through the day before, running up to the wood and back, collecting fuel for their fire. Julia could not do that too well with her bad ankle, and anyway Nathan wanted to show he was useful again.

She clucked round him like a mother hen, the morning he set off. She made him wear his anorak, though the day was quite warm, and privately he decided to take it off as soon as he was out of sight, and tie it round his waist by the sleeves as usual.

Just as he was setting off, Julia had a thought. She had almost forgotten; she had meant to mention it before. 'Nathan,' she said, 'you don't need to take all your money, do you? Why don't you bury most of it like I done, like I showed you – under the tent?'

Nathan frowned, and shook his head. 'Nah – I rather carry it.'

'Suppose you lost it.'

'I won't lose it. How can I lose it? I rather carry it.'

He felt safer with the money on his person, where he could touch it, feel its comforting bulk in the lining of his coat. There was no way the money could possibly be lost. Nathan examined the coat every day to make sure no hole was coming through which it might fall out.

Once on the road, which was high above the valley, Nathan realized that the weather was not nearly as warm as he had thought. There was a blustery wind, with little pink scudding clouds in the sky. Nathan decided to keep his anorak on, at any rate for the time being.

He felt well and happy, and strong enough for anything, even Porlock Hill. He walked down the steep part of course, carefully, gripping the brakes as hard as he could. There was a notice halfway down, and Nathan went close to read it. The notice said about looking out for cars out of control.

Nathan imagined a car out of control, and then he imagined a bicycle out of control. Hurtling madly, somersaulting on the bend, breaking its rider's neck, most likely. Nathan shuddered at the thought. It was deliciously horrifying, but not really frightening because of course he, Nathan Browne, was much too clever to risk such a thing. In fact, it was quite marvellous to think how clever he had been all through this adventure. And Julia, of course. Not taking undue risks, not getting caught, outwitting everybody!

Continuing this pattern of cleverness, Nathan looked for a food shop he hadn't used before. He was just about to padlock the bicycle, before going in to make his purchases, when an idea struck him.

Ships!

He hadn't seen any ships for weeks. The sea was near here, wasn't it? Porlock Weir! Nathan had a picture in his mind, from last time, of a stone jetty with a row of cottages on the top. And below the jetty the harbour, with all sorts of fascinating little boats in it. He would go there first, it was only a short way. He would sit by the harbour, and look at the ships. perhaps even. . . ?

There was no need to tell Julia he didn't go straight to the shops and back. She wouldn't understand. Ships weren't her thing, she had never read *Treasure Island*, and probably never would.

Anyway, he wouldn't be long by the sea.

The tide was out, as usual. There were a few people on the beach, making the most of the indifferent weather, but not many round the boats in the harbour. Those that *were* round the boats seemed very busy and occupied, doing things with ropes and paint brushes and so on. No one took any notice of Nathan.

He had his eye on a little motor cruiser, and he walked all round it, assessing its possibilities. Because there was no water, the boat was tipped slightly to one side. Nathan chose the side that leaned towards the ground, reached up to grasp the short rail, and swung himself easily on to the deck. His luck was in; the hatch was not locked. Nathan lowered himself into the cabin, excited to be actually in a boat for the first time in his life.

It was something like the caravan inside, only smaller. There was a tiny kitchen, a table, and a long seat that was probably a bed as well. Nathan sat on the seat, and looked around the shiny interior of the boat. The slight tilt added to the illusion he made for himself, that he was really out at sea, on the tossing waves. Nathan thought himself in heaven.

It was warm in the cabin; quite stuffy, in fact. Nathan took off his anorak, and tied it round his waist. He didn't double knot it, as usual. It was only going to be for a few moments, after all.

For those few moments he was not Nathan Browne at all. He was Jim Hawkins, in *Treasure Island*. No, not Jim Hawkins. Jim Hawkins lived a long time ago, when they didn't have little cabin cruisers like this. He was a modern pirate then, off to the Caribbean in his own ship, to search for sunken treasure. Or better still – he was a lone yachts-man, sailing round the world, braving sharks and storms. . . .

Lost in his dream, Nathan was unaware of footfalls on the deck above. He had no idea he was not alone on the boat until the hatch suddenly yawned open, and an angry red face regarded him from above.

'You thieving little brat!' roared a voice. 'What you doing in my boat?' The owner of the face, and the voice, was clearly not pleased to see Nathan.

Nathan jumped as though he had been shot. For a moment he had difficulty in remembering where he was, the fantasy had been so real. But he was *not* on the high seas coping single-handed with a hurricane. He was in the har-bour of Porlock Weir, trespassing on someone else's boat.

218

And what was more, the owner of the boat now stood between him and freedom.

'Come on, come on out of it, you little pest.'

Nathan obeyed, with a sinking heart. He stood on the deck, frightened and penitent, the owner of the boat towering over him.

'What did you steal then?'

'I didn't, I didn't steal nothing.'

'Come on, turn out your pockets.'

'I didn't steal nothing, I didn't.'

'You're not going till you've proved it. Your pockets. Or do you want me to get the police?'

'No, not the police, not the police!'

Fear was robbing Nathan of the power to think. He was aghast at what had happened. He looked round wildly, but there was no escape.

'Pockets then, hurry up.'

There were only the pockets of his jeans, and not much in them. Two ten pence coins, a few coppers, a shell and a pebble from the beach.

'All right – what about your coat?'

'There ain't nothing in my coat. There ain't, I swear, I swear.'

'Don't bother to swear, show me.'

Without untying the sleeves, Nathan turned the pockets of his anorak inside out. The pockets were empty, but the hole in one of them was very apparent, and the big man did not miss it.

'You put something through that hole? In the lining?'

'No, no.'

'Yes you did, you little liar, I can see the bulge.'

'There ain't nothing. It's mine. It's my own.'

'Let me see.'

'No.'

The big man put out his hand. Nathan saw his intention,

but was not nearly quick enough. He dodged, but the man's hand had already closed round the hood of the coat. Frantically, Nathan wrenched himself away from the big man's grasp. He grabbed at the edge of the open hatch, struggling and pulling. Suddenly feeling himself free, he lunged over the side of the boat, falling painfully on to the stones in the empty harbour. He scrambled to his feet, and with weak and sagging knees ran to where he had left the bicycle. He fumbled with the padlock – would it never come undone? But it did, and no one had chased after him to catch him, and he was on the bicycle at last, pedalling as fast as his shaky legs would carry him.

Nathan had escaped. But the owner of the boat was still holding his coat. The anorak with more than eight hundred pounds in the lining.

The journey back to the camp was a nightmare. One part of Nathan could not believe that such a calamity had actually befallen him. He must be dreaming it. He kept putting his hand down, hoping to feel the anorak still there, tied by the sleeves around his waist. But of course, the sad truth was that it was gone. Meanwhile, the other part of Nathan was mortified at the thought of having to face Julia, having to tell her the dreadful news. No food, and half their money lost.

She'd warned him of course, and he hadn't listened. If only he had! As he pushed the bicycle up Porlock Hill – an easier matter this time, of course, since it was carrying no weight –Nathan re-wrote the sequence of events in his mind. In this version he had taken Julia's advice, and buried his money under his tent. Now it didn't matter that the big man had his coat. It was nothing but an old anorak, and he had plenty of money to buy another.

Only, of course, that was just make-believe. It hadn't *really* happened like that.

Julia would probably be angry. She would probably say, 'I told you so,' and be all self-righteous about it. Well, she wasn't so perfect herself! Who was it worked out how to get the bikes up the hill, for instance? And how to stow away in the caravan? Who did Julia Winter think she was, telling him off for just losing his coat? Pedalling over the moor, Nathan played out in his mind a scene in which he and Julia exchanged angry words. There was a nasty bitter quarrel, and it ended with each of them going into their own tents and not speaking.

Only, of course, *that* hadn't happened either. *That* was only make-believe too. As Nathan neared home the silly trumped-up rage left him, and numb despair took its place. The tears came to his eyes and he couldn't control them. They blurred his sight worse than ever, rolled down his cheeks, and trickled into his mouth as he rode. They were salty and warm, the only warm thing on this moor today – this cold, windswept moor, that had been so friendly, but had turned so bleak and cruel.

Julia was waiting for him, with the pan already hot for tea. As she saw him bumping the cycle down the grassy slope, she gave him a bright smile of welcome. Through his misery, as he came near, Nathan saw that her hair really was growing again. He could see it sticking out, from under the cap. Soon she would be able to look quite nice again, like she did in Brighton. It was a shame, it really was a shame, to have to wipe that smile off her face.

The smile disappeared anyway when she saw that he was crying.

'Nathan, what's the matter?'

Nathan tried to tell her. He *wanted* to tell her and get it over with, but the words would not come, only great gulping sobs.

'What *is* it?' Thoroughly alarmed now, Julia looked for clues. 'Where's the food? Haven't you brought none?'

Nathan shook his head, the sobs now a torrent of grief.

'Nathan! Stop it! Where's your coat?'

Nathan sprawled on the ground, and wept.

'You lost it!'

Nathan did not deny the awful truth.

'You did. You lost your coat. You lost all your money!'

'I'm sorry, I'm sorry, I'm sorry, I'm sorry—'

'Oh shut up!'

'What?'

'Shut up keeping on saying you're sorry. It's all right, you can have half mine.'

'What!'

'You heard. You can have half mine. I'll get it now.'

She turned to go, but Nathan stopped her. 'Wait a minute.'

'Don't you want it?'

Nathan's whole self was a tumult of feelings he couldn't define, and couldn't express. Shame, gratitude, affection – all churning around together inside him.

'You keep it for me, Ju,' he said humbly.

It was the only spoken thanks she got, but she knew what he meant.

The big man had taken his car, and gone straight to the police station in Minehead.

'There was all this money in the lining,' he said, handing over the coat and the bundle of notes. 'The kid went off on his bike. I couldn't have caught him.'

'And the money's not yours, you say, sir?'

'Oh no, I wouldn't ever leave that much in the boat.'

'He must have been scared, to leave all that money behind.'

'I didn't bully him,' said the big man.

'I'm sure you didn't, sir,' said the police officer, feeling

222

pretty sure he had. 'I meant – it looks as though the boy had no right to the money, wherever it did come from.'

He was examining the coat as he spoke. The inked-in name at the neck was so faint it was almost illegible. The policeman took it closer to the light. 'Looks like an "N", and something "BOURNE". No, "BROWN". Wait a minute – by George, it is! It's "NATHAN BROWNE"! Well thank you very much, sir, for bringing this in. Looks like you've helped us find one of those London kids that've been missing from home – nearly a month now. You didn't see where he went on his cycle, you say?'

The big man shrugged. 'Back towards Porlock is all I can tell you.'

'Right. We'll get a police car over there straight away. Excuse me.'

In Porlock there were plenty of people who remembered, when pressed to try, a small black boy on a bicycle loaded with camping equipment, going up towards the moor. On two occasions he was alone, the police learned, but at the first sighting he had been with a much taller child. A white girl, or it might have been a white boy. It was hard to tell these days, wasn't it, with both sexes wearing the same sort of clothes.

17

Hunted

Next morning Nathan said he would have to go back to Porlock, since there was hardly any food left. Julia was worried that the man from the boat might see Nathan if he went back to Porlock, but Nathan pointed out that the boat was at Porlock Weir, not Porlock town itself, and he didn't think there was much danger.

He had another worry, a private one. Suppose the man from the boat had found the money in the lining of that anorak – he might have taken the money to the police. He might have taken the *anorak* to the police, with 'Nathan Browne' written inside it. On the other hand, he most likely kept the money for himself. Almost certainly he kept the money for himself, so there was nothing to worry about, after all.

Julia went with Nathan up to the road, and as it was such a lovely morning she thought she would like to go with him, just a little way. 'Let me ride on your carrier, Nathan,' she begged. 'I can walk back, no problem.'

So they wobbled, two on a bike, towards the turning on to the Exford road.

'This is all right, isn't it, Ju,' said Nathan, beginning to feel happy again.

'Stop!' said Julia, in sudden alarm.

Nathan stopped. They straddled the bike, their feet on the road. 'What's the matter?' said Nathan.

'Look!'

'What? I can't see nothing.'

'Over there – on the other road.' Julia's sharp eyes had picked out the car crawling along the skyline. 'Oh Nathan, I think it's a police car.'

'Are you sure?'

'I think so. I think I can see that light thing on top.'

'It might not be a police car, it might be a ordinary car.'

'Why's it going so slow then? They're looking for something.'

'Us!'

'Do you think so? Oh I'm frightened, I'm frightened, what we going to do?'

'Get back to the camp,' said Nathan.

'Yeah let's do that quick. They can't see the camp from the road.'

Back in the valley with the great silent slopes all around, the children felt momentarily safe.

'Perhaps it wasn't a police car after all,' said Julia.

'It was,' said Nathan, accepting the bitter truth.

'How do you know? You couldn't see it even.'

'My coat,' said Nathan.

'Oh I know what you mean – with the money in it!'

'And my name in the neck.'

'That man must have took your coat to the police station, Nathan.'

225

'Why didn't he just keep the money? *I* would have.'

'Anyway, the police won't find us here, will they?'

'Oh yes they will.'

'They will?' she echoed him, terrified.

'They'll see the river like we did. They'll come down, and look for the tents.'

'We'll pack them up,' said Julia, running on trembling legs to do it.

'No,' said Nathan, 'there might not be time. Let's just hide.'

'Where?' Julia looked round in fear. 'Where can we go, so the police won't find us?'

'I dunno. What about the wood?'

'Won't they find us in the wood?' said Julia. 'Won't they look?'

'I dunno. If they see we left the camp, maybe they'll think we've gone. Gone away.'

'Oh yes – perhaps they will think that, Nathan. Let's go quick, quick, before they come.'

'We can watch what happens.'

'Yes, yes.'

'Where you going?' said Nathan.

'To get the money.'

'Oh yeah. . . . Leave your bike, Ju. We can't use the bikes. We can't go on the road.'

'But we got to hide the bikes. If they see the bikes they won't think we're gone away, will they!'

'Yeah, that's right. That's right, I didn't think of that . . . Where you going now?'

'My coat. And the biscuits.'

They dragged the bicycles up the slope. 'I can't push,' said Julia. 'My legs are all shaking.'

'Try,' said Nathan. 'We nearly there.'

They reached the cover of the wood, and hid the bicycles

in the thick undergrowth. They lay with twigs scratching their arms and faces, peering through tickly foliage into the valley.

'I hope the police didn't see us on the road,' said Julia, fearfully.

'Nah – they'd have been here by now.'

'How did they know we was on the moor? How do they know we got tents?'

'Easy. They asked questions in the shops, didn't they. Somebody told them we got camping things, didn't they. Somebody saw us going up the hill.'

Of course! She could have worked that one out for herself if she hadn't been so flustered. She waited for her heart to stop thumping, and her breath to stop coming in such painful gasps, and her chest to stop hurting from the panic. 'Nathan,' she said at last, 'what are we going to do?'

'Hide, of course, till the police go away.'

'But after that, what are we going to do? Now they know about the camp?'

Nathan said nothing.

'What, Nathan? . . . What we going to do?'

Nathan hesitated. He didn't want to say it. His dream was so fragile, he didn't want to expose it to the pitiless light of day. 'I have got a *sort* of idea.'

'Tell me.'

'Nah – you wouldn't like it.'

'Tell me, I said.'

'I don't think you'd want to do it.'

'Tell me what it is, and I'll tell you if I want to do it.'

Nathan took a deep breath. 'All right. You remember when we was in Watchet?'

'Where the cave was? And the bus to go to – where was it? – Taunton?'

'Yeah, and the harbour. Remember the harbour?'

'What about it?'

'Remember that big ship that was going to Norway?'
'No.'
'Well *I* remember it.'
'So?'
'Let's stow away on that ship, and go to Norway!'

There – it was out! The dream he had nursed all these weeks. Born of his reading, nourished by his imagination, and launched now by reason of the dire peril they were in.

Julia turned to look at him, her face aghast. 'You must be mad!'

Well, he'd expected her to say *that*. 'I knew you wouldn't like it.'

'Stow away on a ship? Us?'

'We done it on the caravan. *That* was all right.'

Julia considered. 'The ship might not be there any more.'

'Then we get another one. We wait till there is one. There will be one though, I just know there will.'

Julia dropped her head on to her arms. Everything was moving so fast. The little bit of security she had enjoyed, in the tent this past couple of weeks, had suddenly vanished, dissolved into thin air. And in its place, what? 'I don't want to go to Norway,' she said, in a very small voice.

'It might be nice when we get there.'

'But it won't work, they'll just send us back.'

'They might not. There might be a way. Let's just try it, Ju, eh? Eh?'

Julia chewed a piece of grass, gazing sadly down at the little camp. 'I wish they'd leave us alone. . . . What's it like at Norway, Nathan?'

'Don't you remember? Mr Abbot told us about it when we was in his class. It's all mountains, with snow on them, and forests.'

'Is it cold?'

'We can buy warm clothes.'

Cold. And discomfort. And terrifying, unknown perils. And all the while there was a cosy little flat in London with a warm bed, and the television, and three square meals a day.

'I want to go home,' said Julia.

'*What*?'

'I want to go home. I don't want to go on no ship, I want to go home.'

'What about they going to put you away? And your mum's going to beat you?'

'I don't believe they going to put me away. And I don't believe my mum's going to beat me either. Well, not *hard*. I think she just said that, I don't think she meant it. I want to go home.'

She was serious. Nathan struggled with himself. 'Go on then.'

'What do you mean, go on?'

'Go down in the camp and wait for the police. They'll take you home.'

'Ain't you coming?'

'No, I said. I'm going on the ship. I *always* wanted to go on a ship. This is my best chance.'

Julia turned a piteous face towards him. 'But I'm scared to go without you. I'm scared to go down there and wait for the police all by myself.'

'Well, you'll have to, won't you.'

'But what will they do to me, Nathan?'

'That's your problem,' said Nathan, roughly. 'I'm going — before they come.'

He started to wriggle out of the hiding place, suddenly terrified that the police would arrive, and Julia would announce herself thus forcing him to join her anyway.

'Don't leave me,' wailed Julia. 'Don't leave me, Nathan!'

Nathan dragged his bicycle out of the undergrowth and

charged out of the wood on to the wide open slope. He bumped his way over the uneven ground, and Julia with her bicycle followed behind. 'Wait for me, wait for me, Nathan!' Parallel with the stream they ran, until it curved out of sight of the camp, and fear lent strength to both the children. Nathan was terrified of losing his chance, and Julia was terrified of losing Nathan.

They were heading away from the road, deeper into the moor. Nathan knew where he was going. He knew this little part of the moor quite well – he had wandered it enough times during the peaceful days. He was going where the police would have no reason to search unless they had seen him running. Julia could come or not, as she pleased, but anyway *he* would be safe.

As long as Julia didn't tell. But Julia could *still* tell. She could, couldn't she! She could go back and tell them which way he went! Nathan turned and shouted at her, 'Are you coming, then?'

Julia staggered towards him, the brief surge of energy almost exhausted. 'Course I am.' It was all she had breath to say.

'All the way? On the ship?'

'Yes, yes I am! Wait for me, Nathan.'

He hesitated, still unsure.

'Why did you run away from me?' said Julia.

'I thought you was going to tell.'

'What!' She was amazed, and deeply hurt, that he could think it.

'Well, you wanted to go home, didn't you?'

'But I wouldn't tell of *you*, Nathan. I wouldn't tell of *you*.'

Her sincerity was transparent. Nathan felt mean and ashamed. 'Come on,' he said, holding her bicycle too to make up for it. They went up, and over, and round, and down, and they hid in a valley where the slopes were all

wooded, a valley which Nathan thought perhaps only he
knew about. Where no one had ever been before.

The police had found the camp. Touring the road above in
their car, they had seen the little stream. The tents were not
visible from the road, but the stream was. This was a most
likely place for two runaway children to set up camp. The
two police officers left their car, and scrambled down to the
valley to investigate.

They were delighted to find the children's camp, but disappointed that it was so evidently abandoned. They radioed
their colleagues to look out for two kids on bikes, almost
certainly heading west, since otherwise they would have
already been spotted.

Then the police searched the valley quite thoroughly,
because of course you never knew, the kids might still be in
the area, hiding. They searched the wood where the
children had been, and although there was some evidence
of recent disturbance, that might have been yesterday, or
early this morning, and anyway the wood was bound to
appear disturbed, since the children had clearly been
gathering their fuel there. In any case, it was empty
now.

The police settled themselves in the wood, because it was
such an excellent look-out post from which to watch the
camp. You never knew, the children might return for the
rest of their stuff, or even to take up residence again if they
thought the coast was clear. You never could tell how kids'
minds might work. They could be cunning as weasels one
minute, and incredibly naïve the next.

So far, so good. The children were safe, but making no progress, and Watchet was a long way away.

'I wonder if they found our camp yet. . . . Nathan – how
we going to get to Watchet?'

'I dunno. I haven't worked that out yet.'

'We can't ride on the road, can we? There's probably a load of police cars on the moor.'

'You're right there. Probably hundreds. All talking to each other, with their radios, and their walkie-talkies.'

'Nathan, why did we bring the bikes to this wood then?'

'Why? . . . Oh yeah . . . I dunno. I didn't think. Did you think?'

'No, I just followed you. . . . We *could* use them, you know.'

'On the road?'

'After it's dark.'

'Oh yeah – shall we wait till it's dark then, Ju?'

'I can't think of nothing else, can you?'

'It's the best idea.'

They played I-Spy, to make the time go by, but it got boring after a while, and Julia wished she had brought *The Dawn of Love*, so that she could practise her reading. The afternoon dragged on.

'I'm hungry,' said Julia, sadly.

'There's the biscuits. You did bring them with you, didn't you?'

'In my pocket, but I'm thirsty too. Is there a river here, Nathan?'

'I don't think so.'

'I wish it was time to go. Nathan, do you think you can find the way to the road?'

'Yes.'

'In the dark?'

'I think I can.'

'Perhaps the moon will shine.'

'Ju, we don't *want* the moon to shine.'

'Oh yeah – that's right.'

'Ju, I forgot to say, my bike's got another puncture from

all them thorns. Look, the tyre's flat as a pancake?'

'We'll have to both ride on mine then.'

'All right, we'll do that.'

'Are we going to ride our bike all the way to Watchet though?'

'We rode all the way to here.'

'But not in one night. It's too far.'

'We'll have to hide in the day then, and ride again the next night. It'll be fun.'

It did not sound like fun. To Julia, it sounded inexpressibly dreary and uncomfortable. 'What are we going to drink?' she asked, but Nathan could not tell her.

When it came, the night was wonderfully black. The clouds had obligingly covered the sky, just when they were wanted for once, blotting out moonlight and starlight. With the instincts of one of his cats Nathan navigated the way to the road, and they were glad they had brought only one bicycle. One between them was quite enough to manage, in the dark.

Once on the road, they felt more confident. Nathan pedalled, and Julia rode on the carrier. She was looking out for police cars, but there were no cars at all, at first. The little car without lights parked on the edge of the road was almost invisible until they were level with it.

'Go – go fast, fast,' Julia shouted suddenly, at Nathan.

He pedalled hard, head down. 'What's the matter?'

'A police car. It *was* – back there!'

'I didn't see nothing.'

'It was all dark. Do you think they seen us? Why ain't they chasing us?'

Nathan calculated. 'They must have not been there. I know, I know, I know where they are? They're at our camp, Ju! They found our camp. This is the place where you go down to the river.'

'What are they there now for though, Nathan? They can't catch us in the camp if we ain't there.'

'Perhaps they only just found it. Perhaps they're waiting for us to come back. Perhaps they're hiding. That's a good joke, Ju, innit!'

'It's sneaky!' said Julia, disapprovingly.

They changed over, and Nathan rode on the carrier for a bit, while Julia pedalled. They were on the other road now, and there were some cars passing, but it was easy to see if they were coming because their headlights showed up a long way off. Every time that happened, the children left the road and lay flat in the heather until the car had passed. Julia was certain that none of the vehicles that passed was a police car. The search of the moor had presumably been called off for the night.

Going down Porlock Hill, Nathan took charge of the bicycle, and Julia walked behind. Porlock itself was dark and sleeping. There was that other hill – up, this time – and at last they were on the Minehead road.

'It's going good, Ju, isn't it?' said Nathan.

'I'm thirsty,' said poor Julia.

She was also very tired. She didn't think her legs would carry her much further, and her ankle, which had seemed well again, was beginning to hurt. 'I'll pedal,' said Nathan. 'You just ride.'

But Nathan was tired also. He had to concentrate really hard on keeping his feet going, and Julia's weight on the back was making the bicycle wobble dangerously. Nathan clamped his teeth together and leaned over the handlebars. They *must* get further than this tonight. Everything hurt, but Nathan tried to think only of straining and pushing, straining and pushing, straining and pushing. . . .

There was a screech of brakes behind them, and a large car swerved into the middle of the road, and came to a halt a short way further on. Startled, Nathan and Julia fell into the hedge, and the car reversed, stopping again just beside them.

The nearside door opened. 'You all right?' said a voice.

'Yes,' said Julia.

'You made us jump,' said Nathan.

'Well what the hell do you think you're doing, riding two on a bike without lights? You're lucky you didn't get killed.'

'I forgot we supposed to have lights,' said Nathan.

'You forgot! Well, the police won't take that as an excuse if they catch you!' The driver slid across to the passenger seat and peered more closely at the children. 'Good lord – it's a couple of kids! What are you doing out anyway at this time of night? Do you know what time it is?'

'No,' said Nathan.

'Half past one in the morning. Where do you live?'

Silence.

'Well come on, where?'

'Watchet,' said Nathan.

'You're not intending to go all the way to Watchet in that fashion, I hope.'

'Yes,' said Nathan.

'Oh don't be ridiculous. Look, I'm going that way. You'd better let me take you. . . . I don't know about the bike, though.'

'It's all right,' said Nathan.

'What do you mean, it's all right?'

'We'll go on our own. Her bike broke, see, that's why we're late. Our mum knows,' said Nathan.

The man scratched his head and frowned. 'But I can't leave you here like this.' He was really a very nice man, and he had three children of his own at home. 'Oh I know, you've been told never to take lifts from strangers.'

'That's right,' said Nathan, gratefully. 'Our mum told us we must never get in a strange car. Our teacher said that too.'

'But this is rather an exception, isn't it? Damn it, I don't know what to do.' The man seemed to consider for a moment and then, in a different sort of voice, a falsely hearty sort of voice, he said, 'Well – you carry on, you carry on. Good-night, then.'

He slammed the car door, and drove off into the night.

'I wish we went in his car,' said Julia, wistfully.

'Julia!'

'Not really. . . . I wish there was something to drink.'

Almost at that moment a large drop of rain fell on the top of her head, followed by another on her nose. She put out her tongue to lick the rain off her nose, and more drops began to come thick and fast, soaking her clothes and running down her face. She turned back her head and let the rain fall into her mouth. Both children made cups of their hands to collect the precious drops.

They were no longer thirsty, but they were very wet.

'Can't we shelter?' said Julia. 'Just till it stops raining?'

'Where though?'

'There's only the hedge. We could go in that field – see if there's a wood.'

'It's too dark to see, there might be bulls.'

They pressed against the hedge.

'Nathan, I think that man's going to tell of us.'

'Who can he tell? There's no police stations here.'

'There must be a police station *somewhere*. He can phone.'

'You're right. They probably coming now!'

'They probably coming in their cars, to find us!'

'Come on,' said Nathan, making for the gate.

'What about the bulls?'

'I rather bulls than the police.'

They climbed a gate and headed away from the road. They crossed one field, and as they were crossing the second they heard the police sirens and saw the flashing lights.

The police found the abandoned bicycle, where the children had left it, but there was nothing to indicate which way the fugitives had gone. There were fields with gates to them on both sides of the road.

'Poor silly kids,' said one policeman to another. 'Out there in all that wet!'

'I quite thought we were going to have 'em tucked up in bed with a hot supper tonight,' said the other. 'No warm beds for them till tomorrow now, by the look of it.'

The police searched with torches, but there was little they could do until morning light.

Like rabbits, Nathan and Julia had gone to ground. Their panicky running had taken them across three or four fields and into the shelter of a thick wood. A wood which sloped upwards, and went on and on. They plunged deeper into the wood, scrambling up the slope to get as far from the road and the police as their aching legs would carry them. Then like rabbits they had burrowed into the dense undergrowth where the rain could not penetrate.

They were wet, and cold, and hungry – but they slept until dawn.

18

The end of
the adventure

Nathan had just one idea in his head, and that was to get to
his ship. The idea was a furnace in his mind, burning up all
other thoughts. He had read about ships, and dreamed
about ships, about adventures on ships – and now *he* was
going to have an adventure on a ship. He *was*. Nothing was
going to stop him. Not the police, not Julia, not anybody.
As far as Julia was concerned, he'd rather she came with
him than not, but if he had to go alone he would. He was
not going to miss his chance, he was going to make it happen,
he *was*.

Julia was in poor shape. She was cold and wet and shivering. She had eaten her share of the biscuits at first light, but
without appetite, even though it was a whole day since her
last meal. She had no enthusiasm for Nathan's adventure,
but she could see no alternative for herself. Her efforts were
now concentrated on one single thing – staying with Nathan
at all costs.

'How we going to get to Watchet, Ju?' Nathan brooded.

'Don't know,' Julia was past thinking, much. Whatever Nathan said she would do, as long as he didn't ask her to leave him.

'The police is going to be watching the road, and anyway we haven't got the bike no more. There *must* be a way.'

Julia could not help.

'I wonder if there's a bus. Do you think there might be a bus, Ju? . . . But we don't know where the bus stop is.'

'The police might have told the bus conductors to watch for us,' said Julia, coming to life a bit.

They might, indeed.

'We could stop a car.' The incident last night had given Nathan that idea. 'We could ask for a lift.'

'Isn't it dangerous though? There's bad people.'

'Not *ladies*,' said Nathan, triumphantly.

'I think there's *some* bad ladies,' said Julia.

'I don't care. I'm chancing it anyway. Are you coming or not?'

'All right,' said Julia, though she knew they really shouldn't.

'We'll have to look out for police – and sometimes they have roadblocks. We'll have to take a chance about that.'

'What's a roadblock?' said Julia.

'Oh, nothing for you to worry about.'

She wasn't really interested anyway. She just wanted the adventure over, one way or another, as long as she could stay with Nathan. 'Look,' she said, not caring very much, 'the police is searching the fields. They're coming this way,' she added, almost casually.

The children crept through the woods, which seemed to go on for ever. And a long way from where the police were searching, they made their way towards the road. At least it wasn't raining. It was daylight though, and they could be seen from the road They crept under cover of the hedges, and peered through the final hedge in case there should be a police car parked, but there was no sign of one. Nathan made for the gate, and was going to climb over. 'Get back,' said Julia quickly. 'Get down.'

'Police?' said Nathan.

The police car was crawling down the road, patrolling.

'Let it go by,' said Julia. She peered into the road again. 'It's clear now.'

'Supposing it comes back?'

'We'll have to run again then, won't we.' She sounded as though she didn't want to run any more, ever.

They climbed over the gate, and watched the passing traffic. There were quite a few cars on the road, that morning.

'You look a awful mess,' said Julia suddenly. 'I suppose I do too.'

They picked twigs and leaves off each other's clothes, to make themselves more respectable for getting into someone's car.

'There's a lady in that one,' said Julia.

Nathan stepped forward and held up his thumb, as he had seen hitch-hikers doing on the telly. The car slowed down immediately, and a very pleasant looking lady put her head out of the window. 'Are you going to Minehead?' asked the lady.

That would do for a start. 'We missed the bus,' said Nathan.

'All right, get in,' said the lady, opening the back door for them. 'My goodness, you are wet! Has it been raining here then?'

'Just a shower,' said Nathan.

Fortunately, the lady didn't seem to want to talk. She had the radio on, and she was listening to some very boring music. She switched it off just before they came to the town, and threw a question into the back of the car. 'You wanted Minehead, you said?'

'We're meeting our mum and dad there,' said Nathan.

240

'O.K. Where do you want me to drop you? I'm going on to Watchet.'

Watchet. This car was going all the way to Watchet. Nathan could not believe his luck. 'Can we come to Watchet with you?'

'I thought you said you're meeting your parents in Minehead.'

'I made a mistake, I meant Watchet.'

'Oh. Well, not to worry. Yes of course you can come. But are you sure? You did say Minehead at first.'

'I meant Watchet,' said Nathan.

The lady turned the radio on again. 'Do you like Beethoven?' she asked.

'What's that?'

'This is. This music. Do you like it?'

'Oh *yes*. It's my favourite.'

'I don't believe you,' said the lady, laughing. 'I think you're just being polite.'

Nathan let her think that. He was not being polite at all, just prudent. While the lady was listening to the boring music, she could not be asking awkward questions, could she. 'I like that bit,' he added to encourage her. 'That twiddly bit.'

The lady laughed again, and there was no more conversation.

'I think this is Watchet,' said Nathan, to Julia. They were coming down a hill, and the little seaside town was spread out before them. Julia was silent. Her eyes were closed. She was curled into the corner, and sleeping. Nathan nudged her to wake her up. 'Come on, Ju, we're here. We're at Watchet.'

'Where do you want me to drop you?' said the lady.

'Oh – anywhere.'

'Well, where are you meeting your parents?'

'By the harbour,' said Nathan, whose thoughts just then were of nothing else.

'All right. I'll leave you here by the bus stop. You know how to get to the Esplanade?'

'Down the shopping street, isn't it?' said Nathan, suddenly wary.

'Well you can go that way. It's quicker along by the station. Here you are then, out you get.'

'Thank you very much,' said Nathan.

'Thank you,' said Julia, struggling to keep her eyes open, and balance on unsteady legs.

'Wake up, Julia,' said Nathan, seething now with impatience to get to his ship.

'All right, I'm awake. Where do we have to go?'

'To the harbour of course, to find the ship that's going to Norway.'

Julia gazed around her, getting her bearings, remembering. 'That's the street where the man was that asked us the questions. In that shop. The man that suspected us.'

'I know.'

'Let's go, Nathan. He might see us again. And that pink woman with the wobbles. The strawberry jelly woman.'

'I know. We don't have to go that way though. We can go by the station. Look – you can see where the harbour is. You can see the lorries and things!'

They hurried towards a messy conglomeration of lorries and warehouse sheds and great bales of wood, behind a high barricade. The harbour would be somewhere to the left of all this, and the ship that was going to take them far away. Nathan seized Julia's wrist and dragged her with him, and she scuffled her tired feet, trying to keep up.

The harbour lay in front of them. It was full of little boats and unsightly mud. But the place by the wharf where the big ship had been last time, was empty. 'There's no ship!'

said Nathan, not believing it. He had been so sure the ship would be there.

'What shall we do then?' said Julia, bleakly.

'Wait till tomorrow. Perhaps it'll come tomorrow.'

'I'm *tired*,' said Julia.

It was a bright morning, but there were grey and pink clouds billowing up from the sea. It was going to rain again soon, and in any case if they stayed in the open, the pink woman might find them, and start asking a lot more nosy questions. They must find shelter, but Nathan did not want to stray too far from the harbour. 'Let's go this way,' he said.

There were some steps leading up to the railway line, and a path running beside it, heading towards some high cliffs to the right of the harbour. Nathan dragged Julia up the steps and along the path. Soon there were more steps, and as they climbed they were looking down on the dockyard. There were piles of things everywhere. Peering with his short-sighted eyes, Nathan could see that there were plenty of places to hide. He would have liked to shelter in the dock-yard, to be handy for when the ship came. But the way to get there was a steep drop over a cliff face, and in any case they would surely be seen if they tried to climb down. The barricade at the entrance was not there for nothing. Clearly, trespassers were not allowed. Nathan went on dragging Julia up the steps and on to a grassy cliff-top, overlooking the sea.

'Let's go in there,' said Julia.

Nathan had been so preoccupied with his survey of the dockyard that he almost missed the perfect shelter, which Julia had seen. It was actually a relic of the war – a look-out post, like a little man-made cave, with a low entrance and a dark interior. Nathan looked around. He didn't want any-one to see them going in. He would feel safer if no one at all knew they were there. But there was no one on the cliff, and the pinky-grey clouds were already obscuring the sun. The rain would be falling any minute now, drenching them. Nathan pushed Julia inside the dug-out, as the first drops began.

It was smelly and dark, but at least it was dry. 'Good as the tent, innit, Ju,' said Nathan, to keep her cheerful. But Julia was sinking into an exhausted stupor, and didn't answer. They both slept, more or less, for two or three hours, and when they woke, Julia moaned that she was hungry and thirsty. She went on moaning until Nathan lost his patience and told her to shut up.

'Well I *am*,' she insisted.

'You are what?'

'Hungry. And thirsty.'

'If I go out to buy something, I might meet the pink woman. It's too risky.'

'You want me to starve, then?'

'Besides, it's raining, and my pullover's only nearly dry from yesterday. I could borrow *your* coat, Ju.'

'Then I'll freeze, as well as starve.'

'You could have my pullover. You Know Who couldn't see me, with the hood up on your coat.'

'I don't want you to have my coat, I want my coat myself.'

'*Julia!* You got to be reasonable. If you want to eat you got to let me have your coat. That fish and chip place might be open, eh?'

'All right, then.'

'You'll have to give me some money.'

Enveloped in Julia's anorak, Nathan felt protected both from the weather, and from the prying eyes of pink ladies. He battled his way through the driving rain, down the steps and across the Esplanade. He noticed that the tide was almost in, in the harbour.

It was lunch time, and the fish and chip place was indeed

244

open. Nathan was so hungry himself he felt he could probably eat everything on the menu, and with a new twenty
pound note in his pocket there was no need to stint. He
bought fried fish and sausages and beefburgers, and four
portions of chips, and four cans of Coca-Cola. The lady in
the shop wrapped the hot food and found a carrier bag for
him to put everything in. Then Nathan turned to go.

It was hot and steamy in the chip shop and Nathan, not
thinking, had pushed back the anorak hood. He had even
taken of the silly Brighton cap, not thinking he was going to
need it since he had the hood of Julia's coat.

And there, standing behind him in the queue, was – not
the pink woman, but the young man with the long nose and
the red hair. The young man who, by all calculations,
should have been safely behind his counter in the grocery
shop. But who, alas, had chosen that minute to come out
and buy his lunch.

Nathan made a rush for it. The young man was thinking
his own thoughts, and if Nathan hadn't been so obviously
in a hurry, and so obviously alarmed, the young man might
not have noticed him, even with his head uncovered. As it
was, he couldn't help but notice. And recognize.

'Hey – you! You'm that runaway kid!'

But Nathan was gone. Pounding through the rain, speed-
ing along the Esplanade, away from the red-haired young
man and back to Julia. Nathan's eyes might be weak, but
there was nothing wrong with his legs. The young man was
a good runner too, but Nathan had a start on him, and it
was as much as he could do not to lose distance. At the end
of the Esplanade, Nathan hesitated a moment. Which way?
The last thing he wanted to do was to lead the young man
up the cliff steps and into their hide-out. Nathan charged
straight ahead, across the railway line, past a little red light
and into a deep dark lane, which looked as though it had
been cut out of the hillside.

As Nathan reached the lane, he heard a shrieking and clanging behind him and turning, he realized the significance of the red light. A great steam train had just turned the corner, and was ploughing towards the station, puffing and clanging its way across the level crossing. The man from the grocery shop was the other side of the train. He would have to wait for the light to turn green, and that gave Nathan an extra precious minute.

Nathan pulled the anorak hood over his head again. There were other people in the lane, but they only thought he was running because of the rain, or perhaps to get home with his take-aways before they should get cold. He was just another small boy running.

The lane carved its way steeply between high walls, and at the end was a providential choice of roads. To the right, to the left, straight on, or parallel with the deep one, but on a higher level. The red-haired man would never know which way he had gone. There were a few people with umbrellas to see, but by the time the young man arrived at the crossroads, they would no longer be there to tell him.

Nathan chose the path that doubled back. It wasn't a road, just a muddy lane. Soon there was another turning to the right and Nathan took that, sloshing through the mud along a path which skirted the backs of other peoples' houses, and which led to a large field with football posts in it. Across the playing field, all by himself in the rain, Nathan drove his flagging legs, and tried to ignore the pain in his chest.

He was winded! He couldn't run any more. But he was out of the wide open field now, and safer in the shelter of another lane. To his left, Nathan could see the grassy cliff-top. He had come round half a circle.

Julia and the hide-out must be to his left again. The cliff-top was quite deserted, as well it might be in this weather. Nathan paused a few moments to get his breath, then started once again, head down, chugging along the cliff-top with the sea on his right and the railway line on his left. The young man from the grocery shop was long since outdistanced. He would never find him now, Nathan thought.

In the dug-out, Julia was fretful. 'Why did you take so long?' she wanted to know.

'There was a long queue in the chip shop,' said Nathan.

'These chips are nearly cold,' she complained, wolfing them down nevertheless.

Nathan was ravenous. He ate as though he had not had a proper meal for days, as indeed he had not. A day and a half, anyway. He felt good in the dug-out. It was cosy with the rain lashing down outside, and the two of them dry and safe and well-fed. It was not until he had almost finished eating that the true nature of the situation dawned on him. 'But he's going to tell the police!' he said out loud, dismay in his voice, and suddenly clouding his face.

'Who?' said Julia. 'Who's going to tell the police?'

'That man from the grocer's shop. He saw me. I wasn't going to say.'

'How do you know he's going to tell the police? He might not?'

'He chased me. He called me runaway kid. He knows. The police is going to be here soon. Any minute probably.'

'Oh.'

'You don't care, do you!'

'Yes I do, I do care,' said Julia loyally, trying to rally a bit. 'How will they find us here, though? In this hiding place?'

'It's a obvious place, innit! It's probably the first place they'll look. Everybody in this town must know about this place. We'll have to go somewhere else.'

'In the rain?'

'It might be too late anyway. The police might be here already.'

He crawled out to see. The rain had stopped, almost, but the cliff-top was still deserted. Wherever the police were, they had not yet arrived here. Nathan stood up cautiously, and peered across the dockyard to the Esplanade, seeking striped cars and blue-uniformed figures. But the distance was all a blur. If the police had been there, he would not have been able to identify them. His gaze travelled over the harbour towards the harbour mouth. And there was something that even *his* defective eyes could not fail to see. Coming into the harbour, on the afternoon full tide, was a beautiful big ship!

'Ju – come and look!'

She came out of the hide and stood beside him. 'I suppose now you want us to stow away on that.'

'It's a miracle,' said Nathan, in awe. 'It's a miracle. It came just in time. There's *got* to be a way. There's *got* to be a way.'

Frantic with excitement, he tried to assess the possibilities. The ship was there, making for the dockside, only a few metres from where the children stood. But they couldn't just go and jump on it. For one thing it was broad daylight, and they would be seen. For another thing, there was no way into the dockyard for them, except down the cliff, glaringly exposed to view, and in any case too steep. If it were dark, on the other hand, and they were already hidden, somewhere in the dockyard. . . .

Perhaps there was another way down, an easier way. Across the cliff-top, next to the sea, it looked as though there might be steps. 'Come on!' Nathan grabbed Julia's wrist, and dragged her towards the steps he thought he saw.

The steps led down to the beach, skirting the far end of the dockyard. Down below were great piles of new wood, and Nathan could smell their fragrance as he ran. Halfway down the steps, he paused. One of the piles of wood was stacked close to the cliff. Between the wood and the cliff was a space. That would be a good hiding place. Nathan peered over, and he couldn't see to the bottom of the space, because the cliff was overhanging just there. If he and Julia were in that space, and the police were coming down the steps looking for them, he didn't think they could be seen.

How to get down?

To his left as he looked, there was a steepish slope of grass and wet earth, and then a wall, perhaps a metre and a half high. Not a very big drop. He could manage it easily. Even Julia could manage that little drop, surely.

Nathan looked to see if they could be seen, climbing down. A long shed jutted from the harbour, almost right across the dockyard. On their side of the shed there were no work people, not one. It was now or not at all, there would never be another chance like this.

'Come on, Ju. Down here!'

Julia followed Nathan without question. She was too tired, and too dispirited to think for herself. She would do whatever Nathan said. He slithered down the cliff slope, on his feet, balancing with practised ease. He vaulted the last drop, landing lightly on the ground, with flexed knees and ankles. Julia tried to do likewise.

She tripped, half way down the slope, and pitched on to her side. She slid and rolled the rest of the way, falling over the wall to the ground with a sickening thud. Her left leg took the full force of the fall.

'Come on, Ju,' said Nathan, who was already crawling into the hiding place.

'I can't.'

'What you mean "I can't"? We have to hide.'

'I hurt my leg. I can't move.'

249

'Course you can move!' Impatiently, Nathan grabbed Julia by the shoulders and dragged her into the lovely little space, between the pile of wood and the cliff. Julia screamed.

'Don't make such a fuss! They'll hear you!'

But Julia's face was white with pain. Her pale eyes were screwed into little slits, and she was biting her lips.

'Are you really hurt, then?'

'Yes I am.'

'Why didn't you come down more careful?'

'I tried to. I ain't good at climbing like you.'

Nathan considered. 'Shall I bandage it for you? Like you done my arm?'

'We haven't got no bandage.'

Nathan took off his tee-shirt, and tried to improvise with that, but Julia screamed again when he touched the leg, so he put his shirt back on again.

'Lie still and rest it, Ju. I expect it'll be better by this evening.'

'It won't.'

'Yes it will. How do you know it won't?'

'I think it's broke.'

'It *can't* be. It *can't* be broke.'

'I think it is though.'

There was a heavy silence.

'Nathan,'

'What?'

'I can't come on the ship, can I!'

Silence.

'I can't, can I, Nathan.'

'No.'

'Are you going to get a ambulance for me?'

'No.'

'What are you going to do then?'

Silence again.

250

'What are you going to do, Nathan?'

'Ju – I have to go on that ship, I have to! It's my only chance! It's my best chance in the world.' He didn't like himself particularly while he said this, but he said it nevertheless.

'And leave me here?'

'Yes.'

'All by myself?'

'You'll be all right, Ju. They'll come and put you in a nice hospital, and look after you. You'll be all right.'

'Oh it hurts, it hurts,' wailed Julia. 'Don't leave me, Nathan.'

'Sh-sh-sh-sh – somebody's going to hear. I ain't leaving you yet. . . . Not till it's dark. . . . We got hours yet.'

Julia turned her face to the wall. Two tears of pain and lonely desolation trickled across her cheeks.

'Julia,' said Nathan, suddenly anxious.

'What?'

'You won't tell of me, will you? When I'm gone on the ship. You won't tell them where I am!'

'No,' said Julia, in a small flat voice.

'You sure?'

'I said. I won't tell of you. . . . You better take the money, didn't you.'

'I'll have half of it.'

'You might as well have all of it. *I* shan't need it no more. You better have it for your chance.'

'All right,' said Nathan, feeling indescribably mean and horrible. 'What will you do, Ju? When I'm gone on the ship? Will you call somebody?'

'I suppose so. Won't I have to wait till the ship sails away? Will it be a long time? . . . Perhaps I shall die,' she added with some satisfaction.

'Don't be silly. You've only hurt your leg. People don't die because their leg's broke.'

251

'What do you know about it? Actually, I think my heart's broke too.'

'Oh don't be stupid! Don't be stupid, Rat-bag! You only thought of that out of them rubbish stories you been reading!'

What did she want to do it for? What did she want to break her stupid leg for? Nathan kicked at the wood in front of him, his face like thunder. Across the dockyard came the sounds of shouting men and clanging metal as the ship came to the harbour wall. *His* ship. What *could* have been his ship.

He looked at Julia, still lying with her face to the wall. He gave the wood a final kick, and with one great painful wrench, he made up his mind. He crawled into the open, and stood up, in full view of the police, who were at that moment searching the cliff-top. They had found the remains of the children's lunch, and very excited they were about it too.

'You can come and get us,' Nathan yelled. 'We're down here. You can come and get us!'

Then he squatted down beside Julia, who was gaping in wonder at this extraordinary behaviour.

'What you do that for?'

'I ain't going to leave you, am I, stupid Rat-bag! I'm going with you, aren't I?'

He glowered at her, still furious, but the look she gave him back was one of pure, shining love.